VANISHING ACT

Also by Laura Martin

The Monster Missions

Glitch

Hoax for Hire

Float

Edge of Extinction #1: The Ark Plan

Edge of Extinction #2: Code Name Flood

VANISHING ACT

LAURA MARTIN

HARPER
An Imprint of HarperCollins Publishers

Library of Congress Cataloging-in-Publication Data

Names: Martin, Laura, author.
Title: Vanishing act / Laura Martin.
Description: First edition. | New York : Harper, [2022] | Sequel to: Float |
    Audience: Ages 8-12. | Audience: Grades 4-6. | Summary: Thirteen-
    year-old Hank must overcome his inconvenient invisibility to save
    Camp Outlier from a saboteur—and win the camp-wide challenge.
Identifiers: LCCN 2021051671 | ISBN 9780063136762 (hardcover)
Subjects: CYAC: Camps—Fiction. | Summer—Fiction. | Ability—Fiction. |
    Fiction. lcgft
Classification: LCC PZ7.1.M3734 Van 2022 | DDC [Fic]—dc23
LC record available at https://lccn.loc.gov/2021051671

Typography by Ellice M. Lee and Catherine Lee
22 23 24 25 26   PC/LSCH   10 9 8 7 6 5 4 3 2 1
❖
First Edition

For all the kids taking the road less traveled . . .
I'm proud of you.

CHAPTER ONE

When I was little, I used to love playing hide-and-seek. I had three older brothers who were 100 percent normal, so they'd hide in normal places. Eddy would squeeze behind couches, Phil liked hiding under tables, and Charlie had a thing for curtains—you get the idea. I, however, would simply disappear. One second a scrawny kid with floppy blond hair would be standing there. The next second the only thing visible would be whatever clothes I happened to be wearing, which is probably why I got in the habit of ditching my clothes at a very young age. What was the point of being invisible if your T-shirt and shorts gave away your location?

If I was having a good day, I could make all of me disappear for the game. However, I didn't have good days very often, so usually just a chunk of me was invisible. If it was just a small chunk that wouldn't go invisible, like a hand or a toe, then I'd just jam the visible bit into a flowerpot or the dog food bowl. If it was something bigger, like my entire leg or head or something, I'd use everything from the trash can to my mom's favorite soup pot. Which, for the record, worked great until she tried turning the stove on underneath the soup pot. At which point I jumped out howling, only visible from the shins down, and got grounded for a week. Apparently, no one wants their kid hanging out naked in the same pot they make chili. After that, my mom tried to add rules to hide-and-seek, but you aren't allowed to add rules to hide-and-seek, even if "no naked kids in the soup pot" is probably a good one.

The games were epic, and I got pounded on for winning a lot. I didn't mind, though. When you're the youngest of four boys, getting pounded on by your brothers is just par for the course. Even when Charlie went to college, the first thing we'd all do when he came home to visit was play hide-and-seek, although I was the only one who hid these days. It was fun, but I didn't want to play today. It was a bad day. It was a day where I didn't exist.

Okay, that was being a bit dramatic, which, according to my mom, is one of my many talents, but still. She should try disappearing for an entire month and then we'd see who was dramatic. One month of looking in the mirror and not seeing myself look back. One month of getting tripped over by everyone in my family. One month of not being able to go out without getting stared at or terrifying the general public. If only my mom would let me tag along naked to the grocery store and the movies, it would be fine. No one would even know I was there, so no one would stare or scream or faint. Plus, as an added bonus, she wouldn't have to buy me a ticket.

"Please? I'm begging you," I said, folding my hands in front of me and dropping to my knees in front of my mother. She, of course, couldn't see the hands. Today I was just a walking-talking pair of Nike shorts and a blue T-shirt. Nike shorts and a blue T-shirt can't win anyone over.

"No," she said as she rubbed the back of her hand across her forehead. It was unusually hot for May in South Dakota, and my dad refused to turn on the air-conditioning.

"But why?" I whined. "I've been invisible for weeks. I'm not going to just become visible again this afternoon for the one hour we're at the mall. I promise."

"You can't promise that," Phil chimed in from his spot at the kitchen table. Of my three older brothers, he was the closest to me in age at seventeen, and he took a special pleasure in making things hard on me. I think he was still bugged about losing his status as the youngest when I'd come along unexpectedly thirteen years go.

"I don't need your help," I said, and stood up. If kneeling on linoleum wasn't helping my cause, I might as well stand. "Come on," I begged. "I leave for camp tomorrow, and I still need a bunch of stuff."

"Should have just ordered it all online," Phil said around a mouthful of pizza. I reached over and swiped a slice off his plate. Thanks to my invisible hand, it took him a solid five seconds to realize it.

"Give that back!" he said, and made a swipe for it.

"I already licked it," I said, "but fine, here ya go." I tossed it back on his plate. He made a face and shoved it away from the rest of his un-licked pizza.

"Mom!" he said.

"I didn't actually lick it," I said when Mom stopped unloading the dishwasher to stare daggers at me. Well, not so much at me, but at the spot where she knew my head was probably located. She was really looking right through me and giving the rooster clock on the wall behind me her signature Mom glare, but that

4

didn't make it any less effective. She nodded and Phil pulled the offending piece of pizza back onto his plate and grumbled something that probably wasn't overly complimentary.

"Mom!" Phil said around his next mouthful. "I think I'd like to go to the mall. You know, just to browse. I'll be back by dinnertime." With that he stood up, jingling the keys to his new jeep in that obnoxious way that made me want to smack him, and taking his pizza with him.

"How is that fair?" I said, anger bubbling inside me as I watched Phil saunter across the driveway toward his car.

"No one said that you couldn't go," my mom said calmly, "but you have to go with clothes on. I don't feel like I should have to explain this to you again."

"You don't," I said. I folded my invisible arms across my chest and stood at the window, debating with myself. I glanced over at the tree where I used to set up the Mountain Dew cans for the squirrels. They'd really loved the stuff, but Dad had made me stop. Sometimes having a veterinarian for a father was fun, like the time he'd brought home a box of kittens for us to bottle-feed, and sometimes it was annoying, like when he lectured you about not giving soda pop to the wildlife. In my defense, I had no idea the crazy critters would get cavities.

"Can I go to the mall with Phil?" I finally asked.

"Sure," she said. "But if I hear about you going naked to fly under the radar, I may just call off camp."

"Whoa," I said, turning from the window. "You don't mean that. I have to go back to camp. The guys are counting on me to be there."

"And I'm counting on relaxing this afternoon without any phone calls from the mall security," she said, matching my tone perfectly. I was about to tell her about how my friend Emerson had accidentally floated all the way up to his mall's ceiling and that they'd needed four security guards and the fire department to get him back down again, but the roar of Phil's jeep interrupted my thoughts, and I realized that my ride was about to leave without me.

"Bye, Mom!" I said, grabbing my flip-flops off the mat by the door and spinning to go.

"Hold it," she said. I froze and turned back to look at her.

"Forgetting something?" she prompted, and I hurried over to give her a quick peck on the cheek. She managed to wrap her arms around my invisible shoulders and give me a quick squeeze before I was out the door and racing after the jeep that was already making its way down our driveway.

"Wait up!" I yelled, but Phil just kept going.

The *kiss Mom* rule was really going to mess things up for me this time, I thought grimly as I doubled my speed.

"Hey," Phil said, without even looking back as I finally vaulted through the open back of the jeep. "That took you longer than I thought."

"You could have slowed down," I wheezed as I fumbled with the seat belt.

"Could have," Phil agreed. "Didn't want to. You took your sweet time leaving the house."

"*Kiss Mom* rule," I said.

"You mean the Hank Rule," Phil corrected me. As the youngest, I should have been able to fly under the radar a bit more than I did. However, as the only family member who had a RISK factor, the government's clever acronym for Recurring Instances of the Strange Kind, I wasn't allowed to avoid any radars—mothers', governments', or otherwise.

Mom had instituted the rule after I accidentally got broadsided by my oldest brother's four-wheeler, and they'd had to spend two days in the hospital trying to instruct doctors how to stitch up my invisible bleeding head. Life was short, life was fragile, life wasn't guaranteed, so you'd better kiss your mother before you leave the house. Period. All my brothers had quickly renamed Mom's new mandate the Hank Rule, since it was obviously put in place for me. They were 100 percent visible all the time and much less likely to die a horrific death. At least in theory, I thought grimly as Phil took a turn faster than was probably safe. Phil drove this jeep like he'd stolen it, and I wondered how long it would take the paramedics to realize there was another, invisible person in the car if he bent it around a tree.

Our family's farm was a good twenty minutes from the nearest mall, and I settled back in my seat as Phil turned up his radio. My hair whipped around my face and into my eyes, and I quickly snagged a baseball hat off the floor of the jeep and jammed it on my head to keep my hair out of the way. Yet another side effect of prolonged invisibility was the inability to get a haircut. Phil had offered to take his clippers to it and just shave the whole mess, but after the lost eyebrow incident two years ago, I wasn't going to allow that to happen again.

I reached into my pocket to pull out the list of supplies I still needed to get before camp the next day and felt the familiar thrill of excitement as I pictured the next few months.

Camp Outlier was my favorite place in the entire world, and after nine months of waiting and preparing, it was almost time to go back. I unfolded the paper and smoothed it out on my leg. It consisted mostly of sunscreen, bug spray, and some new shirts and hoodies. I'd never cared much about my wardrobe, but since it was literally the only thing people could see, I thought I might want to move it up the priority list.

I then pulled the other list out of my pocket, the list of requirements I'd given the guys at the end of camp last summer. I'd instructed them to destroy their list upon memorizing it, but I'd kept my original copy since my memory was absolutely horrendous. My dad always joked that it was lucky my RISK factor didn't involve detachable appendages, or I'd have lost my arms or head years ago. He was probably right. This paper was much more wrinkled and crinkled than the other one, since I'd crammed it in my pocket about a hundred times.

Red Maple men:
Before next summer you MUST, and I repeat, MUST have completed the following items.
Write me an email. Here is my email address. LifeListsRule127@gmail.com. I will then send around everyone else's email addresses so we can stay in touch. Oh, and if you have a cell phone, send me

the phone number too. I don't have one anymore after getting grounded for a prank-calling binge last year.

Be able to hold your breath underwater for at least two minutes. I have a capture-the-flag plan for next summer. Two words. Sneak attack. (Murphy, I know you crossed this one off your list already. Which is actually what gave me my brilliant plan. Thanks!)

Learn to juggle.

Murphy made me add this one. He wouldn't say why, but apparently, it's important that we can all run a six-minute mile. So start running, men. Gary—this includes you.

Learn how to dance. Not like lame dancing either. Go to YouTube. The Monarch girls won't know what hit them.

Age at least fifteen years by the time I see you again. I have my list of where you all left off, so no cheating.

Start lifting weights. No more string-bean arms for us. Chicks dig muscles, so I hear.

Learn how to quack and waddle like a

duck. Kidding. Just wanted to see if you
were still paying attention.

Start brainstorming an initiation night
for when we're in Red Wood, and we get to
harass the new Red Maple boys. It's going
to be hard to beat eighties prom dresses.
Although you have to admit, I looked good
in mine.

Check out the picture I stuck in your
envelope. I pulled some strings and had
Chad make enough copies for all of us, you
know, just in case you forgot how fabulous
we looked.

Sincerely,
Hank
PS After you've read and memorized
this letter, either flush it or eat it.
Whatever floats your boat.

I didn't need the picture in front of me to remember
the glory of those eighties prom dresses. Mine in particular had been spectacularly horrendous, and I was
kind of sad that I'd forgotten to bring it home from
camp. It was going to be hard to top that initiation
night, but I was looking forward to the day I got to
welcome the Red Maple cabin into the brotherhood of

camp by dragging them into the middle of the woods and forcing them to bond on their trek back to camp. The thought actually brought me up short, since the entire school year I'd been thinking about how great it would be to be back at camp and be a Red Maple man again, but I wouldn't be in Red Maple this year, would I? We'd all be moving up to the White Oak cabin. The thought made me a little sad.

Aging in real life had a bittersweet feeling that aging on a Life List didn't. A Life List, which was like a bucket list only way less depressing, was a way I'd come up with to really squeeze the most out of my life. A Life List was a list of everything from the challenges I wanted to tackle to the places I wanted to visit to the talents I wanted to acquire, and for the last couple of years I'd dutifully checked things off my list. Each item that I successfully checked off counted as a year in my Life Listing life. I was an old duffer in Life Listing years, well over a hundred, and I had no intention of stopping.

I pulled my Life List from my pocket. The list spanned five pieces of paper that I'd stapled and then re-stapled together more times that I could count. I ran my finger down the things I'd crossed off this past school year, and felt a bit smug about a few of the more daring items on the list. The thing with the snakes at school had been particularly tricky. I wondered if the other guys had held up their end of things and aged the fifteen years I'd stipulated in their letters. Murphy would for sure, although now that he'd lost the *I've got nothing to lose since I time travel and die before summer ends* mentality, he was probably a bit more cautious these days. Zeke and Anthony were also pretty reliable Life Listers, and I wouldn't be surprised if they aged double the required amount. Gary? Well, Gary was a grump and a half, partially because he routinely got himself stuck to inanimate objects and partially because he had the personality of a constipated toad. Sometimes when you told him to do something, it just made him *not* want to do it. I was pretty sure Emerson would follow through. He'd left camp a different kid than the one I'd met in the parking lot on the first day of camp. I smiled as I pictured my friend who'd gotten the double whammy of uncontrollable floating and a puke-inducing fear of heights.

At the beginning of camp, he'd reminded me of one of those ponies at the carnival that spent their life walking around in circles giving pony rides and had no idea what to do with themselves when they were finally freed. Emerson had been clunking around in shoes essentially made out of bricks and the look of a lost puppy, and I'd immediately liked him. So much so that I'd helped him out and chucked his shoes in the lake on our first day at camp.

I was so engrossed in the list that I didn't notice that we'd pulled over until Phil snatched my list out of my hand.

"Hey!" I said as I tried to swipe it back.

"I thought so," he said, nodding as he handed me back my list. "You still haven't managed to cross cow tipping off your list."

"So?" I said. I quickly refolded my list and crammed it back in my pocket. My brothers refused to buy into the whole idea of Life Listing, and it would bug me until the day I died.

"Well," Phil said slowly, running his hands through his blond hair so it stood up in all directions, "wanna cross it off?"

I looked up to see him grinning at me in the rear-view mirror. In front of him was a large field full of cows.

"You have to tip cows at night," I said. "You know, when they're sleeping and they lock their knees." I'd done my research on this particular endeavor, since death by cow didn't sound like a dignified thing to have on your tombstone.

"Odds are that one of them is sleeping out there," Phil said, jerking his head toward the field.

"This isn't some ploy to get me in trouble, is it?" I said, remembering how he'd helped me get out the ladder so I could sled off the roof two years ago, only to also help me get grounded for a week by telling Mom about it before I could actually do the deed. In his defense, I probably would have broken my neck.

"It's not," Phil promised. "I just kind of want to see you sneak up on a sleeping cow. It's too quiet around here in the summer now that you go to camp and Ed and Charlie stay at college to work. Consider this my parting gift."

I studied him for another long minute and then I quickly shucked off my T-shirt and shorts before vaulting out of the back of the jeep. Mom had said that I couldn't be naked at the mall, but she hadn't said a thing about naked in a cow field. It wasn't until I was halfway across the field, my eyes on a giant black heifer snoozing in the shade, that I heard the engine of the jeep start and Phil's laughter as he pulled away and left me standing, naked, in a field of cows. Sometimes, I really hated having older brothers.

CHAPTER TWO

I stayed up that night filling all of Phil's dresser drawers with cow poop. He deserved it, and since our flight was super early, he wouldn't wake up and discover it until I was long gone. Still, staying up that late the night before I had to wake up at six a.m. to catch my flight to Camp Outlier was probably not one of my best decisions. I yawned as my mom handed the lady at check-in our tickets. Here we go, I thought, and frowned as the lady at the counter called her manager over to discuss how they could verify me as a passenger without actually being able to see me. Those perks were pretty few and far between.

"See, this is why you always leave early," Mom said

with a huff as she finally got our tickets back from the flustered lady behind the counter. "Let's go grab something to eat quick before we have to board." I followed her obediently through the busy airport terminal, making sure to stay right next to her since she always got twitchy about losing me in big crowds. I was wearing clothes, though, so I was pretty easy to spot in my bright red Red Maple hoodie and cargo shorts.

"Why do I keep smelling cows?" Mom mused to herself as she glanced around. "I didn't realize there was a farm so close to the airport." I made a mental note to put on more cologne before we got to camp. The smell of cow poop lingered longer than pig poop on the skin, which was something I kind of wish I didn't know first-hand. The line for McDonald's was long, and I quickly excused myself to go use the bathroom while my mom waited in line for our breakfast sandwiches.

I did my best to ignore the stares of the people I walked past on my way to the restroom, wishing I at least had a visible head. That way, by grinning back at their startled faces, I could show them I didn't care that they were staring. I used the bathroom quickly and was just bending over the sink to wash my hands when I felt someone grab my shoulder. I glanced up in the mirror, but the only reflection I saw was of my disembodied sweatshirt and backward baseball hat. No one was behind me. Still, the hand on my shoulder squeezed painfully, and I saw the fabric of my sweatshirt indent around invisible fingers. I'd have screamed, but I froze as my own voice whispered in my ear.

"Don't scream. It's me, Hank."

"Uh, you're naked, aren't you?" I said, which really was one of the weirder things I've ever said to myself.

"I'll explain in a second. Follow me," said my voice, and I obediently let myself get pulled down the long aisle of bathroom stalls toward the large accessible one in the very back. Around us toilets were flushing and people were busy maneuvering their large rolling suitcases into the tiny bathroom stalls, and by some miracle, no one was looking at the invisible kid getting dragged by yet another invisible kid. The door of the accessible stall swung open, and I walked in, stopping in surprise when I saw Murphy and Gary standing there, crammed shoulder to shoulder in the small space. The door shut behind me, and I saw it latch as though doing it by itself, and for the first time I understood how being invisible could really creep out someone else.

"Stay in your corner," Gary barked quietly, and for a second I thought he was talking to me.

"All right, all right," came my voice as it obediently moved into the far corner of the stall by the toilet, where a pair of sopping-wet shorts was picked up off the bathroom floor and put back on invisible legs. "It was your idea for me to be naked for this, remember? We could have sent you out to grab him, but you said it had to be me!"

"Well, I've got my hands full at the moment, don't I?" Gary said, and for the first time I noticed that he had one hand stuck to Murphy's shoulder and the other attached to a rope. A rope that the other invisible me was quickly tying around his own waist.

"What's going on?" I said.

"We're from the future, duh," Gary said, and I realized that he did look older than last summer. A quick glance at Murphy showed a taller, slightly less skinny version of the redheaded time traveler who had become my friend the previous summer.

"Give me a break, guys," came my voice from the corner. "I wasn't there the first time you did this. Remember? You had Emerson along the last time."

"I can't believe we are even doing this again," Gary grumbled. "I swore that if you knuckleheads tried to stick me to things to time travel this summer that I would happily drown you in the lake. Maybe there's still time to do that," he said thoughtfully.

"Quiet—" Murphy said, but before he could go on, I'd thrown my arms around his and Gary's necks and squeezed. So what if they were from the future? So what if this was all utterly bizarre and weird? I was part of a generation of bizarre and weird, and it didn't matter that we were all crammed in a bathroom with the sounds of flushing toilets and people peeing. I hadn't seen them in nine months, and I was pumped.

"You guys are a sight for sore eyes!" I said. "Whose idea was it to visit me by a toilet? This is epic! How far into this summer are you from? Is it amazing? Has Anthony accidentally set anything on fire? Has Emerson had to float and puke yet? How's Eli?" I turned to the corner, still holding Gary and Murphy in overly affectionate choke holds so I could look at where my future invisible self was inconspicuously hanging out wearing nothing but shorts and a rope. I raised an eyebrow no one could see. "Why is there a puddle of water on the floor? At least, that had better be water. Looks like I'm still invisible? Like completely invisible? An ear hasn't even shown up?"

"Why do you smell like cow poop?" Gary asked, wrinkling his nose in disgust as he attempted to pry off an arm he couldn't see.

"Shut up! Will you?" Murphy hissed, his voice barely carrying over the sound of flushing toilets and hand dryers. "I think we must be here to warn Hank about something."

"We are?" Gary said, trying to turn so he could look at Murphy. "Isn't that against the law or whatever?"

"What we are doing right now is against time-traveling law," invisible me said. "So what have we got to lose? Do you really think warning me will do any good? I mean, we still haven't figured it out, and we obviously have survived it all so far."

"So far," Gary said with a sniff.

"Good to see you're still a regular old ray of sunshine," I said to him before turning back to the other guys. "Will one of you please just spit it out? Why did you time travel to a bathroom of all places?"

"That's the thing," Murphy said, biting his lip. "I don't know if warning you about the stuff at camp is going to prevent any of it from happening or just make things worse."

"It definitely didn't prevent this from happening, and that's a crying shame," Gary muttered to himself as he peered around the cramped stall in disgust.

"Shhhhh," Murphy said with a nervous glance to either side.

"Wait," I said as what they were saying finally made its way through my initial excitement at their appearance, "this isn't a planned mission?"

"You know I can't do that," Murphy said. "This is what you call dumb luck."

21

He leaned forward, dropping his voice so low that I could barely hear him over the flushing toilets. "So here's what's been happening . . . ," he started to say, but his words were cut off as he suddenly flickered and disappeared along with Gary and the future version of myself. I stood there, frozen, as I stared at the spot my friends and I had been just moments before. I'd experienced a lot of weird things in my life, but that just topped the list.

"What just happened?" I said aloud. I felt like someone had just turned off a movie right before the most exciting part. I stood there staring around the empty stall, willing my friends to show back up, but of course they didn't. Well, at least not all of them showed back up. I'd just given myself a little shake and was turning to leave when there was a small but oh-so-familiar popping sound behind me. I whirled to see Murphy standing there. For a second, I thought that it was the same Murphy who'd just been stuck to Gary and a very wet, very invisible future version of myself, but it wasn't. Of course, my first clue should have been the missing Gary and Hank, but it wasn't. It was his expression that told me that this was a very different version of my friend. The Murphy from moments before had been nervous but still calm and collected; this Murphy was in a full-on panic. He was also soaked.

"Hey," I said. "Long time no see."

"What?" Murphy said as he whipped his head this way and that to take in the bathroom stall.

"You were just here," I said. "So was I, actually, and Gary. We have got to do something about that kid's disposition. I mean, there's grumpy and then there's grumpy, do you know what I mean?"

"Hank," Murphy said, and there was something in his voice that made me snap my mouth shut. His red-rimmed eyes were suddenly overflowing with tears, and he lunged forward and grabbed me in such a tight hug that my ribs creaked in protest.

"Whoa!" I said as Murphy sobbed hard on my shoulder. "What's going on? Is this about whatever you were just trying to tell me? What was that, by the way? Because you can't just leave a guy hanging like that."

Murphy just shook his head and cried harder, and I felt my stomach sink as I registered the sound of that cry. It wasn't a mad cry or an upset cry; it was the cry of someone who'd lost something—or, I realized, someone. I stood there for a second before wrapping my arms around my friend and hugging back.

"Murph?" I said, and I felt the next words catch in the back of my throat. "I die, don't I?" Because there was really no other explanation that I could think of. Murphy's shoulders went rigid, and he pulled back and looked at me and nodded. We stared at each other for another heartbeat while the world around me seemed to blur for a moment as that nod and what it meant sank in. And then he was gone. My arms fell to my sides, no longer supported by his shoulders, and I was alone for the second time in the bathroom stall.

I stood there while toilets flushed and doors banged open and shut and hand dryers whooshed. It could have been a minute or it could have been a lifetime, but my feet felt like they'd permanently attached themselves to the linoleum. My knees felt wobbly, but I had enough of my wits about me not to let them buckle and send me onto the floor of an airport bathroom. I probably would have stood there even longer if an incredibly familiar voice hadn't come over the airport's speaker.

"Henry Roberts! Please report to airport security now!" said my mother, sounding furious. I cringed. How long had I been in the bathroom? Long enough for my mom to figure out how to work the airport PA system, obviously, I thought as I quickly flushed the toilet. It wasn't really necessary, but it also seemed weird not to flush it. That accomplished, I hurried out of the stall and past the people giving me judgmental looks for not washing my hands and went to find my mom.

CHAPTER THREE

Camp Outlier was in Michigan, which was a two-hour plane ride from South Dakota, but those two hours seemed never-ending. I felt twitchy as I sat next to my mom, watching the clouds zoom past like fluffy marshmallows. She was mad, but she got over it when I told her that I had, in fact, still been in the bathroom when she'd hit the panic button and hijacked the PA system. Now she read her book while I fidgeted in my seat, anxious to get to camp. To say that the back-to-back episodes in the bathroom had me on edge would have been the understatement of a century. I shut my eyes as I tried to recap the conversations again. The one with the second Murphy hadn't really been a conversation, just my name, a lot of crying and snot, and the nod that would be pressed into my memory for the rest of my life. Which, I thought, swallowing hard, might not be all that long.

It was the first conversation that felt like a mystery I needed to unravel. My friends had shown up and debated warning me about something. A future version of myself had actually told Murphy that the warning wouldn't change anything, that they'd all survived whatever it was so far. Those two words, *so far*, felt especially heavy now. The whole thing was equal parts ominous and obnoxious, a rare combination that I couldn't say I particularly enjoyed. It had put a dark cloud over a day that I'd been anticipating for months.

I glared out the airplane window at the clouds and debated telling my mom that I just wanted to go back home. Of course, I couldn't do that, not really. Not only would I miss out on camp, but RISK kids like me weren't allowed to spend their summers just running about willy-nilly. If I wasn't at camp I'd be in summer school or worse. No, I couldn't tell my mom. I'd seen how Murphy's parents had reacted last summer when they'd had to say goodbye to him at camp, believing that they'd never see him again. The thought brought me up short and snapped me momentarily out of my pity party. Of course, Murphy had gone through this exact same thing the previous summer, and he'd lived to tell the tale. I immediately felt better, and I busted open the package of snacks that had been sitting forgotten in my lap. I popped a few in my mouth and chewed, ignoring the wide-eyed stare of the woman across the aisle. I smiled a smile that she couldn't see and popped a few more into my mouth. You couldn't really blame her. It wasn't every day that you saw snacks disappear in midair.

I spent the rest of the flight caught in my own tangled thoughts, and the next thing I knew we were touching down. The minute we got off the plane, I started to feel the effects of Camp Outlier. Unlike the airport in South Dakota, Michigan's airport was packed with RISK kids. It was the closest airport to camp, and since today was check-in day, a bunch of other campers were flying in with their parents and caseworkers. A lot of them, like me, were proudly wearing their cabin's sweatshirt from the previous year, and I quickly spotted a girl in the orange Monarch cabin sweatshirt. However, since it wasn't Kristy or Molly, I turned my attention to the other commotion going on in the terminal. To my left a kid was wearing a head-to-toe plastic hazmat suit, as were the caseworkers walking on either side of him. To my right was a kid who was calmly sprouting leaves directly out of his skin. Which wouldn't have been all that interesting except that they kept turning yellow and red and then falling around him into fluffy puddles. I grinned. These were my people.

RISK kids like me had become more and more common, but we were still only a tiny fraction of the population, and there weren't many occasions when we were all in one spot. The average school had one or two of us, a fact that I'm sure they were extremely grateful for, since just one RISK kid could cost them hundreds of thousands of dollars a year in specialized equipment, aides, and resources. However, thanks to a law that went into effect last year, we now had to be herded together like a bunch of unruly cows and monitored for the summer.

I'd never take for granted that I was one of the lucky ones who got to go somewhere like Camp Outlier, one of the only summer camps specially equipped to not only monitor kids like us, but also let us enjoy summer like any normal kid. I made a mental note to thank my mom again for shelling out the cash so I could go. It was no small amount either, as the rest of the guys and I had figured out when we'd decided to help get Murphy back to camp this summer. It had taken some fancy footwork, but he'd been awarded a special scholarship to allow him to attend camp. At least, that's what his parents thought. Really, we'd scrimped and saved and pooled our resources to ensure that our friend would make it back for another summer. The fake scholarship that both covered our tracks and allowed Murphy to save face had been a work of genius, if I did say so myself. I smiled, grateful for an older brother who was an engineering major and knew his way around a computer well enough to make a fake scholarship completely believable.

Mom and I made our way out of the airport and toward the rental car pickup, and I barely got a second glance. Compared to the kid who was turning everything around him into chocolate, I was pretty boring. The drive to camp was only about fifteen minutes from the airport, and I finally found myself in the spot I'd been longing to be in for the entire school year. Just like last year, the camp had turned the large grassy field where we played soccer and football into a makeshift parking lot, and campers with duffel bags slung over their shoulders were making their way toward the dining hall to check in. It was obvious who was a first timer to camp. Those kids wore looks like someone had killed their puppy, and their parents talked quickly, wearing large fake smiles that weren't fooling anyone.

The car next to us had one of the newbies, and I grinned at a boy who stood clutching his duffel bag like it was a life preserver. He'd be in Red Maple this year, and I would have bet any money that he was going to love it. It was that kid and his terrified expression that suddenly snapped something into place for me. I'd been panicking ever since the airport bathroom about dying, but, really, had anything changed? I knew at some level that I was going to die some day in the future. It wasn't a big secret. In fact, a RISK kid like me had pretty good odds of something tragic happening. I'd known that my entire life, and I'd gone above and beyond to live each day like it was going to be my last, so, really, what did this change? I watched as the terrified kid made his way across the parking lot toward the dining hall and I took a deep breath. I wasn't going to let an unknown future ruin my summer, just like I'd never let it ruin any summer before this one. Carpe diem, YOLO, and all that, I thought with a smirk, recalling the very words I'd told Emerson at the beginning of camp last year.

"HANK!" someone yelled. "Is that you?!" I turned to see Gary getting out of the back of a snazzy black Escalade. Last year his reddish-gold hair had been cut in a floppy sort of way that we had ended up shaving into a rather impressive Mohawk for the last week of camp. This year he'd buzzed the whole thing so close to his scalp that he looked a bit like the Mr. Clean guy. It wasn't exactly a good look.

"Gary!" I called back, and hurried over to say hi.

Gary's dad was still sitting in his car, talking on his cell phone, and he waved in a politely distracted way without actually turning to look in my direction. It was a far cry from the scene Gary had made last year upon his arrival. He'd stuck his hands to the side of his dad's brand-new Corvette and done some pretty impressive damage to the paint job when they'd finally removed him.

"Don't even ask if I learned how to run a stupid six-minute mile," Gary said.

"Hello to you too, my fine fellow!" I said, clapping him on the back and then taking a quick step away. Gary was a bit like a hedgehog or a really grumpy hamster: liable to bite you if you got too close. Unlike me, he hadn't opted to wear his Red Maple gear and instead was in an artfully distressed T-shirt that looked old but was probably super expensive, baggy cargo shorts that were so long they could have been pants on his short frame, and Jordan sneakers that probably cost more than everything in my duffel bag combined.

Gary raised an eyebrow. "What happened?"

"Inconsistently invisible," I reminded him. "I don't get to decide when and what part of me disappears. What about you?" I asked, eyeing the clear gloves covering his sticky hands.

"My mom did it," he said with a frown as he ran a

hand over the top of his head. "I got my hand stuck in my hair, and we had to buzz the whole thing."

"Huh," I said. "Did you try peanut butter? My brother Phil once got five wads of gum stuck in his hair and that worked like a charm."

"Did I try peanut butter?" Gary muttered. "Don't be dumb, and stop smiling. You don't need a visible head for me to know you're grinning like a goon right now. Knock it off." I rolled my eyes and sighed. Good old Gary hadn't changed much since last summer. He was a bit of an acquired taste, like pickle juice, sour and kind of disgusting the first time, but if you kept at it, you'd eventually like the stuff.

"Not the haircut," I said, "which I must say makes your head appear wonderfully lumpy. I meant the snazzy new hand gear that looks a lot like clear cellophane. What happened to the black elbow-length jobbers you had last summer?"

"Oh," Gary said, holding up his hands as though he'd just remembered that they belonged to him. "These are supposed to help me blend in more with normal kids, because, ya know, normal kids walk around with their hands wrapped in cellophane."

"Normal is overrated," I reminded him. Before he could respond, a bush at the far end of the parking lot suddenly went up in flames. There were a few yelps of surprise followed by a man yelling, "No worries! I got it!" This shout was followed by a burst of foam from a fire extinguisher.

"Oh good!" I said. "Anthony's here."

"I'm *not* sharing a bunk with him again this year," Gary growled as he opened the trunk of the Escalade.

"With your charming personality, I'm sure you can share a bunk with anyone you choose," I said.

"Charming," he scoffed. "Speaking of charming. Watch this." He turned back to the car and called, "Hey, Dad! Don't bother getting off the phone. Aliens have arrived and are going to escort me into camp, but you might want to get out before they shove your car down the hill into the lake!"

"Sounds good!" Gary's dad called distractedly with a wave of the hand. Gary rolled his eyes and hit the button that shut the trunk. "He wouldn't notice if aliens *did* arrive and shoved it down the hill," he said.

"I think he'd notice when he hit the lake," I said. "Phones don't like water very much." Gary snorted as I turned to scan the parking lot. "Have you seen any of the other guys yet?"

"No," Gary said. "Technically, I haven't seen you either."

"Technically, you could be the twin of my bald uncle Seymour," I replied. "Or a very large egg."

33

"Think that's Murphy?" he said, and I looked where he was pointing and saw an impressive, very official-looking black SUV with the TTBI logo emblazoned across the side—the Time Travel Bureau of Investigation—pull into the parking lot. The driver had a grim no-nonsense look, and I felt my stomach do a nervous flop as I remembered my friends ambushing me in the bathroom earlier that day. I turned back to Gary and quickly ran a hand over his head.

"What was that?" Gary said, ducking and smacking at the air above him.

"Sorry," I said, "I was just checking something. How fast would you say your hair grows? Like, do you think you'll have a whole inch by August?"

"Good to see you're still weird," Gary muttered without answering me, and before I could ask him again, a skunk came trotting across the parking lot to greet us. There were shrieks of surprise as parents and campers alike jumped behind their cars, inside their cars, or for one kid who apparently had a problem with gravity, over the car. However, those of us who'd been around the year before knew that the tiny white-striped animal sporting a rather snazzy red collar was completely harmless. He also had a thing for marshmallows.

Gary bent to pet the creature he'd called "the rat" all last summer, and I smiled at Zeke's service animal he'd

34

appropriately named Mr. Stink. I crouched down and held a hand out to Mr. Stink, but since he couldn't see me, he ignored me and snuffled his nose into Gary's pockets in search of a treat. I huffed in exasperation and narrowed my eyes at Gary's noggin. The Gary I'd seen earlier that day had had subtle differences from the Gary I was standing in front of now. He'd been tanner, for one thing, while the Gary currently running a hand down Mr. Stink's back was so pale that it was obvious that he'd spent most of the last nine months indoors. His hair had also been longer, and I realized that I could use Gary's head like my own personal clock to mark the time until my friends and I time traveled.

"Hey!" Zeke said, walking up a minute later carrying his duffel bag. I spotted his mom talking to my mom over by our car, and I waved when she looked in my direction. Of course, my wave is really just a shirt sleeve flapping, but people usually get the general idea, and I knew that my mom knew what I was doing even if Zeke's mom looked a tad confused. Zeke turned to see who I was waving at and smiled. "Sometimes I think the moms like drop-off even more than we do," he said.

"Think they ever secretly compete over who has the weirdest kid?" I pondered out loud.

"You'd win," Gary said, and I snorted. Zeke flashed a grin. His black glasses were the same as last year, so thick that they made his honey-brown eyes appear too large in his bronze face.

"Really? I figured I'd win that one," came a voice from behind us, and we whirled to see Emerson heading our way. He grinned and ran a hand through dark brown hair that was gelled and swept to the side over wide-set blue eyes that were crinkled at the corners from his huge ear-to-ear grin.

"You're not even close!" I said, throwing an arm around his vest-covered shoulders.

"You may be right there," Gary said dryly as he turned to take in the parking lot. "There seems to be a pretty impressive new crop of strange and stranger coming to camp this year."

We turned to survey the parking lot, and I had to admit that he was right. Between the kid oozing something neon orange and the kid who appeared to be covered in frogs, we looked downright tame.

"Have you spotted anyone else yet?" Emerson said.

"We think that's Anthony," Gary said, pointing to the far end of the lot, where something was still smoking.

"And that hot mess of official nonsense is probably Murphy," Zeke said, pointing to the SUV that had ignored the No Parking signs in front of the dining hall and parked there anyway. For people whose job it was to enforce the rules, the TTBI certainly didn't seem too concerned about following them.

"At least he's here," Emerson said, and we all nodded.

"I didn't think we'd be able to raise enough money to pay for his admission after somebody refused to sell his Xbox," Emerson said, and we all turned to look accusingly at Gary, who scowled back at us.

"I don't know why I had to pony up the most money," he said. "It's not fair."

"Probably because you had the most stuff?" Zeke said.

"Whatever," Gary said. "He's here, isn't he? So lay off."

"Yeah," Emerson said. "No more talking about the Murphy project. I think he feels a little weird about us helping pay for camp."

"And if anyone asks, we didn't help pay for camp," I said with a big exaggerated wink. When everyone just shot confused looks in my general direction, I sighed. "I was winking," I explained flatly. "Real big and over-exaggerated, as in *this is a secret, dumb-dumbs, so stop talking about it.* For all anyone knows, including the goons from the TTBI, Murphy was given one of the Camp Outliers scholarships since he was such an outstanding camper last year."

"Someday, you'll have to tell us how you pulled that one off," Emerson said.

"A magician never reveals his secrets," I said, and then stopped short as a car pulled into the parking lot with two girls in orange hooded sweatshirts. I elbowed Emerson hard in the ribs and jerked my head toward the car.

"Ouch," he said, rubbing the side of his weighted vest. "What was that?"

"My elbow," I said. I thought about pointing out that his weighted vest should really give him some elbow protection as well as prevent him from floating away, but there were more important things to focus on at this particular moment. "Look." Emerson seemed confused for another half second, and then he spotted Molly getting out of the car, followed closely by Kristy, and his face lost all color. For a moment he looked like the pasty-faced nervous wreck I'd met in the parking lot last summer, but then he seemed to shake himself a little bit, and the confident Emerson from the end of the summer was back.

"Think they remember us?" he said.

"Let's find out," I replied, and before he could protest, I'd grabbed his arm.

"Do my eyes deceive me," I called loudly as I hauled Emerson across the parking lot toward the girls, "or are those the marvelous Monarch ladies, looking more lovely than they did last year?"

"Let me guess," Kristy said, putting a hand on her hip. "Hank?"

"See!" I said to Emerson. "We are unforgettable!" I elbowed him again and hissed out of the side of my mouth, "Bow, man, bow!" I stepped back, and with the biggest flourish I could manage, bowed low as the girls watched with expressions of polite amusement. I knew that since I was invisible a lot of the impressiveness of the gesture was lost, but I didn't let that stop me. I'd watched a YouTube video on how to bow correctly, and I was pretty sure the queen of England would be impressed. Kristy, however, was no queen of England. She snorted and turned from me to Emerson.

"You're Emerson, right?" she said. "The kid that got the Red Wood cabin's flag, time traveled, and then barfed everywhere?"

"Now that's a legacy," I said.

"Hi," Molly said from next to Kristy, and I turned my attention to her. She was shorter than Kristy, with big brown eyes and curly hair pulled back in a ponytail. I'd had my sights set on her at the beginning of camp the summer before, but after I'd realized that Emerson did too, I'd done the gentlemanly thing and stepped back. Besides, Kristy was an intriguing challenge, and I liked intriguing challenges.

"May we escort you ladies to the dining hall for registration?" I said with another grand flourish. The girls ignored the flourish, and I remembered that all they were seeing was a red sweatshirt flapping around. I gritted my teeth in frustration. How were you supposed to make an impression when you didn't even have a shadow?

"I don't think that's possible," Kristy said.

"Why not?" I said.

"Because you will be too busy escorting your mother," said a voice from behind me, and I turned to see my mom standing there with her arms crossed and her eyebrow raised. The girls covered their mouths to stifle their laughter. The guys made no such effort, and I could hear them hooting and cackling gleefully as my mom marched me toward the dining hall. So much for making a great first impression.

CHAPTER FOUR

"**H**ank!" said a familiar voice the minute my mom hauled me into the cavernous dining hall. I turned to see Eli, my counselor from the year before, striding toward us. At least, I was almost positive it was Eli. This guy had brown curly hair, bright blue eyes, and dimples, and I saw multiple girl campers stop what they were doing to watch him. The guy then suddenly shot up four inches, his hair turned blond, and his eyes morphed into a dark brown. The only things that stayed were the dimples, and I grinned. It was Eli all right.

"Hey!" I called, and shrugged out of my mom's choke hold.

"No more spectacles," she whispered in my ear, and I mumbled something I hoped sounded like an agreement but wasn't legally binding.

Eli nodded a polite greeting to my mom before turning to me.

"Are you my counselor again this year?" I asked, but to my disappointment, he shook his head.

"Nope. I'm with the Red Maple cabin again this year. The White Oak cabin has a new counselor named Aaron." He jerked his chin to the left, and I looked over to see a tall Black guy who looked like he was in his early twenties talking to Murphy's parents and the TTBI agent who had escorted Murphy to camp. Aaron had broad shoulders, and his military-style buzz cut accentuated his high cheekbones and serious eyes. He reminded me a lot of one of the G.I. Joes I used to play with before our dog had chewed off its legs.

"He seems . . . serious?" I said, glancing over at Eli for confirmation.

"He is serious," Eli said.

"Good," my mom said approvingly. "You could use some serious in your life, Henry."

"You can drop off that packet right over there," Eli said helpfully, pointing to a long table where some of the camp workers were busy talking to parents and going through impressive amounts of paperwork.

"Thanks," my mom said, and then she turned to give me the stink eye. "No shenanigans while I'm gone." She didn't wait for my response before turning and hurrying to get in line behind two parents with a kid whose head was completely encased in an astronaut-like dome of glass.

"She's got your number," Eli said with another of his wide grins. "It's good to see you—or what there is of you."

"I've been invisible for weeks," I said. "It's getting very old very fast." Eli's eyes widened as he spotted something behind me, and I turned as a kid walked in covered in what looked like large soap bubbles, a befuddled-looking caseworker at his side.

"That's one of mine," he said. "I need to go talk to them."

"Are those bubbles coming out of his ears?" I said, a little impressed.

"Hank," Eli said, and there was something about the way he said my name that had me snapping to attention. The only other time I'd heard him sound like that was at the end of last summer after Murphy, Emerson, and Gary had managed to time travel together and the TTBI agents had been swarming all over the camp like flies.

"Yeah?" I said.

"Aaron isn't someone you mess with," Eli said, his voice dropping so that I was sure I was the only one who could hear what he was saying over the general chaos and clamor of the overcrowded dining hall.

"What do you mean?" I said.

"Just behave, okay? Follow the rules—like, all of them," Eli said quietly as Aaron turned to stare at us.

"Okay?" I said, still not quite understanding his meaning. Before he could elaborate, someone screamed, and we turned to see that a camper had slipped on the large puddle of bubbles the boy we'd seen had left all over the floor, and Eli sighed.

"Got to go," he said, and with that, he was gone, jogging over to the new camper, who was now turning a very interesting shade of neon green. I watched as Eli helped up the kid who'd fallen, my brain working overtime on what he'd just said. I felt a twist of unease as I realized that this was the third warning I'd gotten in less than twenty-four hours, and the summer hadn't even really started yet.

"Done," my mom said, rejoining me. "You don't have anything to drop at Nurse Betsy's, so I think that's it." She glanced around. "Did you see where your new counselor went?"

I nodded and pointed to where Aaron stood with Murphy.

"Good," my mom said, turning to me with a sad smile. "I guess there's nothing left for me to do then except tell you I love you."

"Love you more, Mom," I said as she pulled me into a too-tight hug. I hugged her back, committing her sugar cookie and hair spray smells to memory. I wouldn't be homesick this summer, but was it possible to be Mom-sick? She finally let go and stood back with her hands on my shoulders as she looked at the space above my disembodied sweatshirt.

"Gosh, I wish I could see your sweet face," she said. "I hate that I have to say goodbye without actually seeing you."

"Sorry," I said, but she just brushed the tears out of her eyes and shook her head.

"Don't you dare apologize," she said. "You never apologize for who God made you."

"Right," I said, and smiled. "Sorry."

She gave an exasperated laugh before her face got serious again, and she held up an accusing finger and shook it less than an inch from my nose. "And if I get another call from Mr. Blue about you being naked, you will be in for a world of hurt. Naked isn't funny."

"It's a little funny," I said.

"Henry . . . ," she said, my name both a command and a warning.

"I know, I know," I said.

"And don't do anything too crazy. A little crazy is fine; a lot of crazy isn't."

"Okay, Mom," I said.

"And nothing dangerous," she said. "I've seen that Life List of yours, mister, and I don't want to hear that you were tobogganing off the dining hall's roof."

"Mom," I said. "I'm not stupid. That only works if there's snow!"

She groaned and shut her eyes before opening them to shake her head at me. "Just, use the brain you were born with, okay? And leave those poor girl campers alone. Remember that you're a gentleman. And wash your hands a lot, and don't forget to wear deodorant, and remember poison ivy has three leaves. Or is it four?"

"Mom!" I said, glancing around. "I got it."

She sighed, gave me one more quick, tight hug, and then headed out of the dining room and back to her car.

"I was really hoping she was going to let slip an embarrassing nickname of yours," Emerson said, coming to stand next to me as his own mother hurried for the door.

"Tough luck, Boo Boo," I said with an evil grin as I reminded him of the nickname his mother had been

46

flinging around the previous summer.

"Watch it," Emerson said. "Or I'll tell everyone your nickname is Snuggle Bunny."

"You underestimate me," I said. "I could totally pull off Snuggle Bunny."

Emerson snorted.

"Are you Emerson and Hank?" said a voice behind us.

"Humble Henry and the fabulous, floating Emerson at your service," I said, turning with a flourish only to come face to face with Aaron's no-nonsense face.

"Right," said our new counselor. "The rest of the White Oak cabin is already heading up the hill. I'd get a move on because one of you is going to find yourself on KP duty for a week."

"Aw, crap," Emerson said, and then to my surprise he showed an impressive self-preservation instinct by giving my duffel bag a swift kick that sent it careening across the floor in the opposite direction. That job done, he grabbed his own duffel and took off.

I dashed after it before hurtling out the door after my friend. Maybe chucking his iron shoes in the lake last summer hadn't been one of my brightest ideas.

CHAPTER FIVE

I was the last one into the cabin. It turned out that Emerson had taken seriously my initiative to learn how to run a six-minute mile, which, considering he'd had to do it while wearing a weighted vest, was pretty impressive. My too-long hair was stuck to my head in sweaty chunks, and I shoved it back and out of my eyes as I took in the cabin that was a mirror image of the one we'd stayed in last year. The boys' cabins were all on one hill while the girls' cabins were on their own hill on the opposite side of camp. In the middle of the two were the dining hall, rec buildings, lake, and boathouse. There were technically six boy "cabins" but only three buildings. There were two cabins per building separated by a shared bathroom. Last year, we'd been on the opposite side of the building in the Red Maple cabin, but this year, we weren't Red Maple men, I reminded myself. We were White Oak men.

"Honey! I'm home!" I called, thumping my duffel bag on the floor.

"Hey!" Murphy said. "Want the bottom bunk with Emerson?" He was already spreading his sheets over a top bunk while Zeke spread his stuff out across the bottom.

"Sure!" I said, giving my duffel a well-aimed kick so it went sliding underneath the bunk in question. "Emerson?" I said, turning to where he was carefully attaching his ropes and tethers to the top bunk.

"Yeah?" he said, glancing up with a guilty expression.

"Well played," I said. "Next time, kick it harder. I like a challenge." The next ten minutes were a flurry of helloing and chattering and general chaos as we all claimed bunks and unpacked. Mr. Stink wandered around from bunk to bunk inspecting our open duffel bags for treats and accepting praise and pets wherever they were offered. There was a bit of a tense moment when Gary pitched a fit about getting stuck bunking with Anthony, but Anthony quickly demonstrated that all the bunks were flame-retardant by attempting to light a mattress on fire, and Gary calmed down.

"No TTBI officials shadowing you this year?" I said to Murphy as he carefully placed his T-shirts in the dresser next to our bunk. I believed in the scoop, dump, and shove-it-shut method of unpacking, so I'd been done for a while now, and I was spending the extra time attempting to put my hair up with a twisty tie I'd found under our bunk. I succeeded, sort of. It wasn't quite the man-bun Hollywood made look so good, but since no one could see it anyway, I couldn't care less.

"Nope," Murphy said happily. "Apparently when you aren't doomed, they aren't nearly as twitchy. They practically just dropped me and left. It was a little weird, honestly. I almost felt like any other RISK kid." I flinched at his comment, but thanks to my invisibility he was none the wiser. Despite my excitement about being back at camp and my resolution not to let my own impending doom ruin the summer, twitchy was a pretty good description of the way I felt. I looked at my happy friend and felt my heart give a painful tug. The minute I told him about his second time-traveling trip to that airport bathroom his happy-go-lucky attitude was going to disappear. So, I decided on the spot not to tell him. Not now and probably not ever. There was no way I was going to be able to keep secret the first-time traveling visit to the bathroom where he'd dragged

Gary and me along. I didn't want to get my hopes up since I knew it was the longest of long shots, but if the guys and I could unravel the mysterious warning from that first trip, maybe Murphy wouldn't have to take that second trip. It was definitely worth a try.

"No sob fest from your parents either, I bet," I said, remembering the scene they'd made last year when they'd thought that it was Murphy's last summer before death by time travel.

"Not even one tear," Murphy said proudly.

"My mom is throwing a party tonight," Gary chimed in from across the cabin. "The theme is freedom, and she's bringing in some guy to juggle knives and swallow fire."

"Hmm," I mused. "Juggling knives . . ."

"Don't even think about it," Gary said with a shudder. "Can you imagine? We wouldn't be able to see your hands, just a bunch of knives flying around."

"Thinking doesn't hurt anyone," I protested. "Besides, I already know how to juggle turtles. A knife would be a piece of cake."

"You learned how to juggle turtles?" Emerson said.

I shrugged. "I wanted to use frogs, but those suckers are slicker than snot."

Everyone paused to stare at me, and then Zeke kind of shook himself and looked over at Gary. "How'd you find out about the party?"

"The cake got delivered before I left," Gary said with a scowl.

"Don't feel too bad," Anthony said, nonchalantly stamping out the small fire he'd accidentally started on Zeke's duffel bag. "I think all our parents are secretly relieved to have us off their hands for the summer."

"Probably as relieved as we are to actually *be* off their hands," Emerson agreed. "My mom is going to a month-long yoga retreat to calm her nerves."

"Given her any panic attacks worth noting?" I said, always up for a good Emerson story. Next to Gary's rants about getting stuck to inanimate objects, they were my favorite, and really, I probably only liked Gary's stories best because he turned red and used some interesting vocabulary.

Emerson cringed. "I may have almost gone out the sunroof of the minivan the other day. I caught the rim of the car on the way out, though, so I was just flapping away on the freeway while my mom screamed bloody murder. I got grounded."

"She may need more than a month at that retreat," I said.

"What about you?" Emerson said. "What trouble have you been getting into? You haven't been making any appearances in any book clubs, have you?"

I snorted and smiled as I relived the moment that I'd gone from completely invisible and completely naked in our pantry to completely visible and completely naked clutching a bag of barbecue potato chips in front of my mother's entire book club. It was in that moment I'd realized that, no matter what the situation, bow and make the best of it. It had kind of become a motto that I lived by. I'd also done a jig that day, naked, but that was not something I felt needed to be repeated in my life ever again.

"Does naked cow tipping count as trouble if I didn't manage to actually tip the cow?" I said.

"So that's still on your Life List?" Gary said, eyebrow raised.

"Yup," I said. "Still there."

"Just to clarify," Gary said. "Do you have to be naked to tip the cows?"

"Nope. The naked part is optional. Who knows? The summer is young; maybe you can check that one off your list too!"

"Fat chance," Gary said with a snort.

"That's the name of the cow I tried to tip!" I said. "She was standing right between one named Chubby Bubby and her sister Large Lucy."

Gary stared at me blankly and then turned to Murphy. "So Murph, I'd ask you if you'd been anywhere good lately, but ya know, I don't feel like getting imprisoned for life."

"All good," Murphy said.

"Didn't want you to feel left out," Gary said. Something out of the corner of my eye brought me up short, and I elbowed Murphy in the ribs.

"Ouch," Murphy said. "Emerson wasn't lying: you do have freakishly sharp elbows."

"Who's that?" I said, and he turned to where a boy was standing in the doorway. He was tall, probably even taller than me, with dark brown hair that had been expertly highlighted and styled into twisted spikes all over his head. He was probably around our age, thirteen or so, but there was something about the way he carried himself that made him seem older somehow.

"Who are you?" Gary said loudly, and the kid turned to look at him.

"Hudson," he said. "Is this the White Oak cabin?"

"It is," Gary said. "What cabin are you looking for?"

"This one," Hudson said. "What bunk is still open?"

"Um, that one," Zeke said, pointing to the empty bunk closest to the bathroom that no one else had taken, mainly because the smells that came out when you opened the bathroom door could be pretty brutal at times.

"Thanks," Hudson said as he adjusted his duffel

bag and strode across the cabin to the empty bunk. The rest of us looked at one another, eyebrows raised. Apparently I wasn't the only one surprised to discover that we had a new cabinmate. I'd thought our original six was it.

"What do we do?" Murphy whispered as the kid dropped his duffel and bent to unpack it.

"What do you think we do?" I said. "We give him a Red Maple men welcome!"

"But," Murphy whispered, "we aren't in Red Maple anymore."

I flapped a hand at him. "Details shmetails."

"Hey!" I said, striding over to the new kid. "Welcome! You took us by surprise before. We were all in the same cabin last year, and we didn't realize we'd be getting a new cabinmate!"

"That makes two of us, then," Hudson said as he lifted the entire contents of his bag out and crammed it into the top drawer of his dresser, where it overflowed out onto the floor. He surveyed it and gave the drawer a shove. It slid halfway in before getting stuck, and he shrugged and gave his empty duffel bag a kick that sent it sliding under his bunk.

"Weren't planning to come to camp, then?" Gary said, coming over with his arms crossed over his chest to survey the kid.

"Nope," Hudson said simply, and sat down on his bunk to pull out a cell phone. He pressed a few buttons, his forehead wrinkling in frustration. "What's the Wi-Fi called here?" he said without looking up.

"Dream on," Gary said. "Capital D, capital O."

The kid nodded, still not looking up and searching for the Wi-Fi.

"I don't see it," he said. "You sure that's it?"

"Yup," Gary said. "And the password is 'sorry about your luck.' No capitals."

Finally, the kid looked up. "You're messing with me, aren't you?"

"Definitely," Gary said. "But only because I did the same thing last summer. I'll save you some time. You can carry that brick of technology all over this place, and you aren't going to find even a whiff of a signal. I have no idea how they do it, but we are about as off the grid as it gets here. No phones. No video games. No internet."

"Yeah," Anthony chimed in. "We have to write letters on paper with a pencil. When we have movie night on Fridays, they use a projector. Like an honest-to-goodness projector with film rolls and stuff."

"So there's no phones here at all?" Hudson asked.

"Depends," Zeke said, shoving his glasses farther onto his nose. "There is a phone in Mr. Blue's office and in Nurse Betsy's, but they are connected to the wall with a cord, and you can't just use one whenever you want. Right, Gary?"

"I learned that lesson the hard way," Gary said. "Landed KP duty for a week, and trust me, you don't want KP duty for a week." Hudson just stared at us like we were speaking a foreign language.

"This is Gary," I said. "We like to call him Mr. Positivity and occasionally Mr. Sunshine." Gary snorted. "I'm Hank. Inconveniently invisible, although lately it's been more like completely invisible."

Emerson stepped forward and smiled. "I'm Emerson. I float." All the other guys took that as their cue to chime in.

"Anthony. I self-combust occasionally. Don't worry, though: most of the stuff at Camp O is at least flame resistant, and I don't usually set other people on fire."

"I'm Zeke. X-ray vision impairment." Zeke pointed to the thick black glasses that took up most of his face. "My regular vision isn't so great either, but every now and then I have episodes and can only see through stuff. That's why I have Mr. Stink." Mr. Stink was currently inspecting Hudson's shoelaces, and Hudson looked up at Zeke with a confused expression.

"What kind of cat is that?"

"The kind that's a skunk," I said.

"I'm Murphy," Murphy said. "Time traveling."

Hudson looked up from Mr. Stink to stare at Murphy. "Did you say time traveling?" he said. "For real?"

"No, for fake," Gary said, rolling his eyes. He gave Hudson the once-over again from top to bottom and then raised his eyebrows in surprise. "Wait a second," he said. "I know you."

"I doubt that," Hudson said.

"No!" Gary said, snapping his fingers. "You're that YouTube kid. Handy Hudson or Hello Hudson or something, right?"

"Handsome Hudson LLC," Hudson said.

"What's the LLC mean?" Emerson said.

"It means that no one else can use that name without paying for it," Hudson said.

"You should trademark Grumpy Gary!" I said, clapping Gary on the shoulder. He gave me a stiff-armed shove without even looking in my direction, and I tripped sideways into Emerson, who lost his balance and took out Anthony. The result was a small fire that we stamped out quickly. Hudson watched all of this with a strangely blank expression on his face. His eyes kept flicking down to his phone and then back to us.

"So, phones really don't work here?" he said, and I could have sworn I heard a hint of actual panic in his voice.

"Really," I said.

"That can't happen, though," he said, clutching his phone tighter.

"It can because it did," Gary said unhelpfully.

"No," Hudson said. "I have content that needs posting. Comments I need to respond to. How will I know what's going on?"

"Content?" I said, turning to Gary. "Do you speak this language?"

"Yeah," Gary said. "He means posts and stuff. He has like a million followers or something crazy, and he posts all these videos of himself levitating stuff. Everyone loves them."

"Huh," I said. "Well, sorry about that, Hudson, but even without your phone I think you'll like it here. Gary had to do a bit of a detox last year too, didn't ya, Gare Bear?"

"Call me that again and you lose your teeth," Gary said. "I don't care if they're invisible. I'll find a way."

"I could pull off toothless," I said. "I've got spectacular gums."

"I showed up with bags of electronics last year," Emerson piped up. "I thought I'd spend the entire summer hiding out in the cabin and playing video games."

"And?" Hudson said, sounding hopeful.

"And I thought wrong," Emerson said with a shrug.

"I sold it all after camp last year."

"You guys are weird," Hudson said, glancing around. "Like weirder than I expected you to be. You mean to tell me that all summer, you don't have access to any technology?"

"None. Squat. Zero. Nada. Zilch. Zip," I said.

"Well, it looks like you guys have done the introductions for me," said a voice behind us, and we all whirled around. "I'm Aaron, and I'll be your counselor this summer," he said. He seemed even taller and more intimidating up close than when I'd spotted him at registration. Eli's words rang in my head, and I made yet another mental note to talk to the guys in private. The mental notes were really starting to stack up and make my brain feel cluttered. I resolved that a midnight meeting would have to happen tonight, despite the fact that it was our first night at camp and we had no clue what the new kid was like. The door to the cabin suddenly popped open again, and Eli's familiar, grinning face looked in.

"Hey, guys!" he called. "I need to steal Aaron for a second. It's time to figure out capture-the-flag territories!"

"Right," Aaron said with a nod before turning back to us. "You guys better get geared up. Flag hiding starts in twenty minutes." With that he dropped the bin full of capture-the-flag gear on the floor and left, leaving the cabin door open behind him.

"You heard the man," Gary said. "Time to put on camouflage gear and stomp around the woods."

"Aw, you know you love it," I said, slapping Gary on the back a tad too hard in retaliation for his shove. He stumbled forward and almost pitched headlong into the box of gear on the floor.

"Wait," Emerson said, turning back to where Hudson still sat staring gloomily at his phone. "What did Gary mean by 'levitating stuff'?"

Hudson looked up from his phone, sighed, and stood. We waited for him to do something, but first he walked over and carefully propped his phone on a ledge. He took a full minute to double-check the image reflecting in the screen and then hit the record button and stepped back. Suddenly the Hudson that had seemed vacant and bored moments earlier came to life, and he flashed a blindingly white smile at his phone and held out his arms.

"It's my first day at Camp Outlier," he said, his voice projecting so it rang out around the cabin. "And my new roomies just asked about my RISK factor. Should I show them?" He leaned forward with his hand to his ear, and I glanced over at Emerson with my eyebrow raised. Was this kid for real?

61

"You know," Gary muttered quietly, "this is much more impressive when you watch it on a tiny screen."

Hudson was ignoring us as he turned and held out his hands to the door at the far end of our cabin, which Aaron had left wide open. We all turned to follow Hudson's gaze, and the door suddenly banged shut of its own accord.

"No way!" I said. "That's awesome!" Hudson turned his focus to the bathroom door to his right, and it flew open, revealing an unfortunate kid sitting on one of the pea-green toilets in the center of the room.

"Sorry!" Hudson called, and he quickly slammed the door shut again. I turned back to Hudson and grinned.

"What else ya got?" I said.

Hudson's lips curled up into a half smile, and he gave his phone a big overexaggerated wink before glancing to his left. A heartbeat later the shutters outside our cabin suddenly slammed shut over the floor-to-ceiling mesh screens that acted like our windows and then banged open again. On a roll now, Hudson continued showing off. Duffel bags shot out from under bunks before zooming across the floor to slide under different bunks; clothes came flying out of dressers before slam-dunking themselves back into the dresser. Mr. Stink even found himself on top of a levitating sleeping bag before Zeke snatched him from the air with a disapproving scowl. I was thoroughly enjoying the show when suddenly things took a turn. The lights flickered once, and then the light bulbs all exploded with ear-splitting pops. I threw my hands over my head as glass rained down around us.

"You can stop now," Emerson said as he jumped into one of the bottom bunks to avoid the glass. But one look at Hudson's face and I was pretty sure that he couldn't stop.

"Uh-oh," I said as the bunk beds suddenly started to shake. I grabbed Emerson and yanked him out right before the bunk he was sitting on toppled over, scattering sheets and bedding across the floor. A second later the dressers followed suit, upending themselves as drawers clattered out. Absolute chaos ensued as everyone tried to duck and cover.

The door to the cabin burst back open, and Aaron came running in, Eli and another counselor hot on his heels. They didn't pause to take in the situation; they just bolted right for Hudson, who sat with his hands gripping the sides of his head as though he was worried that his brain was trying to escape through his ears. Anthony's foot caught on fire and ignited a pile of someone's clothes, and smoke started to fill the small cabin quickly. The buckles on Emerson's weighted vest

63

exploded or shattered or something because suddenly it was slipping off his shoulders as he started floating toward the ceiling. For the second time in my life, I made a flying leap and landed on my best friend before he could float away. Gary's gloves went flying off his hands just as Murphy suddenly doubled over and disappeared, and for the first time since I'd been at Camp O, I was terrified.

CHAPTER SIX

"**I** can't believe we don't get to hide our flag," Zeke said glumly as he used the broom in his hands to sweep up the shattered glass that liberally coated the floor of our cabin.

"I can't believe I almost floated away on our first day," Emerson said, shaking his head. "Again!"

"I can't believe Murphy still isn't back yet," Anthony said as he hefted a fallen dresser up off the floor.

"Will everyone stop with the *I can't believe* stuff? It makes me want to smack you, and I can't really do that at the moment. Which makes me even madder," Gary said grouchily from where he sat on the floor nursing his bandaged hands. He'd managed to get stuck to a dresser drawer and a bunk bed leg during the chaos, and Nurse Betsy had needed to use the corrosive acid to remove them from his sticky palms. A process that had really creeped me out the first time I'd seen it last year. Still, I was pretty sure he could help clean up if he'd really wanted to, but I wasn't going to be the one who suggested it. Hudson, the kid who had caused all the issues, was nowhere to be seen. I'm not sure what Aaron and the other counselors had done after they came charging in—I'd been too busy saving Emerson's life—but whatever they did had knocked Hudson out cold. Nurse Betsy had shown up and levitated him right off the floor and out the door without even looking at the rest of us.

"It's my fault," I said. "I asked him what else he had."

"In your defense, you probably didn't think that he had a tornado," Zeke pointed out. "Mr. Stink is still shaking!"

"It's my fault too," Emerson said. "I asked him about his RISK factor."

"What would you call that RISK factor?" Zeke asked.

"Chaos," Gary said. "I hope they send him home."

"No way," I said. "They probably sent him here because he was too dangerous to be home. Let's cut him some slack, guys. It's not like he meant to almost kill half of us."

"Right," Anthony said. "I didn't mean to light Zeke's clothes on fire either." He grimaced. "Sorry about that."

"It's fine," Zeke said. "You didn't torch my sweatshirt, and my mom can ship me some more socks and underwear." He turned and quickly shooed Mr. Stink away from the circle of red rocks that Aaron had set up in the spot where Murphy had disappeared. I felt a tug of worry for my friend, even though he wasn't the doomed time traveler he'd been last summer. This summer I was the one who was doomed, I reminded myself.

"Think he's okay?" Emerson said, coming to stand beside me. I glanced over at his nervous expression and forced a smile that he couldn't see.

"He'll be back, but man, old habits die hard, don't they?" I said. As though I'd summoned him, there was a loud pop and Murphy reappeared. He gave himself a shake and looked around at the wreckage of our cabin.

"Betcha never time traveled and been more nervous about what you were coming back to than where you went," I said, leaning on my broom.

"Where did you go?" Gary said.

"He can't tell you that," said a voice behind us, and we all whirled to see Aaron walking in, a hand on the shoulder of a very solemn-looking Hudson.

"Right," Gary mumbled. "I knew that."

Aaron glanced around the cabin and then looked down at his watch. "Dinner starts in fifteen," he said. "And if this place isn't spotless, you won't be going to dinner, so I suggest you hustle. I'll do an inspection when I get back from filing some paperwork." And with that he turned and left again.

"Thanks for the help," Gary muttered.

"*You* aren't even helping," Zeke pointed out.

"Why should I help?" Gary said. "The new kid made this mess. He should have to clean it up."

"Hey now!" I said, glancing around at my friends, each looking more dejected than the last. "We're at Camp O, remember? The place we've been looking forward to being all school year!"

"You guys seriously looked forward to coming here?" Hudson said, and we all turned to look at our new cabinmate a bit warily.

"Yeah," Emerson said. "It's kind of hard to explain." He turned to me with a questioning look.

"It's not hard to explain at all," I said, turning to Hudson. "You do know there are girls at this camp, right?"

"Girls we won't get to see if we miss dinner," Anthony pointed out.

"Good point," I said, looking around at our wrecked cabin. There was no way we would be able to get this mess cleaned up in fifteen minutes.

"Sorry," Hudson said quietly.

"No apologies necessary," I said. "Anthony doesn't apologize when he lights something on fire. Murphy doesn't apologize when he time travels, Gary definitely doesn't apologize when he gets stuck to stuff, and if I apologized for my invisibility, I'd never get to talk about anything else. My mom says that we should never apologize for who God made us to be, and my mom is a brilliant woman."

"Apology or no apology, I'd really hate to miss dinner," Anthony said.

"And I really don't want to get stuck with KP duty on the first night," Gary said.

"Really?" I said. "What if I told you that I had a plan to make our first KP duty memorable?"

"Then I'd tell you to dream on," Gary said.

I turned to Emerson and gave a big exaggerated wink. "What?" he said, and I sighed, remembering yet again that he couldn't see my face. I hadn't realized how much I relied on things like the overexaggerated wink or the raised eyebrow to get my point across. I just shook my head. The plan I'd been cooking up all year wouldn't work if we didn't make it to dinner, and at this rate, we wouldn't get to eat all summer.

"Here," Hudson said. "I can help."

The remaining two dressers suddenly righted themselves, their dislodged drawers sliding across the floor before levitating to slide into place. A bunk bed followed suit, as did a large pile of clothes. Everyone watched warily as an upended trash can did a backflip before landing in its original spot. The whole process took less than a minute, and we found ourselves standing in a cabin that, while still wrecked, was definitely much better.

"Now this we can handle," I said approvingly as I surveyed the remaining mess. Hudson shrugged and picked up the phone that he'd strategically placed to capture the cleanup. He stared down at it, swiping this and tapping that.

"What are you doing?" I said. "I thought you didn't have a signal."

"I don't," Hudson said, not bothering to look up. "But that doesn't mean the camera stopped working. I'll just have to film a ton of content and post it after this summer is over."

"Exploding an entire cabin should make excellent content," Gary said sarcastically while putting the word content in air quotes with his bandaged hands.

"Yeah," Hudson said absentmindedly, still not bothering to look at us.

"So, your content is you wrecking stuff?" I said.

"No," Hudson said, finally pocketing the phone. "It's me moving stuff. I can edit that video down so it looks like it all went according to plan. No big deal."

"Huh," I said, not sure what I thought about that. I was going to say more when I spotted the time on the broken clock on the wall.

"Shoot! It's already almost dinnertime. We need to move it, men, and unfortunately that means no time for showers," I said as I ruefully ran my hand over my head and remembered that I'd pulled the front chunk of my hair back with a twist tie. It was a sweaty mess, and I was sure that my face was covered in the same dirt and dust I saw on everyone else's faces. Apparently, you couldn't survive a human hurricane and not look a bit battered on the other side. Under normal circumstances I wouldn't have been caught dead going to the first dinner of the year looking like this, but I reminded myself that no one could actually see the mess, so it was probably okay. Besides, we didn't have a whole lot of options at this point. I gave myself a quick sniff and really wished there was time for that shower. I debated saving my big plan until the next night, but I knew it just wouldn't be the same. I quickly snagged my deodorant off a pile of clothes on the floor and swiped some on. Emerson watched this process with his eyebrows furrowed.

"What?" I said. "It's not like you haven't seen an invisible guy put on deodorant before."

"Yeah," Emerson said slowly. "But that's *my* deodorant." I glanced down and realized he was right. I gave it a sniff—not bad if you liked smelling like a Christmas tree.

"Sorry," I said, and tossed it to him. He attempted to catch it, missed, and the deodorant went sailing right into the back of Gary's head.

"What was that for?" Gary barked.

"It was a not-so-subtle hint," I said. "I didn't pack my *I'm with Stinky* shirt this year."

"There's a kid in the Red Wood cabin this year that smells exactly like rotten tomatoes," Zeke chimed in. "I saw his dad wearing that same exact shirt today at drop-off like it was their own personal joke."

Gary grumbled something, but he swiped some deodorant on too before tossing it to Zeke.

"It's fine," I said, flapping a hand dismissively. "Deodorant's like soap. It's self-cleaning."

"Also, flammable," Murphy chimed in as Anthony's hand caught fire and the deodorant melted into a puddle of plastic and toxic green goo on the floor.

"Awesome," Emerson said dryly. "My mom was right. I should have packed a backup."

"You can borrow mine," I said. "You'll smell fantastic."

"At least something will smell fantastic," Gary said as he flapped his hand in front of his face. I wrinkled my nose: he was right. The entire cabin now smelled like burnt plastic and Christmas trees. I glanced around at my friends' disgruntled faces and felt a flash of disappointment. This was *not* how I'd pictured our first day back at camp. We needed to rally. We needed to get a second wind. We needed to juggle! I grabbed someone's abandoned sneaker, a hairbrush, Hudson's phone, a flashlight, and just to keep things interesting, an open soda can and tossed them into the air.

"Hey, guys," I said, and everyone turned to look at me. "I hope you all learned how to juggle." There were various grunts of acknowledgment, and I deftly caught the flying objects one by one, managing to slosh only a little soda over Gary's shoes. I off-loaded my assortment of random junk into Emerson's unsuspecting arms and crouched to look under my bunk, where I'd shoved my bag of supplies. It wasn't there. However, someone's underwear was, and I chucked it onto the pile of clothes no one had claimed and continued my hunt on all fours for my missing duffel.

"Um," Hudson said. "What exactly is he doing?"

"That is a question you are going to be asking all summer," Anthony said.

"Found it!" I said, grabbing the bag that had somehow wedged itself underneath a dresser. I tugged open the zipper to reveal sparkly red vests with matching bow ties, top hats, and pants. I grinned, thankful that Dad had not only been in a barbershop quartet in college but that he'd saved all the costumes from his Christmas extravaganza performance. "Suit up, men," I said as I tossed Emerson one of the outfits. "Operation Make a Splash has begun."

CHAPTER SEVEN

Hudson went along with it, which was kind of shocking since he'd just met us. Apparently almost killing us all had made him feel like he owed us—either that or he thought it would be worth filming for his YouTube channel. All I knew was that I'd managed to harangue everyone into costumes and out the door in less than two minutes, which had to be some kind of record. We looked good, if I did say so myself. Even Gary looked sort of dashing in his vest and bow tie, although he probably could have used a bigger size. To his credit, he hadn't killed me when I'd crammed the thing over his head.

"Maybe we should have waited for Aaron to come

back?" Zeke said with a nervous glance up the hill toward our cabin. We'd cleaned things up, but they were far from spotless, and rather than risk Aaron telling us we had to miss dinner, we'd instead opted to head to dinner without Aaron.

"He'll catch up," I said. "Now, listen. When we get to the dining hall, we wait outside until everyone else is in. If we don't get KP duty, this doesn't work."

"I already hate this plan," Gary said as he ran a finger under his too-tight bow tie. "Although maybe I just hate you," he muttered. "It's really a toss-up at this point."

"Just trust me," I said. "First impressions matter, and we are going to make an epic first impression."

"What are we juggling?" Anthony said nervously. "Nothing flammable, I hope?"

"Nothing flammable," I promised while quickly rearranging my plan to accommodate my easily ignited friend. We were almost to the dining hall now and were starting to get noticed. Some of the older guys who remembered our memorable initiation in prom dresses the previous summer called out to us, and I waved back, wishing again that I was more than just a floating vest and tie.

"Everyone is staring at us," Emerson hissed, and I grinned.

"That's the point," I said. "Own it, man." To his

credit, Emerson tried. He'd opted to wear the sparkly vest on the outside of his weighted vest instead of underneath, and the effect was interesting. Still, he threw his shoulders back and lifted his head.

"Well done," I said approvingly just as Murphy sidled up to walk beside us.

"So, what do we think about the new kid?" he whispered with a quick glance to his left, where Hudson was walking in a hunched-over position, his phone out in front of him. We watched him navigate his way around three rocks and a log without even glancing up, and I had to admit I was a bit impressed.

"He's a zombie," Gary said from my other side.

"Huh?" I said, glancing back at Hudson. "He looks alive to me."

"Not like a *zombie* zombie, you loon," Gary said, rolling his eyes. "He's a tech junkie. He's hooked. Addicted. Zoned in. Whatever you want to call it. He's got tons of followers on his YouTube channel, and he's super cool and charming or whatever, but he doesn't seem the same in real life."

"All actors are short in person," I said.

"Huh?" Emerson said.

"It's something I heard once," I said. "That actors are all short, but in the movies or whatever, they don't ever seem short."

"Do you have a point?" Gary said. "Or do you just like the sound of your own voice?"

"My point is that we need to give the new kid some grace," I said, "and keep your voice down. He's right over there."

"You could light a rocket off in his back pocket, and he probably wouldn't even twitch," Gary said. "Now, take that phone away, and you'd see some fireworks. I bet he doesn't even realize he's wearing a sparkly vest right now." Gary glanced back over at Hudson and jammed his hands in his pockets. "I wonder if his parents handed him a phone to shut him up too," he said. Just then the dining hall came into view, and I held out a hand to slow the rest of the group down a bit. Gary grabbed the back of Hudson's vest to stop him, and he looked up in surprise and did a quick double take at the vests. Maybe Gary was right and Hudson hadn't been fully aware of what was happening.

"What exactly is the plan?" Emerson said as he adjusted his weighted vest for a third time.

"You think he actually has a plan," Zeke said. "That's cute."

"So . . . ," Hudson said slowly as he glanced at the boys from the other cabins making their way down the hill in shorts and T-shirts, "is this something you guys do every year?"

"No," Gary said, "sparkly vests are a first."

"I actually do have a plan," I said, and then paused. "Maybe it's less a plan than a general idea of how I'd like this to play out."

"The day couldn't really get much worse," Hudson said as he looked down and went back to tapping at his phone.

Emerson winced. "You really shouldn't say things like that."

We purposefully trailed behind the other cabins, lingering by the stairs that led down to the lake as Eli came racing down the hill with his new ragtag band of Red Maple recruits. The kids around him all looked bug-eyed and worried, and I wondered what the Red Wood cabin had planned for them tonight. They sped past us, and I noted that one of the kids seemed to be glowing. That was new. The pause gave me some time to fill the guys in on my plan. Thankfully, they were well versed in their Disney songs, and everyone but Hudson had perfected how to juggle, per my instructions at the end of last year. At first they all seemed a bit skeptical, but I assured them that epic entrances were a thing, and we needed to make one this summer. Finally, the rest of the campers were inside, and we headed for the dining-room door. We were almost there when I caught sight of the girls from the Monarch cabin striding down the girls' hill.

We stopped as they approached. Kristy was in the lead, per usual, and it took me a second to realize that they were all wearing bright yellow T-shirts instead of the orange I'd expected. Of course, I realized. If we weren't in Red Maple, then they weren't in Monarch. I did a quick mental shuffle and remembered that the thirteen-year-old girls' cabin was Swallowtail. This was going to take some getting used to.

"Ladies," I said, dropping my lowest and grandest of bows.

"Please tell me you didn't miss hiding the flag because you were practicing to be in a boy band," Kristy said, eyeing our outfits.

"No," I said, standing up. "We missed hiding our flag because our cabin experienced a very small but very mighty hurricane." I saw Hudson twitch beside me as he glanced up from his phone. He didn't need to worry. I was the last person who'd ever call someone else out on their RISK factor.

"Who's the new kid?" Kristy said with a jerk of her chin at Hudson. She stared at him for a second, and then her eyes went wide and she squealed. "Handsome Hudson?" she said. "No way!" It took the rest of the girls a second, but soon they were all in a flutter, smiling, giggling, and asking rapid-fire questions of our newest cabinmate. Hudson just smiled, obviously enjoying his celebrity status.

Kristy kind of shook herself after a minute and flapped her hand at the rest of the girls to quiet them down. "Hurricane or no hurricane, you guys should have been out there to help hide the flag."

"Wait a second," I said as I noted the irritation in Kristy's voice for the first time. "What do you care if we missed hiding our flag? We won't face off against you guys until the final week of camp."

Kristy huffed impatiently into her thick bangs and crossed her arms. "You don't know yet?" she said.

"I know you are even more beautiful this summer than last summer," I said, hoping that by laying on the charm extra thick I could make up for my utter lack of a visible body.

"Oh barf," Gary muttered, but I ignored him.

"So, you have no flying clue about the new challenge format?" Molly said, and I glanced over at the rest of the guys, who were looking just as baffled as I felt.

"Enlighten us," I said.

Molly opened her mouth to do just that, but the dinner bell rang at the exact moment that a group of girls in bright blue T-shirts came sprinting down the hill.

"Move!" Kristy bellowed, and the Swallowtail girls

practically ran us over in order to get through the door before the approaching cabin.

"What was that about?" Zeke said.

"I have a feeling we'll find out soon enough," Emerson said, turning to me. "Now, before we go in there, how sure are you that this is a good idea?" He gestured to the vest, and I quickly stepped forward to adjust his crooked bow tie.

"Positive," I said, although that may have been a bit of an exaggeration. "Does everyone remember their table assignment?" Everyone nodded. It was showtime.

It didn't take much to make magic happen, but it helped if you had an in with the guy who worked the sound system. It also really helped to have the foresight to burn the song you need onto a good old-fashioned CD before you reached the Wi-Fi wasteland that was Camp Outlier.

The rest of the cabins had barely sat down when Disney's "Be Our Guest" came blaring over the loud-speakers. All eyes turned to us. I flashed my widest grin that no one could see and together we all bowed. Then, as though we'd practiced it a thousand times, we moved over to the long countertop where each of the cabins had a tray with a pitcher of water and glasses waiting for the unlucky cabin assigned KP duty to deliver them to the tables. Each of us grabbed six glasses and tossed them skyward. There was a moment when all the glasses shimmered, suspended in the air, and I wondered if this was going to go horribly, horribly wrong, but then every single guy caught their glasses and started juggling. I hooted in triumph, and with one eye on my glasses and the other on the guys, I made my way over to the table with the girls in the blue T-shirts and stood there belting out the lines, "Try the gray stuff, it's delicious! Don't believe me? Ask the dishes!" And on the word *dishes* each of us caught the glasses one at a time and distributed them to our designated table. This was met with a smattering of applause, and I whirled to go back for the water pitcher per part two of my loosely formulated plan, but Hudson was already spinning all the water pitchers around and around in complicated loops and arcs above his head. I was so surprised that I stopped dead in my tracks and watched as he expertly sent pitcher after pitcher cartwheeling through the air before landing it smoothly on one of the tables. There was a moment of stunned silence while Lumiere the candlestick sang about how sad it was to be a servant who wasn't serving, and then every table was on their feet and clapping. Hudson gave a crooked grin and shoved his hair back. A dimple I hadn't noticed before popped out on his cheek, and I heard a collective sigh as the entire girls' table next to me fell instantly in love.

The sound system suddenly screeched to a halt, and our grand entrance was over. Mr. Blue, the head of the camp, gave us a look that made it clear that, while he was amused, he was also very much done with our shenanigans. We quickly made our way to our assigned table and slid in. We'd barely sat down when a very disgruntled-looking Aaron came busting through the dining-room door, his eyes scanning the room for us. His expression made it abundantly clear that we were in big trouble for leaving the cabin wrecked. However, his expression changed from anger to one of confusion when he saw what we were wearing. Mr. Blue adjusted his microphone and the sound system squealed like an angry pig as Aaron made his way over to our table and sat down.

After a few more squawks from the sound system Mr. Blue finally got his microphone working and Aaron had to swallow whatever he was about to say. Everyone turned their eyes to the front of the dining hall, where a small wooden platform had been set up like a stage. Mr. Blue seemed even bigger and bluer than last year, and I grinned at the man who'd handed me a tooth-brush and made me scrub down a bathroom the year before. The fact that he was still one of my favorite people despite that particular misadventure said a lot.

"Welcome back to Camp Outlier!" Mr. Blue boomed jovially. "I'd like to thank the White Oak cabin for that, let's say, ambitious beginning to camp. I didn't realize that I needed a rule about not juggling the tableware, but for future reference, gentlemen, don't juggle the tableware." Everyone chuckled and glanced over at us. I waved back like a Texas beauty queen on a Fourth of July float. I was feeling pretty good about all the looks we were getting from the girls' cabins before I realized that they weren't looking at me. They were looking right through me at Hudson, who was flashing that dumb dimple again. I huffed, and the twist tie that had been holding my mop of too-long hair back broke so it flopped across my forehead. I let my hands fall onto the tabletop, and I felt my left one land on the plate of garlic bread. I glanced down, thinking that I wouldn't mind another piece, but the plate wasn't on the table anymore. Weird, I thought. I could have sworn it had been right under my hand.

Shoving thoughts about garlic bread aside, I settled back to listen to Mr. Blue's customary *Welcome to Camp Outlier, where everyone is weird so therefore no one is weird* speech that I was pretty sure he gave at the beginning of every summer. I half listened, not because it wasn't a great speech—it was—but because I was pouting. I could feel the puckered *just sucked on a lemon* look on my face and the metaphorical rain cloud that was sitting over my head, but I wasn't sure exactly why. At first I'd thought the feeling was from this morning's encounters with time travelers, but that had settled into a nervous throb in my gut. This was different, and it didn't make sense. I mean, I was in my happy place. I was with my people. I was exactly where I wanted to be, doing exactly what I wanted to do, but I still felt disgruntled and grumpy. What in the world was my problem?

"You know something?" Gary said, leaning over. I could tell he was trying to whisper in my ear, but since he was about three inches off the mark, he whispered directly into my nose.

"I know a lot of somethings," I said. "What particular something were you wondering about?"

Gary snorted. "I was just thinking that for a kid who spends a lot of his time being invisible, you sure hate not being seen." He sat back, and I debated wiping the smug look off his face with my plate full of spaghetti but decided against it. For one thing, I was hungry. For another, he was absolutely right.

CHAPTER EIGHT

'm not one to pout. My brother Charlie was the pouter in the family, so I made an effort to shake off the mood that had hit me like a ton of bricks. Nothing was going to ruin camp for me, and that included a new camper who had successfully stolen my thunder via pitcher floating. It rankled me that a skill I'd spent hours practicing and perfecting he could do without even trying especially hard. I sat up a bit straighter and tuned back in to Mr. Blue's speech, remembering how he'd almost brought me to tears last year.

"So, this year," Mr. Blue said, "I'd like to end my speech by quoting a poem called 'The Road Not Taken' by Robert Frost."

"Seriously? A poem?" Gary muttered, and I gave him a quick jab in the ribs with my elbow.

"Shhh," I said. "I want to hear this."

"'Two roads diverged in a yellow wood,'" Mr. Blue began, and I sat back and listened as he described a traveler finding two paths in the woods. One was well worn from other travelers, but the other, to quote the poet, "wanted wear." The traveler stood there a long time, knowing that he could take only one of the paths.

"'I shall be telling this with a sigh,'" Mr. Blue said, his voice low as he made eye contact with camper after camper.

> "'Somewhere ages and ages hence:
> Two roads diverged in a wood, and I—
> I took the one less traveled by,
> And that has made all the difference.'"

There was a smattering of applause when he finished, but it was just polite applause without any real feeling behind it.

"Did you understand that?" Emerson whispered in my ear.

"I think so," I said. "And I think I like it."

"That might not mean much to you now," Mr. Blue said with a wide smile, "but words like Mr. Frost's have a way of weaving themselves into your soul after a while. The life of a RISK kid is certainly the road less traveled, but I think this poem can mean more than that for a lot of you. This camp," he said, holding his arms out, "is my road less traveled. My mother wanted me to be an accountant."

A few people chuckled, and there was a short burst of applause.

"Can you imagine him as an accountant?" Emerson whispered, and I shook my head.

"So, this summer, I challenge you to take the road less traveled," Mr. Blue said. "May it make all the difference!" Everyone clapped, and I put two fingers in my mouth and let out an ear-piercing whistle that got us a few more looks.

"Ouch," Gary said. "You just blew out my eardrums." I ignored him and whistled again. Mr. Blue nodded and smiled happily, motioning for everyone to quiet down. When we finally did, he stood up a bit straighter and forced a smile.

"Now, before we discuss the exciting changes to the camp competition this year, I would like to introduce you all to a special visitor who will be with us this summer." He turned to his left and motioned for someone to join him onstage. "Ladies and gentlemen, please welcome Mr. Marvin Munkhouser. He will be helping with the supervision of camp this year." A small mousy-looking man took the stage next to Mr. Blue, and the difference between the two was almost comical. For one thing, Mr. Blue stood a good foot taller and foot wider than Mr. Munkhouser. For another, while Mr. Blue wore a pair of ragged khaki cargo shorts and a white Camp Outlier T-shirt, Mr. Munkhouser was wearing a very proper brown suit and tie with shiny brown shoes. He was also sweating, probably unaware that, while Camp Outlier was many things, it was not air-conditioned. He took the microphone out of Mr. Blue's hand and cleared his throat. Everyone quieted down and stared at the newcomer expectantly.

"Now, that guy could have been an accountant," Emerson whispered in my ear, and I nodded.

"Hello," he said. "I'm Mr. Munkhouser, and I'm in charge of the summer regulations department of the RISK branch of the United States." He paused, as though this revelation should merit a reaction of some sort. When everyone just continued to stare at him, he cleared his throat again and ran a finger under his sweat-drenched collar. "As you know," he went on, "Camp Outlier is the first of its kind. As the only camp specifically designed to accommodate RISK children such as yourselves, it was given a special provincial license to act as a monitoring apparatus for the summer months." Again he paused and waited, but the only thing that happened was a low nervous mutter as a few people whispered to their neighbors. "I am here to observe how well Camp Outlier is functioning in that role," Mr. Munkhouser said. "So just consider me another camper here at Camp Outlier. Does anyone have any questions?"

To my surprise, Zeke's hand shot into the air.

"Yes, young man with the cat," Mr. Munkhouser said, pulling a pair of small gold-rimmed glasses from his front pocket and perching them on the end of his long thin nose.

"Mr. Stink is a skunk, not a cat," Zeke said, "and I was just wondering what *your* RISK factor was?"

"Pardon?" Mr. Munkhouser said.

"To be a camper or a counselor here, you need to have a RISK factor," Zeke said. "So what's yours?"

"Oh," Mr. Munkhouser said, obviously taken aback. "Well now, no. I don't have one. I'm just part of the governmental branch in charge of regulating RISK kids such as yourself."

"Then you're not just another camper," Gary called out. "So you probably shouldn't pretend to be one."

"That's enough, Gary," Mr. Blue said as he took the microphone back out of Mr. Munkhouser's hand. "Mr. Munkhouser is an honored guest here at Camp O, and he should be treated accordingly. Is that understood?" There was a general muttering of agreement. "All right, now that those instructions are out of the way, let's return our focus to the camp challenge!"

These words were met with cheers and applause. Mr. Blue turned his back to us to face the large wall-to-wall corkboard that usually held the capture-the-flag statistics, but this year, the board was different. I leaned forward to get a better look. Across the top of the board were the pictures of leaves that represented the boys' cabins and the butterflies that represented the girls'. Last year the girls had been on the left and the boys had been on the right, but this year every leaf picture was paired up with a butterfly picture.

"Wait a minute," I said, grabbing Anthony by the shoulder and giving him an excited shake. "Are we teamed up with the girl cabins this year?! Ouch!" I said as the shoulder I'd been shaking sparked.

"Sorry," Anthony said.

"It's fine," I said, and I stuck my stinging hand directly in our pitcher of water.

"Everything okay there, Anthony?" Mr. Blue called, and I realized that half the cabins had turned to watch us.

"We're good!" I called.

"As I was saying," Mr. Blue said. "We decided to

change things up this year from our traditional capture-the-flag format. This year the girls' and boys' cabins will be partnering up to compete against one another. You should have already met with your new teammates to hide your flag, but in case you were, um, detained," he said with a meaningful glance in our direction, "then please make sure you touch base with them before lights-out tonight. Capture the flag will be just one part of the competition, though," he said, turning back to the board. "Each team will be working all summer to collect points. The two teams with the most points at the end is the winner." Everyone broke into applause again, and I yanked my hand out of the pitcher to whistle again.

Unfortunately, that move knocked the pitcher over, spilling ice water over the entire table. Everyone jumped to their feet, grabbing for napkins, but Hudson stayed seated. A moment later I found out why. The pool of water that was flooding across the table suddenly reversed, and I watched in amazement as the water flew back toward the pitcher. The rest of the guys had frozen mid-napkin-clutch too as a moment later the upturned pitcher righted itself and the water sloshed back inside.

"That was like watching real life hit the rewind button," Zeke said. "Cool." A few of the other cabins had noticed too, and they let out appreciative whistles. Hudson just shrugged nonchalantly, like putting water back in a pitcher was no big deal. If I hadn't seen him lose control in our cabin, I'd have wondered why he was even at camp. As a general rule RISK kids had very little control over things. I stared gloomily down at where my hands should be and wished I had a bit more control over my issue. I'd gone completely invisible before, but it had never been for this long. What if I never reappeared? Maybe that's what the second Murphy in the bathroom had been trying to tell me. Maybe it wasn't that I die; maybe I was going to just disappear forever? Would I be able to live my life completely invisible? Would I be able to go on a date when a girl couldn't even see what I looked like? I shoved the idea aside and refocused on Mr. Blue.

"There are two different types of challenges. Some of them will be whole-camp challenges. These are generally worth more points and will happen every Friday. There will also be smaller challenges worth less points available throughout the week, so keep an eye on the challenge board as these options can change daily," Mr. Blue said, pointing to the bulletin board closer to the door. I squinted at the pieces of paper pinned there, but they were too far away to see what they actually said. I'd check out the board after I properly introduced myself to our new teammates, the Swallow-tails, although I knew most of them from last year.

Kristy, the tall blond with the high ponytail, was their unofficial leader and she was hot, both figuratively and literally. Her skin ran at a toasty one hundred and fifty degrees. It was enough to blister your lips if you kissed her but not incinerate them, something I'd discovered last year when she'd given me a fleeting kiss before leaving camp. I'd felt my heartbeat throb in my blistered face for a week afterward, but it had been worth it. It had been my first kiss, although I'd never tell the other guys that.

Molly had chestnut-colored curls and a thick smattering of freckles over a turned-up nose. She turned into a cocker spaniel when flustered or excited, which was pretty cool if you asked me.

Gabby was short with long brown hair she wore in two thick braids and looked normal, unless you tried to pick her up, at which point you'd discover that she weighed about as much as your friendly neighborhood sumo wrestler. It was like her tiny body was made of lead instead of flesh and bone. She was sitting in one of the heavily reinforced, specialized chairs the camp had provided for her since she'd been known to smash the regular variety into splintered pancakes on more than one occasion. I always found it a tad hilarious since she was so petite it looked like you should be able to carry her around in your pocket.

There was another girl with gingerbread-colored skin, who I think did something with electricity, if the tiny lightning bolts crackling around her thick black ringlets were any indication. There were two other girls I didn't recognize from last year, and their RISK factors weren't ones you could guess just by looking at them. One of them had stick-straight black hair she wore under a baseball hat and wide-set, almond-shaped eyes that seemed a tad unfocused. The other was a tall redheaded girl with braces who seemed a bit twitchy. I hoped that whatever they did was something useful because I was going to be in this to win.

"But remember," Mr. Blue said. "You can also lose points for bad behavior. Your counselors as well as any of the camp staff are allowed to deduct points from your team's overall score, so remember to follow camp rules. Camp Outlier isn't just a camp," he said with another meaningful look at our table, "it's also a government-approved facility charged with keeping you safe. We can't do that if you go around breaking rules and, I don't know, lighting lakes on fire."

"Message received," I called as the other cabins chuckled.

"Everyone is starting at zero, unless any cabins have already lost points?" Mr. Blue said with a questioning glance at the counselors. Aaron stood up.

"No," Emerson said. "He wouldn't."

"He is," Gary said, crossing his arms as Aaron made his way up to the platform and marched over to the picture of our White Oak leaf and the girls' yellow Swallowtail butterfly. Mr. Blue handed him a marker, and Aaron erased our big black zero and wrote in a minus symbol followed by a five.

"Negative five?" I yelped. The Swallowtail girls were looking at us again, but this time they weren't even a little bit amused.

"Geez," Anthony said as we returned their stares with guilty ones of our own.

"Thank goodness none of them shoots lasers out of their eyes or something or we'd be dead meat," Zeke observed.

"Way to go, Handsome Hudson," Gary said with a glare at our new cabinmate.

"That's not fair," Anthony said as Aaron sat back down. "We didn't know anything about points!"

"Life's not fair, boys," Aaron said. "It's about time you learned that little lesson."

"We're RISK kids," Gary muttered under his breath.

"I think that's a lesson we're all fairly familiar with." I glanced over at Aaron, who had turned his back to us to watch Mr. Blue wrap up his speech. Gary was right, but I had a bad feeling that Aaron was going to teach it to us anyway.

CHAPTER NINE

I lay in my bed after lights-out rehashing the day in my head. I replayed the weird interaction with the time travelers in the airport bathroom, Hudson's introduction to our cabin, the new rules of the summer challenge, Aaron taking our points away, and our glitter-vested performance. I grimaced as I remembered the way the girls had all stared at Hudson after he stole the show by sending those water pitchers pirouetting through the air.

For a kid who disappeared a lot, I sure hated not being seen, I thought, repeating Gary's painfully accurate observation from earlier. I didn't like that particular observation about myself. I wanted to believe that I didn't like it because Gary had said it. He was born with the rare gift of rubbing everyone the wrong way, but I knew that wasn't it. I actually enjoyed Gary's crusty, curmudgeonly outlook on life. It was funny most of the time. No, I knew the real reason I didn't like it was because it was true. I'd always loved being the center of attention, and my invisibility had never gotten in the way of that before. In fact, sometimes that helped me claim the spotlight.

I'd never been scared of my RISK factor like Emerson or resented it like Gary. I'd never tried to hide it because, well, you couldn't exactly hide the fact that you were missing a right leg or a large chunk of your head, now could you? So instead I'd taken the opposite approach. I'd owned it just like I owned my large hooked nose that took up way more of my face than it had a right to. Anytime one of my brothers attempted to poke fun at it, I'd just inform them that I made this nose look good, thanks, and they'd stop teasing me. That was the secret to getting teased. You had to make it clear that you couldn't care less about the thing they were teasing you about. If they couldn't make you care, they couldn't get under your skin. It was like taking a balloon and sticking a pin in it. Pop, bang, pow, there went all the power the person thought they had over you. It was magical, really.

I was interrupted from my thoughts by the sound of someone whispering across the dark cabin. I thought it might be Zeke, but before I could figure it out, Aaron's voice rang out.

"Quiet!" he barked. "Lights are out. That means mouths are shut." Whoever had been whispering stopped immediately. While the other cabins got an hour of free time to swim or check out the nature cabin's newest collection of baby bunnies, we'd had to clean our cabin. Again. I'd barely managed to get my message to Kristy before Aaron had yanked us out of the dining room and frog-marched us back up the hill. A feat that was made surprisingly easy when he decided to finally showcase his own RISK factor for us. Aaron was strong. Although strong might be an understatement. He could lift an entire table if it was in his way, which was something he demonstrated when he came over to haul me away from the Swallowtails' table.

"Super strength," I said as he grabbed me by the back of my vest and lifted me a solid foot off the ground. "Impressive."

"Thanks," Aaron had said dryly. "It comes in handy. Now, move it or lose it."

It had taken almost until lights-out to get the cabin put back together to Aaron's exacting standards. The laughter coming in through our windows from the nearby tetherball court just made it all the more painful. I was awesome at tetherball. We'd been told to take off the sparkly vests and bow ties, and I'd crammed them back in my bag. You never knew when something like that was going to come in handy.

I glanced at my watch. We needed a midnight meeting tonight, but Aaron was going to make that tricky if he was going to stand guard over us like this. Suddenly the door to our bathroom opened, and Eli's familiar head poked inside. He glanced around our darkened room in surprise.

"Early lights-out tonight?" he said to Aaron.

"Trust me, they deserved it," Aaron said.

"I don't doubt it," Eli said with a rueful smile. "I could use a hand for a second, though. One of my new campers just got himself stuck under one of the bunks."

Aaron nodded and turned to us. "If I hear one peep out of you guys, you will lose all free time tomorrow as well." With that he followed Eli out the door. Everyone lay still and silent for a second as the bathroom door swung shut behind the two counselors, and then as one, each and every one of us sat bolt upright in our beds.

"What's the plan?" Emerson whispered from above my head. I craned my head out of the bunk to look up to where he was tethered and floating two feet over his bed.

"Midnight meeting," I said. "Wait for my signal."

"Can't we just talk now?" Zeke asked with a yawn. "Why does it have to be at midnight?"

"Two reasons," I said. "The first is that Counselor Crabby could be back at any moment, and the second reason is that midnight meetings are much more epic."

"Haven't we gotten in enough trouble today?" Hudson asked.

"Probably," I said. "But if it's a midnight meeting, it's technically tomorrow."

"How do we get past Counselor Uptight?" Gary said.

"That's a good question," I said. "I'm working on that."

"He really missed his calling," Anthony mused. "He'd have made one heck of a prison guard."

"Just wait for my signal," I said. "He has to go to bed sometime." We heard the sound of footsteps, and we all dived back under the covers. I lay there waiting for Aaron to give it up and go to bed. He did eventually, but not before sliding a long metal bar through the door handle to lock it. Now, that was new. Eli had never locked us in our cabin, even after we'd snuck down to the lake and lit it on fire. I wondered if this was part of what Eli had been hinting at this morning at registration. We needed a private powwow, and we needed it yesterday.

I stripped off my T-shirt and shorts and slipped naked and invisible out of my bunk to do a quick investigation of the window directly behind my bed. To my surprise I spotted a small metal box attached to the bottom screen, not a lock, I realized, but an alarm. I sat back and with a critical eye studied the sturdy mesh screen that was letting in the cool night air. If we had to, we could bust through it, but that wasn't exactly the stealthy exit I'd had in mind. I did a quick loop of the room, and it didn't take the guys long to figure out who was walking over them in order to study the windows, but to their credit, not one of them said a word. Although Hudson was under the covers playing his game, so he might not have even noticed.

Unfortunately, all the windows were wired with alarms, and the only door that was open was the one that led to the bathroom. I pulled on my clothes and climbed back in bed with no clue how I was going to pull this off. I was still wide awake when I heard the ruckus next door of the Red Wood guys kidnapping the newest Red Maple men for their night of initiation. I knew I wasn't the only one lying there feeling a bit jealous of the campers getting blindfolded and thrown in the back of a rusty blue pickup truck. That was when the light bulb went off in my brain. I stripped out of my shorts and T-shirt for the second time that night and carefully wadded them up in a ball and chucked them toward the bathroom door. That job done, I slid out of bed and made the rounds to the other guys' bunks. Hudson was the only one who jumped in surprise when he felt my invisible hand tap his shoulder as I whispered, "Meet me in the bathroom," directly in his ear.

"Right, because that's not weird at all," Gary whispered back when I got to him, and I had to stifle a snort with my hand. One by one the guys rolled out of their bunks and crept through the dark to the door that led to the bathroom. I grabbed one of Emerson's tethers and dragged him along behind me like my favorite carnival balloon. We were almost through the door when I paused to grab his weighted vest and realized that there was still a faint glow underneath Hudson's covers. I pulled them back to discover him staring at his phone as he carefully manipulated little pieces of candy on the screen. I plucked it from his hand, and he rolled out of bed and followed like the proverbial horse following a dangling carrot. We slipped through the door to find the rest of the guys all standing in the dimly lit room. Emerson quickly buckled his vest while I tiptoed around the guys and stashed Hudson's phone inside

105

one of the many shower caddies lined up on the shelf. That done, I threw my shorts and shoes back on.

"Wait, so was he naked?" Hudson asked Emerson.

"Also, something you should probably get used to," Zeke said. Mr. Stink had decided to come along, and he sat looking up at me as though he was awaiting further instructions. Man, I'd forgotten how much I loved that skunk.

"If Aaron catches us, we are in some serious trouble," Gary said.

"Which is why he won't catch us," I said.

"I don't think I want to come," Hudson said. "I was almost to level thirty-seven."

"Midnight meetings aren't optional," I said with a glance at Murphy. "Right?"

Murphy nodded. "I got dragged along on one last year that ended up with the lake getting lit on fire."

"That isn't convincing at all," Hudson said, and then shook his head, resigned. "Just hand over the phone, and I'll come. Maybe there will be something worth filming."

"No phones allowed at midnight meetings," I said. "Rule number one of breaking the rules is that you don't document the breaking of the rules."

"Interesting," Emerson said. "What's rule number two?"

106

"Don't get caught," I said.

"Well, count me out, then," Hudson said, crossing his arms over his chest.

"That's fine," I said. "But I'm not going to tell you where your phone is until we get back." I turned my back on him to address the rest of the guys.

"Follow me." With that I hurried across the bathroom and opened the door of the Red Maple cabin. Just like I'd known they would be, every bunk was empty. The sheets and pillows strewn across the floor were the only evidence of the struggle the campers had made when they were kidnapped for their initiation by the oldest boys' cabin. We tiptoed across the room and past Eli's bed. I saw his eye open briefly and then snap shut again as he pretended to be asleep. Good man, Eli. We made it out the door, and I saw the taillights of the truck full of Red Maple men about to have the night of their lives.

"Where are they going?" Hudson said.

"To get dropped off in the middle of the woods," Zeke said.

"Probably in some ridiculous getup," Anthony added.

"Lucky dogs," Gary said.

"You guys are weird; do you know that?" Hudson said.

"Yes," I said at the same time everyone else did too, and I grinned.

"Where are we headed?" Emerson said.

"You'll see," I said, and together we crept down the hill. I led them over to where one of the rusty camp trucks still sat parked next to the dining hall, and climbed quickly in the back. No one followed me.

"What?" I said, turning around to see my friends looking up at me warily.

"Initiation was great and all," Emerson said, "you know, except for the part where I almost died and you yahoos floated me into a tree to get that compass, but I don't think I want to do it again just now."

"We aren't going anywhere," I said, taking a seat in the truck bed with my back to the cab. "Does it look like I know how to drive? This just seemed like a good place for our midnight meeting." Seeming appeased, the rest of the guys clambered into the back of the truck and found a seat.

"One of these days someone is going to *have* to tell me what exactly happened on your initiation night," Hudson said.

"Shhh," I said, "we don't have time for chitchat. We have some serious stuff to discuss."

"Serious?" Gary said. "Have you ever been serious about anything in your entire life?"

I ignored him and quickly filled the guys in on the weird warning Eli had given me about Aaron at registration.

"You dragged us out in the middle of the night to tell us that our new counselor is a jerk?" Gary said. "I think we all figured that out already."

"Not just a jerk," I said. "A suspicious jerk."

I turned to Murphy with a raised eyebrow. "Does our resident time traveler have anything to add?"

"I don't know," Murphy said, and I saw his eyes flick nervously over to Hudson and back again. I instantly grasped the problem.

"Hudson," I said, turning to him. "Can we trust you?"

"Um," Hudson said nervously. "Yeah? Why?"

"It's not that easy," Gary protested. "Of course he's going to say we can trust him. No one says, 'Hey, nice to meet you. I'm a two-timing, untrustworthy slug.'"

"He's right," Murphy said with an apologetic glance at Hudson.

"Did you guys, like, rob a bank or something?" Hudson said nervously.

"I wish," Gary muttered.

"No," I said. "It's just that last summer was, let's say, eventful, and some stuff happened that we can't really talk about with just anyone."

"I'm not going to jail because Tom Tornado over there couldn't keep his mouth shut," Gary grumbled.

"Don't call me that," Hudson said, and even though it was dark out, I could tell his face was turning red. His hands balled into fists, and a second later we were surrounded by levitating sticks and rocks as Hudson glared at Gary.

"Uh," I said, glancing around, "you know the whole *sticks and stones may break my bones but words will never hurt me* thing?"

"I've heard that," Gary said, and even his voice had a nervous edge to it that we didn't hear very often.

"Well, I think maybe words could get us hurt this time via sticks and stones, so why don't you apologize?"

"Sorry," Gary said. The sticks and rocks around us vibrated ominously.

"Say it like you mean it, man!" I said, eyeing the new kid. It felt like he was two separate people. Sometimes he was zoned out with his phone, and other times he was a tornado just waiting for an opportunity to level a town.

"I'm sorry! I won't call you Tom Tornado again!" Gary said, throwing up his bandaged hands in surrender. "If it makes you feel better, you can call me Sticky Steve!" This brought Hudson's impending tantrum up short as he suddenly snorted with laughter.

"Who calls you that?" he said.

"Not anyone I like," Gary said.

"Well, no one that I like calls me a tornado either," Hudson said.

"Point made," Gary said. "Won't happen again."

"Gary struggles with speaking kindly to his friends," I said, as though I was his kindergarten teacher at a parent-teacher conference. "We're working on it."

Gary snorted.

"Gary has a good point, though," Emerson said. "No offense or anything, Hudson, but we kind of just met you. How do we know if we can trust you? If something happens, you're not the one who will end up in jail for the rest of your life."

"Jail?" Hudson said nervously.

"Worse than jail," Murphy said.

"What's worse than jail?" Hudson said.

"He's cool," came a voice from inside the cab of the truck, and we all yelped and jumped to our feet in surprise as the truck door opened and another Murphy stepped out.

CHAPTER TEN

"**R**elax," said the new Murphy. "It's just me."

Like we always did when a time-traveling Murphy showed up, everyone did a quick double take just to confirm that we still had the original Murphy sitting beside us. I did more than a double take this time, though, because unlike the rest of the guys, I'd seen two other time-traveling Murphys in less than twenty-four hours, and I needed to know where this guy fell in the timeline of events. Was he a Murphy from before or after the time traveling to the bathroom with Gary and me? And if he was from after the first bathroom time-traveling episode, was he from after the second one too? Did this Murphy know why that second Murphy in the bathroom had been sobbing so hard? Did he know that I died? I swallowed hard as the D word that I hadn't allowed into my brain since I'd stepped off the plane flitted through my head.

"You're sure he can be trusted?" said our original Murphy, snapping me from my own thoughts before they could spiral out of control. I glanced at our original Murphy, who was still standing in his pajamas next to Zeke.

"He can," said the new Murphy, who was wearing a bright green White Oak sweatshirt I'd never seen before but had a feeling I would see in the near future.

"Wait a second," Hudson said as he looked from the Murphy in the sweatshirt to the Murphy in his pajamas and back again. "I thought you couldn't run into a future version of yourself."

"It's fine," Zeke said, waving a hand.

"That's just in science fiction movies," Anthony added.

"Another thing you need to get used to," Emerson said with a shrug.

"Like, we can tell him everything?" original Murphy asked himself.

"Not only *can* you tell him everything, you really *should* tell him everything," future Murphy said. "The future of Camp Outlier depends on it!"

"What do you mean?" Hudson said.

"I can't tell you anything else," future Murphy said. "These guys can explain about that."

"It's real annoying," Gary said to Hudson. "Feels a lot like hanging out with a walking, talking fortune cookie." He wiggled his bandaged fingers in front of his face and made his voice sound spooky. "A pleasant surprise is waiting for you. An important person will offer you support. Bide your time, for success is near."

"I do *not* sound like that," future Murphy said, crossing his arms over his chest. "You should try time traveling, and we'll see how you do."

"I've tried it," Gary reminded him. "Emerson puked all over me, and I almost got shot by a couple of trigger-happy deer hunters with a strong dislike for RISK kids. You keep your RISK factor, and I'll keep mine, thanks."

"Are you just here to vouch for Hudson?" Emerson asked future Murphy. "Or can you tell us anything else about the summer? Is Aaron trustworthy? Do we win the camp challenge?" Future Murphy suddenly looked ill. He glanced over in my direction and grimaced. Well, that answers that question, I thought as my stomach churned. This Murphy knew that something was going to happen to me, but he seemed in more control of his emotions than the Murphy who'd ambushed me that

114

second time in an airport bathroom.

"Emerson," I said, forcing a cheerfulness into my voice that I didn't feel, "let the man answer the important questions first." I turned to future Murphy and raised an eyebrow. "Do I get another kiss from Kristy? I forgot to pack burn ointment, and I need to know if I should ask my mom to send some."

Future Murphy rolled his eyes. "You'll never change, will you, Hank?"

"If I did, you wouldn't be able to see it anyway," I pointed out.

"He's got you there," Emerson said.

"Seriously, though," Zeke said, leaning forward so far his glasses almost slid off his nose. "Can you tell us anything?"

"Hmmm," Murphy said thoughtfully. "I don't think so. Nothing important at least, since telling you would inevitably change the future. Oh," he said, brightening. "At one point Hank juggles our cabin's bowls of ice cream and accidentally drops one onto his own head."

"Nice," I said. "Glad I've got something to look forward to. By the way, have you kidnapped me in the airport bathroom yet?" I asked, and everyone except future Murphy looked at me in confusion.

"Who kidnaps someone in a bathroom?" Gary asked.

"Well, you do," I said. "It happened this morning at the airport. Future me showed up with future you and Murphy and hauled me into the accessible stall to warn me about something."

"What did we warn you about?" original Murphy said.

"I don't know," I admitted. "You guys disappeared before I could find out."

The Murphy in pajamas sitting next to me turned to ask his future self something else, but he was gone. "Nuts," he said.

"So," Hudson said slowly, "does someone want to fill me in on what exactly happened last summer?"

"I don't know," Anthony said nervously. "It's kind of a lot."

"No offense," Hudson said as he eyed the small fire that had just erupted on Anthony's shoulder, "but you guys are all kind of a lot."

"He's not wrong," Zeke said.

"Future Murphy vouched for him," Emerson said. "I think that's good enough. Don't you?"

"It will have to be," I said, turning to Hudson. "So, last summer," I began, "Murphy was supposed to die." Hudson's eyes grew wide as I explained how Murphy had time traveled to the future and discovered that he didn't survive the summer. In fact, he'd only been allowed to come to camp the year before because it was his Make-A-Wish, a fact that he'd accidentally let slip to Emerson and me after one particularly rough time-traveling trip. Of course, we'd been bound and determined not to let that happen. It had been Emerson who'd landed on the idea of sticking Gary to Murphy to tether him to the here and now. However, the plan had backfired, and Emerson and Gary had gotten hauled through time like a couple of unlucky hitchhikers. Lucky for Murphy that they did too, because otherwise he'd have ended up a victim of some nearsighted hunters.

"Wait," Hudson said, holding up a hand. "So, you almost got shot? Because you were wearing an eighties prom dress?"

Murphy shrugged. "It was brown with white polka dots so I looked a lot like Bambi."

"And why were you wearing a dress again?" he said.

"It was Hank's idea," Murphy said.

"Guilty," I admitted. "Hang around, Huddy man, and maybe we'll find you a dress too!"

"I think sparkly vests and bow ties are my limit, thanks," Hudson said.

"What do you think you meant by 'Camp Outlier depends on it'?" Emerson asked Murphy.

"No flying clue," Murphy said, throwing up his

hands in frustration. "Future me kind of sucked tonight, to be perfectly honest. But I don't like the sound of it." He paused and scowled down at his hands. "In fact, the whole thing makes me kind of mad."

"What do you mean?" Emerson asked.

"What I mean is that I didn't want something hanging over my head this year," he said. "Last summer was all about me potentially dying, and I wanted to move past that. I wanted to just have an epic summer at camp without worrying about the future."

"You *will* have an epic summer at camp," I said, glad that I'd kept my mouth shut about his second visit to the bathroom. "Even if I have to make you sing Disney songs in a sparkly vest daily."

Murphy snorted, but he didn't cheer up like I'd hoped; in fact he seemed to get even sadder somehow. This was not my normal effect on people, and I wondered if being invisible had something to do with it. I mean, it was hard to cheer someone up when you couldn't make eye contact or smile, and I swallowed a huff of frustration.

"Look at it this way," I said, deciding to try a different approach. "We knew that there might be some leftover mess after you managed to take Emerson and Gary through time with you. It was wishful thinking to believe that you guys could prevent something bad happening to camp just by keeping your mouths shut to those TTBI officers who investigated you when you got back. We will figure things out as they happen, the same way we did last year, but we won't let anything stop us from having an amazing summer."

"I agree," Emerson said. "I've been looking forward to camp all year."

Everyone quieted down, and I leaned forward conspiratorially. "Here's what we know," I said. "Aaron can't be trusted. Eli as good as told me that, so we need to be careful what we say around him." I turned to Gary. "Think you can manage that?"

"I'll try," he said.

"We're screwed," Anthony said.

"While we're at it, I think we should probably watch our step around that guy Munkhoosier or Munkeyhutter or whatever his name is," Emerson said. "He seemed pretty serious too."

"Do you think either of them have anything to do with the whole *Camp Outlier depends on it* thing?" Hudson asked.

"Maybe," Emerson said. "When we time traveled last year, we saw a future where kids like us spent our time locked up in juvenile detention centers instead of camp, and Mooknoser seems like the kind of guy who would be on board with that plan."

"Hmm," I said, remembering the future that Gary and Emerson had accidentally landed in where we weren't accepted or allowed to be around people without RISK factors. It was a future that frankly terrified me.

"I think it's Munkhouser," Anthony said, and then gave a decisive nod. "Yes, definitely Munkhouser."

"Can we please call him Mooknoser?" Gary said with a snort. "It's so much better!"

"So, I guess it's up to us to make sure that Munkhouser doesn't bring about that future that you saw," I said, ignoring Gary as he gave another snort. "If something bad is going to happen to Camp Outlier, we will just have to stop it. Simple."

"And how do you suggest we do that?" Anthony asked.

"We make Life Lists," I said with a grin.

"Seriously," Gary said.

"Seriously," I replied. "We map out all the amazing things we want to accomplish this summer, and then we go for it. You can't live the same summer over and over and call it a life, my friend."

"And how does that help save camp?" Emerson asked.

"It doesn't," I said. "But we don't even know what we're saving camp from at this point. Murphy's right. We can't let this hang over our heads. We are here to have an awesome summer, and that's just what we're going to do." I didn't mention to them that, for all I knew, this was my last summer, and I didn't intend to waste even a second of it.

"I guess the time travelers only visited *you* in the bathroom," Gary mused. "Maybe you're the only one in danger."

"That's the spirit!" I said, thumping him on the back. "Look at it this way. All we know is that letting Hudson in on the events of last summer was important to saving camp. We did that. Check!" I made a check mark in the air with my invisible finger. Of course, no one could see it, so I grabbed Gary's arm and made him do the same motion.

"Knock it off," he said, pulling his arm away from me.

"Never!" I proclaimed. "Now, let's see those Life Lists, men. I want to see what you accomplished this school year." Everyone pulled their crumpled lists out of pockets, while Hudson looked on in confusion.

"I'm sorry to say, my new friend, but you are the youngest of the bunch. Everyone starts at zero." I went on to explain quickly what a Life List was and the theory behind it. Hudson listened attentively and then asked to see the other guys' Life Lists, which they handed over willingly.

"You lassoed a pig?" he asked Murphy, eyebrow raised.

"I wouldn't recommend it," Murphy said.

"Well done, men," I said. "Good to see you didn't loaf about while we were apart. However, I propose something different this year with the lists."

"What?" Zeke said, sounding wary. Even Mr. Stink, who'd tagged along per usual, was giving me a look that made it clear he didn't quite trust me, and I smiled.

"Well," I said. "Last year everyone wrote down a whole bunch of different stuff, and while we made progress on some of them, we didn't cross off as many things as we could have. I suggest we brainstorm and come up with a list of things we can all agree on and we go after them together. I think winning some of the camp challenges should be priority." Everyone agreed, and we ended up with a list of ten things to add to our Life Lists. Just to be nice, we let Hudson add a few more, since only aging up to age ten seemed a bit disappointing.

"I've always wanted to go parasailing," Hudson said, looking up from his list. "There's this video game where you do it virtually, and I'm really good at it. Do they offer parasailing here?"

I was about to answer when the sound of someone approaching brought me up short. We froze as the voice got louder, and I realized that it was several someones. Girl someones, if I was being specific.

"Gentlemen," I said, "I believe our teammates have arrived."

The guys shot me confused looks that disappeared as the girls of the Swallowtail cabin made their way around the side of the truck. The guys sat up straighter, and I imagined we looked like a bunch of prairie dogs popping out of their holes.

"Geez," Zeke said, pressing a hand to his chest. "This truck is like a jack-in-the-box. Who or what is going to pop out next?"

"Hopefully nothing," I said, thinking uneasily of Aaron asleep in our locked-down cabin. "I knew about the girls," I added. "In fact, I invited them."

"If you consider a message written in ketchup on a napkin an invitation? Then yes, he invited us," said the girl with dark hair and a baseball cap. I made a quick mental note to find out her name as all the guys scooted over to make room. Molly sat down next to Emerson and he grinned.

"Okay," I said. "First of all, the men of White Oak would like to formally apologize for the loss of five points. In our defense, we had no idea that there was a point system this summer." I saw Gary scowl as his eyes flicked over to Hudson, but I gave him a quick kick to the shin before he could say anything. We'd all agreed to keep our mouths shut about the Hudson hurricane, just like we'd kept our mouths shut the time he'd accidentally gotten stuck to a toilet last summer. Maybe I should remind him of that particular incident, I thought with a smirk.

"How about an apology for not being around to help hide our flag?" Gabby said, eyebrow raised. "The capture-the-flag game is worth twenty points, you know."

"Actually, we don't know," I said. "I'm sure you noticed that our lovely new counselor, Aaron, who has the unfortunate personality of a porcupine with poison ivy, didn't exactly give us a chance to check out the challenge board. So, if you could be so kind and fill us in, ladies, I know we'd all appreciate it."

The girl with the black spiral curls with the tiny lightning bolts all over them rolled her eyes. "Do you always talk like that?" she said.

"Yes," I said, unapologetically and without any further explanation. "What's your name, my dear lady? I don't believe we met last summer."

"Emily," she said. "I wasn't here last summer. Neither was Amy," she said with a jerk of her head at the girl in the baseball hat.

"Hudson is new too!" I said, clapping him on the shoulder.

"Thanks for the introduction," Hudson said, shrugging my hand off and giving Emily a megawatt smile that made a few of the girls giggle.

"Right," Emily said with a shake of her curls that sent out tiny sparks of electricity crackling around her.

"So, there are five challenges up for grabs right now that we can choose to tackle as a team other than the whole-camp challenges like capture the flag. They are a marathon hike, which is worth ten points," Kristy continued, holding up one hand as she counted them off on her fingers. "Build a treehouse—that one is worth twenty points—the ropes course is worth five; something called the treasure dive, which is worth five; and a survival hike, whatever that is, which is also worth ten."

"So, we can pick and choose which of those we do, right?" Zeke said.

"Right." Molly nodded. "The other five are camp-wide games or challenges, and there can be only one winner."

"So, we have to do all the optional ones and win at least a few of the camp challenges to win this thing," I said more to myself than to anyone else.

"We also can't afford to lose any more points," Kristy pointed out. "So, do us a favor and try not to do anything else that makes your counselor mad."

"Have you met Gary?" I said. "That may be easier said than done."

"Try real, real hard," Kristy said dryly.

"So, what are the camp-wide challenges besides capture the flag?" Anthony asked.

"All the camp-wide challenges are worth twenty points," Molly said, taking over where Kristy had left off. "There's a scavenger hunt, a duck hunt, a canoe race, and something they called the race to home base."

"Got it," I said, rubbing my hands together in anticipation. "So, what are we going to do first?" The next half hour was spent joking around and planning with the girls, who, thankfully, seemed to have forgiven us for losing five points right off the bat. There was a fairly heated debate about whether it was better to go whole hog and tackle one of the challenges worth more points or carve away at some of the smaller, easier challenges that were worth less but could be accomplished quickly. Eventually we decided that we'd start with the ropes course, since almost all of us were pretty familiar with it from last summer. It was well after one in the morning when we snuck back up the hill and tiptoed through the trashed Red Maple cabin and into our own. Thankfully, Aaron was still where we'd left him, snoring on his bunk. I'm sure I wasn't the only one who sighed in relief as I eased myself back under the covers.

I lay there staring at the bottom of Emerson's bunk and listened to the sound of my friends falling asleep as my brain rehashed everything the girls had said. I felt simultaneously energized and excited to tackle this new challenge, and wary about the newest warning from yet another time-traveling Murphy. He'd said that the future of Camp Outlier depended on us filling Hudson in on the events of last year. Why? I glanced over at Hudson's bunk and saw that he'd fallen asleep holding his still-glowing phone.

I thought back to that morning in the airport bathroom and frowned. It somehow already seemed like a lifetime ago that my mom had hollered over the airport sound system. I felt a twinge of homesickness at the thought of my mom. I always missed home a little bit when I was gone, whether I wanted to admit it or not. If I'd been forced to spend my summer anywhere other than Camp Outlier, I was sure I'd feel more than a twinge.

Camp Outlier was special. It was the first and only place where I'd felt like I fit in, invisible neck and all, and I knew that it had done that and more for the rest of the guys. It had to be here next summer and the summer after that and the summer after that. Heck, when I had a kid someday, who would undoubtedly have combustible burps or something else equally interesting about them, I wanted them to come here too. Somehow the danger to camp felt more real and present than the danger I knew I was in. It was more tangible, fixable, and thinking about it didn't make me want to vomit. That was what I'd focus on, saving camp, and if I got saved too, well, that was an amazing bonus. I felt a familiar resolve solidify in my chest. It was the same resolve that I'd felt last year when I'd dragged Emerson out in the middle of the night to brainstorm ways to save Murphy. If I was going to die, saving Camp Outlier was a legacy I could live with. That was that. End of story. Tomorrow is a new day, I thought as I finally closed my eyes, and I was ready for it.

Dear Mom,
Hello from camp! Can you believe it's already been a week since you dropped me off? Time feels like it flies here, and each day goes by faster than the one before it. Guess what? We aren't doing just a big capture-the-flag game this summer. Instead it's a bunch of challenges. It's different, but I think it's going to be fun to work with the boys. (Don't tell Dad about the

working-with-the-boys part. I know he
really wishes that camp wasn't coed.) It's
been nice to hang out with them more
this summer. Last year they just seemed
to show up and make a scene (serenading
us, quoting Shakespeare, sinking canoes),
but this year I think we'll get to know
them a bit better. Unfortunately, we
haven't had a chance to tackle any
of the extra camp challenges yet, but
I think we may have an opportunity to
finally try the ropes course tomorrow.
Don't worry, there is a safety tether, so
even if I transform, I'll be fine. That's
a nice thing about camp: they have all
these built-in safety measures for kids like
us. Oh, and we have a couple new girls in
our cabin this year, which was kind of a
nice surprise. I always love hearing about
what everyone's RISK factor is since
everyone's is so unique and different. One
of the new girls, Emily, has an electrical
imbalance, which came in pretty useful
when we lost power the other day. She
just grabbed on to a couple light bulbs,
and we had enough light to brush our

teeth and read before bedtime. It
didn't work perfectly—she accidentally
exploded one of the light bulbs all over
the bathroom floor—but it was still pretty
cool. Sometimes I wish my RISK factor
was useful like that. Maybe you should
let Rob enter me into an obedience
competition just for kicks. KIDDING!
Tell him I miss him even if he is obnoxious
and smells like feet. I almost wish he
had a RISK factor too so he could see
what camp is all about. It's so nice to be
here around a bunch of other kids that
have so many of the same struggles as
me. At home I always feel like I stand
out, like the moment I turn into a dog, I
stop being me, but I don't feel that way
here. Camp is awesome. Thanks again for
sending me.
    Molly

CHAPTER ELEVEN

"**R**ise and shine," Aaron called out as he flipped on the harsh overhead fluorescent lights. I sat bolt upright, blinking in surprise. It didn't matter that he'd woken us up this way for the last seven days; it still felt as jarring as someone tossing ice-cold water over your head. I'd forgotten how exhausting the first week of camp could be. Even though I was pretty active in my normal life—you kind of had to be if you lived on a farm—camp felt like a major shock to my system. The camp bed, which felt like it was stuffed with golf balls and rocks every night before I went to bed, now felt like a cloud, and I snuggled back under my blankets, thankful for my invisible head. Maybe if Aaron couldn't see me, he would forget about me and I could get another hour of sleep. I'd just drifted off again when my covers were yanked away and the cold morning air hit my skin like an electric shock.

"That means you too, Sleeping Beauty. Now hustle or we'll be the last cabin down for breakfast!" Aaron yelled. Goose bumps erupted down my arms, and I got to my feet and fumbled around groggily for a sweatshirt. I found one and yanked it over my head, only to discover that it was about three sizes too big and hung on my thin frame like a potato sack. I glanced down to see that it was black with the words "Sorry I'm late. I didn't want to come" written across the front.

"Gary," I called. "I think this is yours." I pulled it off and flung it in his general direction and continued the hunt for a sweatshirt I recognized. I finally found it balled up underneath Anthony's bunk—my favorite gray hoodie with the hole in the elbow. Unfortunately, Anthony reached for it at the same time I did, and it caught fire.

"Dude!" I said as I stomped on the small flame before it could become a big flame. "That was my favorite!"

"Sorry," Anthony said. "Here, you can wear one of mine." I took whatever he offered me and yanked it over my head. It smelled a bit like charcoal, but everything

Anthony owned smelled a bit like charcoal. I started to stumble toward the bathroom to do something about my morning breath, which, from the taste alone, I was guessing could knock out Mr. Stink.

"No time for that now," Aaron called, and I found myself being hauled out the cabin door after the rest of the guys. I blinked at them, still half asleep, and realized that everyone else had managed to get themselves somewhat put together. Emerson's hair was wet and combed to the side, Hudson had definitely spent some time with a mirror and hair product, and I could smell Gary's deodorant, which, considering how he usually smelled, was an improvement. Meanwhile my hair was in my face and ratted into some sort of bird's nest configuration since I'd given up brushing it a while ago, and I was wearing someone else's sweatshirt. I paused as I realized I wasn't even sure what color it was. I glanced down at a yellow sweatshirt that read "Nelson Family Reunion." Nifty.

I hunched up my shoulders against the early-morning chill and decided that I was too tired to care. My mood lifted as we walked—it was hard for it not to. Camp Outlier was one of those breathtakingly beautiful places that made it almost impossible to be grouchy. I let my hunched shoulders start to relax. Birds were chirping cheerily in the trees, and fat squirrels scampered across the path in front of us. Mr. Stink arched his tail over his back as he waddled ahead of us. All we needed was a singing princess and we could be in a Disney movie, I thought with a wide yawn.

Every morning at camp seemed just a bit better than the morning before, and I smiled as I remembered our first morning at camp. It had been cold just like today, and we'd been extra tired from our successful midnight meeting with the girls. I'd barely been awake when the Red Woods had come walking into the dining hall with ear-to-ear grins and dark circles under their eyes. It had clicked then that it was initiation morning, and I'd instantly felt more alert. We'd sat down at our table as the Red Woods brought around heaping bowls of scrambled eggs and pancakes. I dug in. I may have the body type of a piece of linguini, but I could pack it away like the prizewinning pig at the South Dakota State Fair. At least that's what I'd been told.

Breakfast was well underway when the dining-room door opened and the men of the Red Maple cabin walked in. I dropped my fork and stared along with everyone else as I saw red. Like, literal red. Somehow the Red Wood guys had managed to dye the Red Maple boys the exact shade of a stop sign from the tops of their heads to their red-shoe-covered toes. To comple- ment their tomato-red skin, they were also wearing red shorts, red T-shirts, and red socks. Their skin was the real showstopper, though, and I leaped to my feet and stood on my chair to clap my hands as they made their way sheepishly through the dining hall to their table and a smiling Eli. They'd barely sat down when the door opened again and the Monarch cabin walked in sporting the electric orange of a traffic cone from head to toe. I clapped again as they made their way to their table before plopping back into my seat.

"Not as good as eighties prom dresses," Emerson had said as he tore off a bite of toast and popped it in his mouth, and I'd had to agree.

Now, it was hard to believe that morning was over a week ago and the poor Monarchs and Red Maple guys were *still* orange and red. It turns out that whatever dye was used was more permanent than anyone had anticipated.

This morning the smell of French toast was wafting from the dining hall as we hurried down the hill. The food at Camp O was the best I'd ever tasted, although sometimes I wondered if it was because I was always starving by the time meals came around.

We settled down at our table and dug in. I was just reaching for my third helping when I noticed that everyone at the table was staring at me.

"What?" I said in confusion as I glanced around.

"Good to see you again, Hank," Emerson said with a wide grin.

"What do you mean?" I said.

"Wait, you're not invisible all the time?" Hudson said, looking up from his phone to peer at me. "I thought that was your thing, like you were the invisible boy or something." I finally caught on and held a hand up in front of my face, and there, for the first time in what felt like forever, was my hand. I grabbed a spoon and held it up to see my reflection staring back at me out of its distorted surface. I whooped, and a few of the other cabins glanced our way before returning to their breakfasts.

"What in the world is going on with your hair?" Anthony said. "It looks like you have a small animal living in there."

"I might," I said as I made an effort to run my fingers through it and failed. "Anyone up for giving me a haircut?"

"No time for that this morning," Aaron said as he walked over to our table. Unlike Eli, who used to sit and joke around with us at every meal, Aaron had the habit of eating his breakfast standing up while talking to either Mr. Blue, Mr. Munkhouser, or another counselor. It was a habit that we weren't complaining about either, since Aaron's presence always made us feel like we had to walk on eggshells. He wasn't as bad as I'd first anticipated, but he was super strict, which could be a real downer.

"So, that's what you look like," he said, cocking his head to the side. "Not what I pictured." Before I could ask what exactly he'd pictured, Mr. Blue stepped onto the podium with Mr. Munkhouser at his heels. The microphone screeched and everyone looked up expectantly.

"Good morning!" Mr. Blue called, and we chorused the greeting back to him. "It's hard to believe that we are already a week into this glorious summer, and as today is Friday, it's time for the first official Camp Challenge!" This was met with a chorus of cheers. "I hope you've all had a wonderful breakfast," he went on, "because you're going to need it this morning. We thought we'd start off with a bit of a bang and surprise you with a challenge worth a whopping twenty-five points." There was a chorus of excited murmuring, and Mr. Blue gestured for everyone to be quiet.

"When the bell rings," he said, "you and your partner cabin go outside the dining hall, where there are six canoes. Find your team's canoe, and get it down to the lake. Take care not to spill any of the items out of your canoe on the way down, though, since you'll need them for the second part of the challenge," he warned. "After you make it to the lake, your team must work together to get it launched with two members from each of the cabins. So that means two girls, two boys. Got it?"

Everyone nodded, and I leaned forward in anticipation. This was going to be good. "After you launch the canoe, it becomes a two-part race. Part one involves the campers in the canoe. It will be their job to race across the lake and up the river to the Willow Bridge as quickly as possible. The rest of your team will need to use the trails to meet their team's canoe at the bridge, haul it out, and then, as a team, carry it back through the woods to the very spot where you found it. First team back gets the points."

He'd barely finished speaking when a bell rang, and the room erupted as everyone bolted for the large double doors that had been thrown open by some of the camp counselors. There was a general chaotic rush as everyone attempted to squeeze through simultaneously. Of course, there were a few campers like Anthony who purposefully hung back for everyone's protection, and I saw a counselor quickly herding them out through a small door by the kitchen. Meanwhile I was shoulder to shoulder with Emerson and Murphy as we battled our way out the door. There sat the six canoes that Mr. Blue had mentioned, and for a second I wondered how in the world we were supposed to know which one was ours. Then I spotted the decals. On the side of each canoe was a large leaf decal and a large butterfly decal. I quickly scanned down the row until I found the White Oak leaf and the yellow butterfly.

"Over there!" I called as I ran. Anthony had beat me there, thanks to his quick exit of the building, and together we took in the massive canoe. It was twice as big as the ones we were usually allowed to check out down by the lake, and inside were four life jackets, paddles, rope, some water bottles, and a bunch of brown paper sacks. Kristy and the rest of the Swallowtail cabin had arrived along with the rest of the White Oak boys, and I noticed a few of the girls each do a double take when they noticed me. Gosh, I'd forgotten how wonderful it was to be visible. I flashed them a wide grin. This was my moment.

"Ladies!" I said. "Allow me!" I reached down and grabbed the canoe. I meant to heft it single-handedly onto my shoulder, but it was heavier than I'd anticipated, and instead I barely got it up past my waist before something popped in my elbow and I grunted and put it back down.

"Smooth," Kristy said, shoving me out of the way so she could get ahold of the rim of the canoe. "Everyone, grab on," she bellowed, and everyone did. I scrambled to help, and together we hoisted the canoe.

Unfortunately, there were already two teams ahead of us, and we fell in line behind them as we made our way down the narrow dirt trail toward the lake. Camp Outlier was built on a series of hills, at least that's what it seemed like, and the lake was at the very bottom of all of those. Usually you got to it by using a rather steep set of concrete stairs that went straight down, but you couldn't exactly do that while simultaneously carrying a canoe that probably weighed well over one hundred pounds. I concentrated on not slipping as we made our way down the dirt trail that zigzagged in switchbacks down the hill.

"There has to be a faster way than this," Gary said.

"There would have been had we managed to get moving a bit faster," Gabby said.

We were only halfway down the hill when we had to come to a complete stop. In front of us the Red Wood and Buckeye teams had stopped too, and I saw them peering around the team in front of them in an attempt to see what the holdup was.

"What are they doing?" Emerson said.

"I can't see anything," Anthony complained as he tried to crane his head to look around the group in front of us without dropping our canoe.

"Hold on," Zeke said, and he took off his glasses and rubbed at his eyes for a second. Mr. Stink, who had opted to ride inside the canoe instead of walking, chittered at him nervously.

"It's fine, buddy," Zeke said as he opened up his eyes again. To my surprise they'd taken on the unfocused look that I'd learned last year meant he was having an X-ray vision episode.

"You okay there, Zeke?" I said, glancing nervously over at the rest of the guys. Everyone with the exception of Hudson was watching Zeke with the same nervous expression that was probably on my own face. Hudson was staring at his phone, completely oblivious to what was happening.

"I'm good," Zeke said. "It's something new I've been working on. Give me a second." He narrowed his eyes and stared ahead of us at the thick pack of campers and canoes.

"What's he doing?" asked Emily.

"Give him a second," Emerson said. "I think he's looking through everybody to see what's going on." A second later Zeke blinked and his eyes came back into focus. He put his glasses back on as Mr. Stink leaned out of the canoe to snuffle his ear.

"So, the canoe at the front of the line just busted into about ten pieces," he said, turning to us. "There's a bunch of counselors up there trying to figure out what happened, but they are completely blocking the trail."

"How in the world does a canoe like this break into ten pieces?" Emerson asked.

"Bad luck?" Kristy said.

"Well, now what?" Gary grumbled.

I glanced around, and spotted the concrete steps that led down to the lake just a few paces through the woods to the left. If we could make it there, we could slide the canoe like a sled down those steps and get around the Red Woods.

"We take the road less traveled," I said as I shoved my shoulder into the canoe and managed to turn us toward the stairs. There were a few shouts of surprise as everyone stumbled off the path and into the weeds.

"Somehow, I don't think this is what Mr. Blue meant!" Emerson said.

"Trust me!" I called over the barrage of protests. "This is going to be great!" The weeds and brambles were waist high, and I felt them scrape against my bare legs as we made our way across the side of the hill.

"There's no way we can carry the canoe down those stairs! We'll break our necks!" Kristy said.

"We're going to slide it," I said. "This thing is built like a tank; it can handle it."

"The one that busted into ten pieces probably begs to differ," Emerson muttered.

"This better work, Hank, or I am going to personally

kill you," Kristy said through gritted teeth.

"I look forward to it," I said. We made it to the stairs, and I quickly pointed the nose down toward the lake. "Think of it as a giant bobsled! We will let gravity do the work!"

"I don't know about this," Gabby said, but we were already making our way down the hill. The canoe made a grinding noise as it slid down the stairs, each of us holding on to the sides to steady its progress. I saw the annoyed faces of the rest of the traffic-jammed cabins flash by us, and I turned and saluted them, because I really like giving things a little flair. Suddenly, Murphy flickered once and disappeared. Emerson cried out in surprise and tripped into Molly, who fell sideways into the canoe and immediately transformed into a cocker spaniel. The poor dog that had a been a girl only moments before lost its footing inside the rocking canoe and fell onto its side, paws flailing. Mr. Stink jumped sideways and out of the canoe onto Zeke's unsuspecting shoulder, causing him to lose his balance and stumble sideways and off the path. The canoe immediately got heavier in my hands.

"A fair maiden is in distress!" I called. "Save her, men!" I lunged into the canoe to grab Molly, and it was at this point that the number of people not holding on to the canoe exceeded the number holding it, and coupled with Molly's added weight, we lost control. I watched in horror as it went bouncing down the steps ahead of us like a runaway train.

"Somebody stop that canoe!" I yelled as we all sprinted after it. Suddenly I had an idea about who that somebody could be, and I spun to find Hudson.

"Hudson!" I yelled. "Do something!" Hudson did. The canoe came to a screeching halt, and I heard the girls whoop as we gained on it. Molly managed to right herself and leaped out of the canoe, fur flying. It looked like the day was saved, and I didn't even care that it was Hudson who had saved it. We were still five feet away from the canoe when it started vibrating.

"Uh-oh," I said, and threw out an arm to stop whoever was behind me. It turned out it was Kristy, and I yelped as her red-hot skin burned my bare arm.

"What are you doing?" she yelled, and was shoving me out of the way when the contents of the canoe exploded. I threw my arms up as brown paper packages, water bottles, paddles, and life jackets were violently ejected from the canoe. A second later the now-empty canoe finished its descent down the hill. We all stood there in horrified silence as it hit the ground at the bottom of the stairs and broke in two.

"Molly! Are you okay?" Emerson called down the hill, and I glanced up to see that he'd somehow caught the worst of the exploding sack lunch shrapnel. He was liberally splattered in chocolate pudding and apple sauce, and half of a peanut butter and jelly sandwich was stuck in his hair. A quick glance down at myself revealed that I hadn't fared much better. Molly barked from somewhere in the bushes to our left, and Emerson took off through the underbrush toward the sound.

"Don't worry," Zeke called as he got to his feet. "I'm good!"

"You okay, Hudson?" I said.

"I'm okay," Hudson said as he glanced around himself. "Have you seen my phone?"

"Not really a priority at the moment, bud," I said, "but if you find us a new canoe, don't keep it to yourself."

"We wouldn't need a new canoe if you hadn't busted our first one," Kristy said as she stomped past me down the hill toward the wreckage. To our right, with their still-intact canoes, the other campers started applauding. Well, so much for redeeming ourselves, I thought glumly as I followed Kristy and the rest of our team down the hill.

Aaron and Mr. Blue rushed over to make sure that everyone was all right, with a sweaty Mr. Munkhouser not far behind. He'd lost the brown suit, but he still looked oddly formal in his stiff blue jeans and collared golf polo. Behind him team after team successfully launched their canoe into the water and then ran past us on their way to the trail. The shattered canoe that had held up the line had apparently been cleared.

"What happened here?" Mr. Munkhouser said, pulling out an iPad in a slick leather case and a small black pen-like thing that he poised over the screen in expectant anticipation. "Did your canoe fall to pieces as well?"

"Well, yeah," Emily said, "but only because we sent it flying down the hill."

"I told ya that's what held up the line," Zeke said proudly, and then turned to Mr. Munkhouser. "Why did it break exactly?"

"Don't worry about that," Mr. Munkhouser said. "I need to know what happened here."

"The White Oak guys happened," Gabby said, crossing her arms over her chest.

"We lost control of the canoe because . . . ," I said. And then glanced back up the hill and smacked my forehead. "Crap! Murphy!"

"Who is Crap Murphy?" Mr. Munkhouser said, scribbling on his pad.

"He's not serious," Gary said, and I saw Zeke slap a hand over Gary's mouth before he could say anything else.

"What he means is that our friend time traveled, and we have no idea where on that hill he disappeared to put his red rocks," Emerson said as he finished making his way down the hill with a human Molly at his side.

"Hm," Mr. Blue said, and immediately left us with our ruined canoe to hike back up the steep concrete steps, Aaron hot on his heels.

"So, a RISK factor caused this accident, then," Mr. Munkhouser said as he continued scribbling on the pad. I saw Kristy's open mouth snap shut, and she glanced over at me with an eyebrow raised as if to say, *What is this about?* I gave my head the tiniest of shakes and flicked my eyes over to where Hudson was still pawing around in the bushes looking for his lost cell phone. She nodded, and I saw a few of the other girls nod in understanding. They were mad at us—well, possibly just me—but they knew where their loyalties lay.

"No," Kristy said. "Hank trying to take over caused the accident. RISK factors had nothing to do with it. That was pure stupidity."

"You wouldn't be mad if it had worked," I said.

"It might have worked," said Amy. When Kristy glared at her, she shrugged. "It's true," she said

147

unapologetically. "If we'd stood in that line another minute, you might have even thought of it." Mr. Munkhouser cleared his throat loudly.

"I'm going to need each of your RISK levels," Mr. Munkhouser said, tapping away at his screen. "This incident will need to be added to each of your records." He hit a few more buttons and then looked up when none of us said anything. "Are there any injuries?" he said.

"That's my job," someone said, and Mr. Munkhouser found himself getting shouldered aside as Nurse Betsy pushed her way through to reach us. Her blond hair was pinned back behind her ears, and she was wearing her signature blue scrubs with their bubblegum-pink polka dots that were at complete odds with her no-nonsense look. Mr. Munkhouser stepped back to give her some space, which told me that this wasn't his first encounter with this small stout force of nature.

"I'm burned," Zeke said, holding up an arm. "Kristy got me."

"Me too," I said, glancing down at the angry red handprint on my arm.

"Sorry," Kristy said, and winced. "I should have worn my gloves. I forgot them at our cabin this morning. I didn't realize we'd have a challenge right off the bat."

"Not wearing government-sanctioned equipment," Mr. Munkhouser muttered to himself as he tapped at his tablet.

"She isn't required to wear them at all times," Nurse Betsy said as she pulled ointment and bandages from her medical kit. "Watch what you put in that computer of yours or your notes are going to throw my data all out of whack. Again."

Munkhouser sniffed and then glanced back at Kristy. "What level are you, young lady?"

"Four," Kristy said, and I saw her confidence waver for a second as a blush colored her sweaty face.

"You're a ten in my book," I said with a wink. She snorted and rolled her eyes, but her hunched shoulders relaxed a bit.

Nurse Betsy busied herself with our burns and then gave each of us a quick once-over, and all the while Mr. Munkhouser continued to question everyone about their RISK number and the equipment we should or should not have on us at the moment.

Once Nurse Betsy was satisfied that we were all in one piece, she brushed off her hands and marched away up the hill, her box of first aid supplies floating behind her like a well-trained dog.

"Well, the rocks are placed," Mr. Blue said as he

came back down the hill.

"So the traveler caused an added complication?" Mr. Munkhouser said. "The one with the special permission to be here?" I felt my hackles rise at the use of the word *traveler*, and I stared Mr. Munkhouser dead in the eyes, thankful that, for once, mine were visible. This guy did not get to make us feel like dirt.

"Didn't your mother ever teach you not to call people by their RISK factors? It's rude," I said, crossing my arms.

Mr. Blue snorted and then covered his mouth and pretended to cough. "Is everyone okay?" he said when he'd composed himself. "I see Nurse Betsy's been here."

"We're fine," Gabby said. "Which is more than we can say for our canoe."

"Well," Mr. Blue said as he walked slowly around the wreckage. "These canoes have been part of camp for the last thirty years. I thought they were indestructible; turns out I thought wrong."

I knew the girls were glaring at me, and I purposefully avoided looking in their direction.

"So, the equipment is from pre-RISK times?" Mr. Munkhouser said, scribbling something into his tablet. "No specialized modifications or adaptations were put in place to accommodate these children and their RISK factors?"

"Now, wait one moment," Mr. Blue said, holding up a hand. "This activity was perfectly safe. The canoes were given a fire-resistant coating and other special reinforcements depending on which team was to use it."

"That doesn't seem to have worked out as planned," Mr. Munkhouser said, his thin lips pursed. "First the catastrophe with the Blue Morpho and Blue Spruce cabins' canoe and now this?" He shook his head in disapproval, and I made a mental note to find out what exactly had happened to that other canoe.

"In our defense," I said, "we accidentally sent ours flying at full speed down a very steep set of concrete steps. I can't think of many things that would come out of that in one piece."

"Is it too late to switch up the teams?" Kristy said. "We'd like to trade."

Mr. Blue chuckled. "I'm afraid not," he said. "But if you guys don't learn to work as a team, you may be in for a very frustrating summer." He looked around at the mess of exploded lunches and gear liberally spread out over the underbrush and turned back to us. "You had better start that working together right now by getting this mess cleaned up. I don't want anyone getting a shard of canoe through their foot when they use these steps to go swimming," he said.

"Everyone look for my phone while you're at it,"

Hudson said, emerging from the underbrush, where he'd presumably been searching for it this entire time.

"I'll help you!" Kristy chirped as she hurried over to stand by Hudson. I thought about pointing out that if she was going to be mad at anyone, she should be mad at the kid that exploded the inside of the canoe, but one glance at Munkhouser had me pressing my lips together.

Just then we heard a pop coming from the hill behind us, and we all turned to see Murphy reappear. He stood there, frozen for a second as he took in his surroundings, reacclimating himself to the present, and then he sat down hard in the weeds. I was halfway up the hill before I realized I was moving. I was quick, but Aaron was quicker, seeming to appear out of nowhere as he crouched down in front of my friend. It wasn't until I saw him that I realized he really should have been there a long time ago. I mean, we were his responsibility. I made a mental note to ask if anyone else had seen him, since it was entirely possible that I was so focused on the canoe disaster that I just hadn't noticed him.

"Are you hurt?" Aaron said to Murphy. Murphy shook his head.

"What happened?" I asked.

"He can't answer that," Aaron said as he grasped

Murphy by the arm and helped him to his feet. Without a backward glance at the rest of us, he turned and marched Murphy up the concrete steps and toward Nurse Betsy's cabin. I watched them go, feeling uneasy. Someday soon Murphy was going to time travel back to that airport bathroom, and when he came back, I might not be here. The thought made my insides do a sickening flip, and I glanced over to see Hudson and Kristy searching the bushes for his phone, their heads bent together as she giggled over something he'd just said. I scowled; this summer was not going even close to how I had planned.

"Nothing you can do for him now," Mr. Blue called up the hill. "Come back down." I started trudging down the hill and felt something hard and square under my foot. I glanced down to see the cell phone in question. I bent over to grab it just as Emerson made his way up the hill toward me, his hands full of torn paper sacks and applesauce containers.

"Everything okay?" he said, and I looked up at him as my hand closed over the cell phone.

"No," I said as I turned to look back at Aaron and Murphy.

"What is it?" Emerson asked, crouching down beside me.

I let the phone go and sat back on my heels. Quick

glances to our left and right revealed that everyone was busy cleaning up the mess while Mr. Blue and Mr. Munkhouser had what looked like a heated discussion about canoes. I turned back to Emerson and took a deep breath.

"Remember how last summer you found out that Murphy wasn't going to survive the summer?" I said. Emerson nodded, his face going pale as he studied my newly visible face.

"Well, this time I think it's my turn," I said. As quickly as I could, I filled him in on Murphy's second visit to that airport bathroom, which, considering all he'd done was cry and nod, wasn't exceptionally difficult. When I was done, Emerson nodded.

"We saved Murphy. We can save you," he said. Something inside me loosened, and the weight that had been sitting on my chest for a week suddenly felt just a little bit lighter.

"Thanks," I said with a rueful grin. "I was really hoping you'd say something like that." He opened his mouth to say more, but Hudson and Kristy were heading in our direction, and he snapped his mouth closed again. I glanced at the ground to grab the phone, but to my surprise, it wasn't there anymore.

"Find it?" Hudson said hopefully as I pawed around

154

in the weeds for the thing.

"I just saw it," I said as my foot hit something and sent it tumbling down the hill.

"Was that the phone?" Emerson asked, and I'd barely nodded before Hudson was shouldering past us to charge down the hill, Kristy at his heels.

"Was it his phone or a rock?" Emerson said.

I shrugged. "I'm not wasting my time looking for it. We better get this mess cleaned up like Mr. Blue asked."

Emerson nodded and, shoulder to shoulder, we got to work.

It took an hour to get the canoe and its contents picked up. By the time we were done we were all sweaty and itchy from poking around in the tall weeds that grew on either side of the stairs, and we'd officially stopped talking to one another since no one had anything very nice to say. Usually I'd have defrayed the tension with some humor, but I couldn't manage it. Between feeling guilty about ruining our first attempt at a challenge, nervous about Murphy's time traveling, annoyed with Hudson's never-ending phone search, and relieved that I'd finally told Emerson the truth, there just wasn't any brain space left for funny. The girls' counselor,

Jessica, supervised the entire thing and then made us all shower with the infamous pink poison-ivy soap. Hudson attempted to protest, still desperate to find his missing phone, but gave in when Jessica pointed out that he'd done some of his most enthusiastic searching in the middle of some poison ivy. By the time we trudged down the hill for lunch, the winning team, the Blue Spruce cabin and their girl cabin counterpart, the Blue Morphos, had made it back to the dining hall with their replacement canoe.

"So, the girls officially hate us now," Emerson said, as though we needed to recap the morning before we could take on the second half of the day.

"To be fair, I think they really just hate me," I said.

"It's my fault," Hudson said. "I exploded the contents of the canoe."

"It's my fault," Emerson said. "I tripped."

"It's not my fault," Zeke said, "but it may be Mr. Stink's. I can't get it through his head that Molly isn't going to eat him."

"It's my fault," Murphy said. "I time traveled and left you guys on your own." He'd come back to our cabin just in time for his own poison-ivy shower.

"Everyone needs to stop trying to take the blame. Y'all are stealing my thunder," I said, forcing a grin I was grateful they could actually see. "I'm the one that had the brilliant idea of sliding the canoe down the stairs, essentially making it into a bobsled. We learned a valuable lesson today. Canoes make exceptionally crappy bobsleds." A few of the guys snorted, but they were halfhearted snorts. "Buck up, men," I said. "This summer is just beginning. The girls can't hate us forever; we'll make it up to them."

"I think they'd just appreciate if we stopped screwing things up for them," Zeke said.

"Good point," I said. "Let's do that, but first let's do something that has absolutely nothing to do with a camp challenge or the girls."

"Like what?" Hudson said, eyebrow cocked. He'd been in a moody funk ever since his phone went missing, and I intended to do something about it.

"Like knock a few things off that Life List of yours," I said. "I have a question for you. If all your friends jumped off a bridge, would you do it too?"

"My mom used to ask me that," Hudson said, his eyebrows furrowed. "So, no?"

"Wrong answer," I said, and grabbed his arm as the guys whooped and followed me out the door. If I didn't know what day was going to be my last one, I'd better start living them to the fullest while I could.

Dear Grandma,

I swear my cabin has the worst luck in the history of the universe. I mean, getting paired up with the White Oak guys hasn't exactly been a treat, and now there is a stupid government official named Munkhouser who seems to show up all over the place. I mean, camp's not huge, but it's big enough that we shouldn't be tripping over the guy. Oh, and did I tell you about the kid who accidentally exploded our canoe? The girls call him Handsome Hudson because of his YouTube channel, but I don't see the appeal. I mean, what's so great about a dimple?

If that wasn't bad enough, we can't seem to win any challenge points to save our lives. I blame Hank. We attempted the tree house building thing about three days after he sent our canoe hurtling down a hill, and after hiking almost an hour to the build site, we discovered that he'd grabbed the toolbox without any actual

158

tools in it. How does that happen!

I'll stop complaining now. Other than the camp challenge being a bit of a bust, the summer is off to a great start. They did a really good job preparing for me this year, and I haven't broken a thing yet. It's refreshing to be able to sit down in a chair and not have it break into bits. Is this what everyone else feels like all the time?

See you in a few days,

Gabby

PS I know I'm not supposed to call anyone stupid or dumb, but sometimes you just have to use words like that. I can put a quarter in the jar when I get home if you really want me to.

CHAPTER TWELVE

"Think today is the day the girls stop hating us?" Emerson said on the way to lunch. We'd been swimming in the lake all morning, and everyone's hair was still wet as we made our way down the hill. The summer was really starting to heat up, and I ran my hand through my hair before putting on the baseball hat I'd taken to wearing to keep it out of my eyes. Maybe I should just buzz it like Gary. I glanced over at him. He didn't pull off the nearly bald look very well, and I had my doubts that it would look much better on me. I ran a hand over the short bristles of his hair, and he turned to glare at me.

"At some point are you going to explain why you

keep petting my head like that?" he said.

"Nope," I said. I couldn't exactly explain that I was using his hair to figure out how close he was to time traveling. I valued my life too much for that.

The last few days had flown by the way most days did at Camp Outlier. Even though Aaron was much stricter than Eli, we'd still managed to have a great time. Despite the mess we'd made of the challenges, I still felt like I spent most of my time at camp on cloud nine. The other guys had no way of understanding what it was like to be invisible for weeks on end—for every wink, grin, nod, and arm motion to go unseen and unnoticed. Now that I was back, rat's nest hairdo and all, I fully intended to make the most of it. The bridge jump with Hudson had been just the beginning, and I smiled as I remembered his bewildered face as one by one we'd leaped into the waiting water below. To his credit, he'd done it, even if he had complained about the fact that he didn't have a phone to record it on. It felt good to be at camp. We hiked, took the yearly swim test to ensure that we were allowed to swim in the lake during free time, and even spent some time reviewing how to correctly construct a log cabin–style fire. Even Hudson seemed to be warming up to camp. At least he'd started dropping the habit of reaching for a phone that no longer existed.

Speaking of things that no longer existed, something odd was going on with my stuff. At first I'd thought that I was just misplacing things like my water bottle and sunscreen, but after the tenth thing went missing, I started to wonder if this was some kind of a prank. I wouldn't put it past the Red Wood guys to swipe all my stuff by the end of the summer just to pile it all on the roof or something. I made a mental note to ask Emerson if he was missing anything too.

The sight of the Swallowtails coming down their own hill jerked me from my thoughts about my missing stuff, and I grinned and waved at them. Instead of waving back they changed their trajectory, heading around the dining hall to the side door to avoid running into us. I felt my smile fade. Apparently, they weren't over my mistake with the toolbox the day before. In my defense, it had never even occurred to me to open the toolbox to check its contents before schlepping it through the woods. How was I supposed to know that it was empty?

"Think they are still planning to do the ropes course with us this afternoon?" Zeke said, biting his lip.

I nodded. "First we apologize, again."

"If we could just get some points on the board, I think that would help," Anthony said.

"It can't hurt," said Emerson.

162

"I think the ropes course is going to be what turns the tide," Murphy said.

Everyone murmured their assent, and we hurried down the hill and into the dining hall. The Swallowtails gave us dirty looks when we walked in, but we walked over to their table anyway.

"Ladies," I said, stopping to bow low. "May I extend a formal apology from the White Oak cabin for the canoe shenanigans and the tree house mishap?"

"What he's trying to say is that we're really sorry," Emerson said. "We realize we keep screwing up."

"Some people keep screwing up," Gary said.

"Gary! We talked about this," Murphy said as he gave the back of Gary's head a playful smack. "We have to be nice if we want to have friends." That made the girls laugh, and even Gary smiled.

"We're going to do better," Zeke said. "Promise."

"You'd better," Kristy said. Mr. Stink chose that moment to jump onto her lap like a very weird cat and curled up.

"Is the skunk sucking up too?" she asked with a smile. She carefully pulled on the gloves that had been sitting on the table before running a hand down the small animal's back.

"He's a very smart skunk," Zeke said.

"He is," Molly said, leaning over to pet our cabin's

furry mascot. "I'm sorry I scared you the other day," she said in that sappy baby-talk voice people liked to use when talking to small furry creatures.

"Please allow us to make it up to you this afternoon at the ropes course," I said.

"You don't need to make it up to us," Molly said. "I think that's where things keep going haywire."

"Yeah, we aren't a bunch of fragile butterflies," Emily said, and then paused. "Well, our cabin name is a butterfly, but you get what I mean. We don't need you to save us. We can do this on our own."

"And we," I said, gesturing behind myself, "are not a bunch of dumb dudes."

"What do you mean?" Molly said.

"What I mean," I said, "is that in every book I've read lately, the guys need to be saved by the gals. Every guy character seems written with a healthy dose of stupid, and the only way he could find his way out of a bucket is if the girl character shows him how. You haven't noticed that?"

"I might have," Gabby admitted. "I get your point, though. No dumb dudes and no damsels in distress, deal?"

"Deal," I said.

"Fine," Kristy said, and then glanced over at Hudson. "Think you can keep these guys in line?"

"I'll do my best," Hudson said. "But I kind of think they're a bad influence." Kristy giggled like he'd just said something hilarious, and I rolled my eyes.

"Easy there, cowboy, you're visible, remember?" Emerson whispered in my ear, and I reorganized my face fast.

"Thanks," I muttered.

"No problem," he said. We chatted with the girls for a few more minutes and then headed across the room to our table and a waiting Aaron.

The morning involved a very long, very hot hike through the woods, and we were sweating hard when Aaron finally dismissed us for free time. The exception to the rule was Murphy, who had time traveled at the very beginning of the hike and not returned until it was all over. While it was a bummer that Murphy had missed out on a fun activity, it was nice to leave Aaron behind watching the red rocks. Hiking with him was very similar to hunting with the game warden, and in his absence, we'd even managed to check another item off Hudson's Life List. I shook my head, still amazed that the kid had gone his entire life without climbing a tree.

We took a quick pit stop at our cabin to refresh the deodorant situation. I headed into the bathroom to wash my dirt-encrusted hands and paused to study my reflection in the mirror.

The Hank staring back at me out of the glass looked different. I'd grown up a bit since the last time I'd slowed down enough to look in a mirror for more than two seconds. I wondered if anyone else ever did this, looked at their face for the telltale signs of aging, and decided they probably didn't. If you saw your face every day, multiple times a day, you'd never spot what I was seeing now. I called it the Aunt Mildred effect. It was why your aunts always gushed about how much you'd grown when they saw you at your birthday or Thanksgiving but your parents always seemed shocked that you weren't still a toddler. If you saw someone every day, you never noticed them growing up, and it held true for seeing yourself as well. I'm sure if I'd been able to see myself in the mirror whenever I wanted, I'd never have noticed that my forehead was just a touch broader than it had been or that my cheekbones were more pronounced. It was an odd feeling, and one I wasn't particularly fond of. I sometimes thought that you weren't supposed to notice yourself growing up, that one day you were just supposed to wake up as an adult and have no clue how you got there. I, however, was very aware of the phenomenon of time. Having a RISK factor meant that there were no guarantees for my future. I had here. I had now. If I hadn't realized that already, having a time-traveling friend pop in and out of my life with ominous warnings pretty much did the trick.

"I almost forgot how big that nose of yours was," Gary said, coming over to wash his hands.

"Thanks," I said. "I almost forgot about your charming personality. And for your information, I make this nose look good."

"Maybe we all just look frumpy compared to the new guy," Gary said, jerking his head toward the open door to our cabin, where Hudson was leaning against his bunk and looking lost. Lost or not, he was still stupidly good-looking.

"He sure doesn't help matters," I said.

I glanced at my watch. "Come on, guys!" I called. "It's not kind to keep ladies waiting!" A minute later we were running for the ropes course.

The ropes course sat on the far end of camp and was situated about twenty feet up in the trees. We'd done it a few times last year, and honestly, it had never gone very well. A fact that we'd failed to mention to the girls. Probably because we'd already stepped in it bigtime on not one but two occasions, and I don't think any of us wanted to make an already bad situation worse.

The ropes course *had* been a disaster last year,

though, between Gary getting stuck to one of the ropes and Anthony almost igniting the entire thing and Emerson hurling his guts out, thanks to his fear of heights. I glanced over at my friends to discover they were all wearing expressions of grim determination.

We ran through camp and down the path in the woods that led us toward the far left side of camp. We finally rounded the corner and the ropes course came into view. I glanced at my watch. We were five minutes late. The Swallowtails had beat us there, and from the way they were all standing around with their arms crossed, you'd have thought we'd stood them up.

"About time," Kristy said.

"Ladies," I said, and performed one of my most elaborate bows. I stayed in the bowing position instead of standing back up and hissed through my teeth, "Bow, men! Bow!" A few of them did. Gary just stood there looking a lot like a grumpy toad who'd just had his favorite rock stolen.

"Bowing doesn't make you any less late," Gabby pointed out.

"But it makes us exponentially more charming," I said with a grin.

"Why are you always this ridiculous?" Gabby added.

"Because I can be," I said, straightening up. "I apologize for our tardiness. In our defense, we got here as fast as we could. And if you'd smelled the alternative, you'd be ecstatic that we took a pit stop at our cabin."

"I don't feel very ecstatic," Kristy said. "Thanks to you yahoos being late, we got bumped." She jerked her thumb behind her, and I saw that there were in fact two cabins' worth of kids already up in the trees.

"Wait a minute," I said as I stepped forward to get a better view of the course, "what am I looking at right now?" The other guys came to stand beside me and together we peered upward at the kids already halfway through the complicated system of ropes that made up the course.

"It's part of the challenge," Molly said. "You can't do the course one at a time this year. Instead you have to be tied to someone from your partnering cabin for the entire course if you want the points."

"Well, that's interesting," Emerson said as we watched a boy and a girl with their wrists tied together traverse what looked like a particularly tricky bit of the course.

"I can't be tied to anyone," Anthony said, and the barely contained panic in his voice made everyone turn to look at him as the small fire that had been perched on his shoulder like a pirate's parrot flickered and doubled in size.

Kristy studied him a second and then walked over

and calmly placed her hand over the fire, smothering it instantly.

"Wow," he said as Kristy stepped back. I studied her a second and then glanced behind her at the rest of the Swallowtail cabin, and I smiled.

"So maybe that's the key," I said thoughtfully.

"What do you mean?" Emerson said.

"The last time we did this course, what happened to you?" I asked Emerson.

"Um, it wasn't great," Emerson said with a self-conscious glance at Molly. "My weighted vest made it hard to balance on those ropes, and my ankle weights kept getting caught on stuff. If I hadn't had the safety harness on, I would have fallen out of the trees or floated away. I also really don't like heights, so—" I held up a hand, cutting him off. We didn't need to know all the gory details, for Pete's sake.

I turned to Gabby. "And how did the ropes course go for you?" I asked her.

She blushed a bright red and then stared down at her feet. "I broke the ropes," she said. "Thankfully they used a special chain for my safety harness, or I'd have fallen out of the trees too."

"Emerson," I said. "You're partnering with Gabby. If you float and she's super heavy, you should balance each other out. Kristy, you and Anthony partner up. If he catches fire, you can help put it out without getting third-degree burns."

"So, what you're saying is, you think we should try this little thing called teamwork this time?" Kristy said dryly.

"Elementary, my dear Watson," I said, bowing to Kristy again. "I think that if I'd realized this a tad earlier, I might not have single-handedly wrecked our canoe and our chances to build a successful tree house."

"Good," Kristy said, rubbing her hands together. "Now, let's do a little RISK matchmaking, shall we?"

Everyone agreed, and together we matched ourselves up in such a way that we counteracted one another's RISK factors. Not all the matchups were as obvious as the Kristy and Anthony combo, but we figured it out. There were seven of us, thanks to this year's inclusion of Hudson, and only six girls in the Swallowtail cabin, which meant that Zeke and Murphy were both paired up with Abby, who did something with mental telepathy. I'm not sure exactly what, but she seemed pretty confident that she could help them navigate their way over the ropes even if one of them struggled with an X-ray vision impairment and one of them decided to time travel unexpectedly. Hudson was paired up with Molly, but I wasn't sure what the theory behind that was. Maybe he could levitate her to safety if she turned into a dog? I was about to ask when I felt a hand tap my shoulder. I turned to see a girl standing there expectantly. She had long straight black hair pulled half back underneath a baseball hat, a small upturned nose, and beautiful almond-shaped eyes that were staring right through me. I felt my heart sink. I knew what it meant when someone looked through you instead of at you. I was invisible again. I glanced down at myself, expecting to see a whole lot of nothing where my legs were supposed to be, but to my surprise, there they were. A quick check of my hands and arms revealed that they were still blessedly visible as well.

"Excuse me one second," I said to the girl, and grabbed the nearest White Oak guy available. It turned out to be Gary.

"What?" he snapped, turning from where he'd been having a conversation with Gabby.

"Quick," I hissed. "Is my head gone?"

"You're all there, at least from the visibility standpoint," Gary said, pulling his arm from my grasp. "Mentally is yet to be determined."

"Great, thanks," I said, turning back to the girl, who was still looking at me as though she could see through me. "Sorry about that," I said. "I don't think we were properly introduced before. I'm Hank. Inconveniently invisible member of the White Oak cabin at your service."

"I'm Amy," she said. "Come on, let's go get ready." With that she turned and headed over to where a set of stairs had been built leading up to the platform where the ropes course began. Everyone else was already ahead of us, chatting with their new partner as they made a strategy for traversing the ropes together. I took my place beside Amy, who was standing almost too still as we waited our turn. There was something odd about the way she carried herself, but I couldn't quite put my finger on it.

"So," I said as we waited our turn to be harnessed up, "what's your RISK factor?" In any place other than Camp O, that question would have been rude. RISK factors were one of those things people weren't really supposed to ask about. People noticed you were different, but they either pretended like they didn't see it, or they just avoided interaction altogether.

"It's kind of hard to explain," Amy said without turning her head.

"Most of them are," I said.

She smiled. "Good point. Well, you could say that I'm blind as a bat, but that wouldn't really be accurate."

"Oh," I said, suddenly feeling like an idiot. So that was why she'd been looking right through me. It wasn't because I was invisible; it was because she couldn't see me. I suddenly felt like a giant putz. I glanced down at my very visible hands and wondered which was worse, to not be seen or to not see? I glanced around at the vivid green of the forest, the blue-gray sky peeping out between sun-blasted branches, and I immediately knew the answer. That was something that Camp O was good at: making you appreciate your own blessings. So often I'd wished away my invisibility, but I'd rarely wished that I could trade it for someone else's RISK. Although there had been a moment when I'd considered trading Hudson, but that hadn't lasted past the cabin combustion episode. Sometimes the hand you were dealt in life was dealt to you for a reason, I thought. I looked back over at Amy and searched for something clever to say.

"I bet you're glad you're paired with me and not Zeke," I finally said with a jerk of my head to where Zeke was currently strapping on a harness while a very disgruntled Mr. Stink stood nearby.

"X-ray vision impairment, right?" Amy said.

"Yeah," I said. "He's got an amazing service skunk. Do you have a service animal?"

"I don't need one," Amy said. Before I could ask her to elaborate, it was our turn. Two counselors were waiting for us at the top, and I smiled when I saw that one of them was Eli. During afternoon free time the counselors were all assigned different parts of camp to manage. Some were down by the lake on lifeguard duty, others were supervising the archery station, while a few were scattered here and there helping campers in the nature center or art department.

"Ready for this, Hank?" he said, taking my hand and helping me up the last step.

"Born ready," I said. "Is your cabin attempting this too?"

"They are just finishing up," Eli said. "They're a good group, just like you guys were, although they haven't gotten in nearly as much trouble."

"Remind me to give them a talking-to about that after I get through the course," I said with a wink.

"Arms out," Eli instructed, and he expertly buckled me into the safety harness while the girl counselor did the same for Amy, and I felt a bit of my nerves subside. I had a lot of confidence in my own abilities to navigate the ropes course, but I had very little confidence in my ability to help a girl who described herself as blind as a bat make her way across too. At least if I failed and she fell, she wouldn't be plummeting to her death.

Once we were both ready, we were handed a small length of rope. I looked over at the course to see that everyone was using their rope in different ways. Emerson was floating above Gabby's head, both of them holding on to their length of rope like their lives depended on it. Abby was towing Zeke and Murphy behind her with her rope, and I was surprised to see Mr. Stink on Zeke's shoulder, his claws dug into the fabric of his T-shirt.

"So," I said, glancing over at Amy. "Should I go first and you follow? Do you want to hold on to my shoulder? I can tell you where to put your feet and stuff."

"Not necessary," she said. "And if it's all the same to you, I'd prefer to lead." I took the remaining two steps to the edge of the platform and glanced down. I didn't have Emerson's barf reflex to heights, but I couldn't say they were my favorite either. I slipped off my shoes and socks and, with a quick glance to make sure they wouldn't take anyone out, tossed them to the ground twenty feet below. I'd done the course barefoot last year, and if I ever needed a bit more grip, it was now.

"Hey, Emerson," I called, hoping to lighten the mood. "Think I could do the course while simultaneously juggling ten pine cones and a squirrel?"

"No," Emerson said, his words tight as he kept his eyes straight ahead.

"What if I ditch the squirrel?" I said. "Does that change your answer?"

"Hank," Kristy said, making my name into both a warning and a threat.

"Joking!" I said, turning to Amy. "Ready?"

"Ready," she said, carefully securing our rope

around one of her wrists so she could grasp the start of the ropes course with both hands. I watched her do this without a moment of hesitation, and I raised an eyebrow.

"I thought you were blind," I said.

"I never said that," Amy said as she stepped out onto the rope with a confidence I wished I felt. "I said I was as blind as a bat, and bats aren't blind." She made her way swiftly down the rope, and it took the tug on my wrist for me to snap out of my amazement and follow her out over the open air.

"Blind as a bat," I muttered to myself as she navigated a bit of rope ladder with ease. I racked my brain for what I knew about bats. It wasn't much. Now, Batman? I'd have had a better shot. I took a stab at it anyway. "So, you use echolocation?" I asked.

"Well done," Amy said as though I was a first grader who'd just spelled the word *cat* correctly.

"That might be the coolest thing I've ever heard," I said.

"Watch yourself here, this rope is loose," Amy said.

I followed her warning and made sure I placed my bare feet exactly where they needed to be. We were the last ones out on the ropes, but I needed all of my focus on my feet as Amy was making her way over the ropes twice as fast as I'd planned on doing them.

I realized that this whole team thing might change a lot about this summer. I glanced up from my feet for a half second to see what kind of progress everyone else was making, and let out a whoop as I saw Emerson and Gabby make it safely onto the platform at the far side. We were going to do this, I thought excitedly, and mentally added five points onto our score. Kristy and Anthony were right behind them, and I saw Kristy bounce over to give Hudson's perfectly styled hair a ruffle with her gloved hand, and he grinned back at her. I tried to remember if Kristy had looked at me like that this summer, and then reminded myself that you actually had to be visible to get a look like that. The rope on my wrist gave a tug as Amy continued, and I refocused on my feet and hurried to catch up. The last part of the course was the trickiest. Unlike the beginning of the course, where there were some rope bridges, ladders, and netting, the end of the course was nothing but a single rope you had to walk on tightrope style while holding on to two ropes on either side of you.

We were only about fifteen feet from the final platform when three things happened almost simultaneously. The first was that the thick rope that hung ten feet above our heads, the rope all our safety ropes were attached to, suddenly broke in half. I stood there in disbelief as it fell past my face to dangle uselessly below us. The second was that my feet, which I'd been staring at intensely almost this entire time, disappeared. But it was the third thing that really threw me for a loop—when the rope underneath my invisible feet disappeared too.

I let out a yelp of surprise, fully expecting to go plummeting to the ground, and froze with a death grip on the still blessedly visible ropes on either side of me. My stomach plunged and then righted itself a second later when I didn't fall. I looked down again at the disconcerting view of nothing beneath me and had to immediately shut my eyes. It wasn't until my eyes were shut that I realized that I felt the rough texture of the rope beneath my bare feet. The rope wasn't gone. It was just invisible. I was still processing this when I felt a tug at the rope tied around my wrist and opened my eyes to the image of Amy moving along through thin air like nothing had happened.

"Um, Amy?" I said as my stomach did an uncomfortable flop. There must have been something in my voice because she immediately stopped and looked back at me.

"What?" she said.

"The rope?" I said, trying to keep the nervous quaver out of my voice and failing. "It's not attached anymore."

"The safety rope?" she said, and I saw her narrow

her eyes as she tried to make sense of what I was saying.

"Yeah," I said, frozen in place. "Like the one that keeps us from dying if we slip. That rope."

"That's not good," she said. "I advise you not to slip. We're almost there."

"Gee, thanks," I said. "But that's not all. The rope we're standing on is invisible too."

"Oh?" she said. "Why?"

"I have no idea," I said. "But it disappeared at the same time that my feet did."

"Your feet disappeared too?" Amy said. "I can still see them and the rope perfectly."

"Interesting," I said. "But not exactly helpful."

"Well," she said after a moment. "Then just follow my lead." She started walking again, but I didn't move, even when the rope around my wrist connecting me to her gave a painful tug. I glanced over at my arm to see that it too had disappeared. I didn't need to ask anyone to know that I was completely invisible again.

"You okay up there?" I heard someone call, but I didn't dare look down or even respond. I felt like my voice was stuck, and I wasn't sure exactly how to unstick it. Instead I just shook a head that no one could see.

"You can do this," Amy said. "Just hold on tight

to the rope on either side. You don't need to see your feet or the rope to know it's there." I barely heard her. It almost seemed like her voice was really far away, and I felt my legs start shaking as I held on to the rope on either side of me with a death grip. My shaking didn't improve matters in the slightest, as it made the single invisible rope we were standing on start to vibrate alarmingly. It suddenly occurred to me that if I fell, I was going to take Amy down with me. She had the rope tied around her waist, and my weight would probably drag her off. I needed to untie it, but to do that, I was going to have to let go of one of the ropes, and that wasn't going to happen.

There was some sort of excited yelling and some screaming coming from below us, but I wasn't really paying attention. My heart was hammering so loudly in my ears, it made it almost impossible to hear anything else. There was another tug on my wrist as Amy tried to make progress while attached to her human anchor. That tug broke through my panic, and I forced my brain to stop hyperventilating for a second so I could think. I had to move. I couldn't live the rest of my life on this invisible rope. For one thing, I really had to go to the bathroom, and wetting my pants on the ropes course wasn't really something I wanted added to my reputation. I moved my feet forward a few inches and then a few more. At this rate, we'd make it across by the end of the summer, I thought dryly.

"How you doing there, buddy?" someone said practically in my ear, and I jumped in surprise, the ropes swinging violently as I heard multiple people gasp. Apparently, I wasn't the only one nervous about how this was all going to play out. I tore my eyes away from the trembling rope to see Emerson floating beside me, a rope tied securely around his waist. I hazarded a quick glance at the ground to see Gary holding the other end of the rope, a look of grim determination on his face. The two-second glance was enough to make my head spin, and I looked back up at Emerson. He had his eyes squeezed shut, and he was flailing about in front of himself, searching for something. I'd seen him do this maneuver a few times before, the most notable being when we'd floated him up into the trees to recover a compass on our initiation night last summer.

"What are you doing?" I said as his searching fingers found the rope attaching me to Amy.

Emerson ignored me, his eyes still shut, and held up the rope. "Is this the right one?" he called.

"That's it!" Anthony yelled back.

"Cool!" Emerson said, and with his eyes still squeezed shut, he began carefully looping the rope around his own wrists with some kind of complicated hitch knot. I watched this performance, feeling equal parts parts impressed and frustrated with my best friend.

"What are you doing?" I said again. "If I fall, now you go down too!"

"No," Emerson said, eyes still shut. "If you fall, I still float, so I'll make sure you get to the ground in one piece."

"Are you sure?" I said.

"No," Emerson admitted, "but worst-case scenario, I'll slow you down so you'll just break your legs and not your neck."

"Well, that's something," I said as something inside me loosened. "Thanks." My voice was hoarse. I knew what this was costing Emerson. He hated heights with every particle of his being, and anytime he floated he took the risk of floating away.

"Told you we'd save you," Emerson said, his eyes still shut. "Now, will you move, please? I'm all for saving your life, but I also really don't want to throw up in front of everyone again."

"Right," I said. "Sorry." I took a step, an actual step this time, not a tentative shuffle. "Would it make you feel better if I puked first?" I asked.

Emerson seemed to consider this for a second and

then shook his head, eyes still shut. "No. Move."

So I did. Now that I had Emerson as my backup, I wanted off this rope, and I wanted off this rope now. Amy moved ahead of me, and I followed, attempting to place invisible feet exactly where they needed to go on an invisible rope. It felt like an eternity, but it was probably only a minute or so later, and I felt the fabulously stable wood of the platform under my feet. I fell onto it gratefully and kissed it like a sailor kissed dry land after surviving a shipwreck.

"Easy there, or you'll be pulling splinters out of your lips for a week," Amy said, and I glanced up to see her watching me. I'd forgotten that I wasn't invisible to her, and I quickly got up and brushed myself off. I turned back to look at where we'd just come from and blinked in surprise to see that the rope I'd been standing on two seconds earlier was no longer invisible.

"Hey," I said as I quickly pulled Emerson down from his floating position by my head. "When did the rope show back up?"

"Huh?" he said, opening one eye as his feet scrabbled an inch above the wooden platform. I yanked him down the last few inches just as Zeke popped his head up and slid me Emerson's vest. I hefted it onto Emerson's shoulders, and he buckled it on gratefully.

"What did you do to the rope?" Zeke said.

"Me?" I said. "You think I did this?"

"Yes," everyone chorused, and I blinked in surprise.

"Well," I said, "only one way to find out." I turned to the left, where another rope setup left the platform, and headed out into the trees. Before I could think better of it, I tentatively placed a bare foot on the rope. It disappeared. I quickly yanked it back and then glanced over at Zeke and Emerson, who both looked just as shocked as I felt.

"Well, that's new," Zeke said. It was then that I noticed the sounds of the cheers and whoops floating up from below us. I glanced over the edge of the platform to see the rest of our team watching as well as the kids from the Red Maple and Monarch cabins. I threw my arms out and bowed, because that's what you did when you were receiving a standing ovation. Since I was invisible, the effect wasn't quite as good as usual, so I grabbed Emerson's arm and held it up in the air in triumph. The cheers below redoubled.

"Lady and gentlemen," I said. "We should head down. Our fan club awaits." I sent the other three down first, waiting until they touched bottom to put my own bare feet on the ladder, just in case it decided to disappear too. Thankfully it stayed visible, and I made my way down and into the arms of our teammates. It wasn't until I was done getting clapped on the back that I realized that Eli and the other female counselor were missing.

"Where did Eli go?" I said.

"He went to get Mr. Blue," Molly said. "He should be back any minute."

"I'm not sure if I'm upset that you thought I was going to accidentally kill myself and Amy in the process or relieved you sent someone for help," I said.

"You probably wouldn't have died," Kristy said. "Maimed horribly, yes. But died? Seems like a stretch. You were only twenty-five feet or so in the air."

"Only twenty-five feet," I repeated. "I'd like to see how you'd do if your rope disappeared."

"I'd have fared just fine," Kristy said with a sniff.

A second later help arrived, and Mr. Blue shoved his way through the crowd to reach me, Amy, and Emerson.

"Are you guys okay?" he said.

"We are," I said. "Thanks to Emerson."

"All right, then," Mr. Blue said loudly, turning to the crowd surrounding us. "Everyone not in the Swallowtail or White Oak cabin, please head back to camp." He raised an eyebrow at the orange and red kids staring back at him and smiled. "I'm sure I'm not alone in hoping that you all change back to your normal coloring soon." There was murmured laughter as they headed back toward camp with Eli, leaving our team standing loosely around the bright blue head of camp.

Mr. Blue glanced behind himself as though he was looking for someone and then turned back to our team. "What happened?" he said, dropping his voice. "Explain quickly, please, before a certain government official gets here. I may have told him to take a left at the big rock instead of a right, but he'll figure it out eventually."

I caught on immediately and did a fast and furious recap of the events, from the rope breaking to my inconvenient invisibility somehow extending to the rope we were standing on. Mr. Blue scratched his chin as he appraised me in all my invisible glory.

"That's a new element to your RISK level, am I right?" he finally said.

"Yes, sir," I said. "That was a first."

"Please report that to Nurse Betsy when we get back to camp," he said. "She'll need to document it."

"What I want to know is how in the world did the safety rope just break? I mean, that thing was as thick as my arm," Hudson said.

"That is an excellent question," Mr. Blue said with a scowl up at the ropes course. His normal royal-blue color seemed to darken into an angry navy as he surveyed the rope that was still hanging limp and useless.

"Need a better look?" Hudson asked, and before Mr. Blue could respond the safety rope was flying through the air.

"So cool," Kristy said breathlessly as Hudson stopped the rope above our heads and began to lower it slowly to the ground.

"Thank you," Mr. Blue said as he caught it in his hand.

"It didn't explode," Gary said, sounding disappointed.

"Things don't always explode," Hudson said, and then he cocked his head and glanced over at Mr. Blue. "In fact, I can't think of the last thing I exploded."

"Trash can," I said automatically. "The morning before you lost your phone during the canoe challenge. You were trying to get a video of yourself sending trash across the room and into the can, and then the can combusted and sent trash into all of our bunks. Which was lovely."

"Um, that was kind of a rhetorical question, but thanks," Hudson said.

"Maybe you're like Nurse Betsy now," Kristy said. "She never explodes anything."

"Nurse Betsy may have a similar RISK factor to Hudson's, but that doesn't mean that they share the same challenges," Mr. Blue said.

"Really?" Zeke said, perking up. "What challenges does she have?"

"That is her business and not yours," Mr. Blue said sternly. "The question at hand now is what in the world happened to this," he said as he turned over the safety rope in his hands.

"Better question," Gary said. "Did we earn our five points or what?"

Mr. Blue laughed and shook his head ruefully. "I believe you did," he said. "The rule was that the teams had to make it across the ropes tethered to at least one other camper. I don't believe that Emerson's assistance changed that in any way." Everyone cheered, and Emerson threw an arm around my invisible shoulders.

"Think you can relax now?" he whispered in my ear, and we both glanced over at Murphy, who was chatting with Amy.

"I don't know," I said, biting my lip. "That felt too easy."

"Easy?" Emerson snorted. "Nothing about that was easy."

"Maybe you're right," I said. "What's more terrifying, do you think? Falling to your death or floating to your death?"

Emerson considered that a moment and then shrugged. "I'm going to say that one's a toss-up since the end result is kind of the same. Although floating to your death takes longer than falling."

"There you are," Mr. Blue said, and we turned as Aaron came jogging down the path.

"Got here as soon as I heard," Aaron said. I expected him to take control of our cabin, but instead, Mr. Blue just handed him the broken safety rope.

Aaron inspected it and then nodded and climbed the ladder up to the ropes course.

Before I could ask what Aaron was up to, a very sweaty Mr. Munkhouser came stomping up the path with his tablet.

"What happened?" he said.

"Nothing to concern yourself with," Mr. Blue said, putting a massive blue hand on the little man's shoulder and steering him back down the path. "Just a little snafu with the ropes course."

I watched the two men head down the path, Mr. Blue striking an air of nonchalance that was at complete odds with the way he'd been looking at that broken rope just moments before. Something wasn't right, and he knew it.

Dear Mom and Dad,
I miss you! Thanks for sending the care package full of cookies. I shared them with

the rest of the girls, and they all agree
that you should probably send a package
at least once a week. Gabby would like
to place a request for chocolate chip
cookies, and Molly would love something
almond flavored. She's not picky.

Camp is great, just like last year, but it's
also kind of different. We attempted to
complete the fire build yesterday, and it
was a complete and total disaster. It was
this challenge where you had to collect
all these sticks and build three different
types of bonfire formations AND light
them before the other teams. Simple,
right? Except it wasn't because this kid
Anthony somehow wore the wrong gloves
or something and accidentally kept lighting
our piles on fire before we could get them
done. I know I should be extra understanding
of other RISK kids—I mean, I scorched
every stick I picked up—but sometimes it's
hard. Why is that?

The first week has gone well otherwise,
and we attempt the next whole-camp
challenge tomorrow. Hopefully the guys
don't screw it up or do something bizarre

like show up wearing ridiculous costumes.
After their musical number in sparkly vests
at the beginning of the year, I wouldn't put
it past them. I'll tell you about that later.
This letter is getting long, and rest time is
almost over.

Lots of love,

Kristy

PS What are your thoughts on getting a
skunk as a pet?

PPS Don't forget about the cookies!

CHAPTER THIRTEEN

"I can't believe we are already two weeks into camp and we still have a giant goose egg on that board," Gary grouched as he bit into his slice of pizza. I eyed the scoreboard at the front of the dining hall, where we still had a big fat zero next to our team's name. It was definitely better than the negative five Aaron had given us, but since the only points we'd managed to win were five points at the ropes course, we still had a zero.

"We've just had a string of bad luck," Emerson said. "It's bound to turn around soon."

"That's one way to put it," Gary said. "I'd say we're cursed."

I didn't comment as I took another bite of the

pepperoni pizza that I couldn't actually see and chewed thoughtfully. My new trick of turning things invisible was obnoxious at best and a pain at the worst. It didn't happen all the time, but often enough that more than once I'd found myself sleeping on an invisible bed and attempting to brush my teeth with an invisible toothbrush. Thankfully everything showed back up eventually, but there didn't seem to be a rhyme or reason to how long things stayed invisible. Nurse Betsy had been trying out different sock and glove options in an attempt to stop my new fun trick from turning our entire cabin invisible, but I kept making them disappear too, which made them really hard to keep track of. The only perk to this new RISK factor discovery was that the mystery of my disappearing stuff was solved. No one was taking my stuff; I just hadn't been noticing that I'd been making it disappear. Some of it had slowly started to reappear, and I was especially pleased to discover my toothbrush, since I'd been borrowing Gary's when he wasn't looking.

I'd also been bumped to a level five, thanks to this new party trick that had entailed a full workup from Nurse Betsy and lots of iPad tapping from Mr. Munkhouser. Neither of those things were as annoying as trying to eat invisible pizza with an invisible hand. Gary was right. We did seem cursed. If it wasn't our

RISK factors getting in the way of succeeding, it was faulty equipment. First our canoe had gone careening down a hill at thirty miles an hour to shatter like a piñata at a kid's birthday. Which, admittedly, had nothing to do with equipment and everything to do with poor decision-making. Although if the Blue Spruces' and Blue Morphos' canoe hadn't fallen apart on the trail and blocked our way, we could have avoided that particular disaster.

Then it had been the empty toolbox with the tree house build, then the ropes course where we'd avoided catastrophe by the skin of our teeth, and the fire-building contest had been a hot mess. Literally and figuratively. Anthony's flameproof gloves had turned out to be very flammable, and the result had been a disaster that would have given Smokey Bear nightmares for a week. It wasn't just our cabins that were having bad luck either. Mishaps seemed to be popping up all over camp, from the Monarch cabin heading out on a canoe trip only to discover that all their canoes had holes to the Red Wood guys who had their bows and arrows malfunction during an archery lesson that led to more than one kid sitting in Nurse Betsy's office.

"It could be worse," Zeke pointed out as Mr. Stink helped himself to the cheese off his pizza. "We could still be in the negative."

"Don't jinx us," I said, glancing around for Aaron. That guy had the uncanny habit of always seeming to be in earshot. It was impossible to say one word to the guys without him turning up. It was a minor miracle we'd snuck out for our meeting with the girls at the beginning of camp.

Speaking of the girls, I let my eyes wander over to their table to discover that they were laughing and having a great time as they took down their own pizza. Kristy looked our way, and I gave her a huge over-size wink and tipped my hat. She didn't even notice. I scowled and was debating having a very small pity party for my poor pathetic, invisible self when I spotted Amy. She was looking right at me, and from the smirk on her face, she'd seen the wink and the tipped hat. Well, that was something, I thought, and then rue-fully lifted my hat to run a hand through my rat's nest of hair. I hadn't even been visible long enough to cut it. Gary had done a spot-on imitation of me the other day while we were getting ready for dinner using some of Hudson's hair gel. It had been funny even if it had made me want to smack him. I turned back to the table and jumped as I spotted a second Murphy helping him-self to a slice of pizza.

"Hey," I said, elbowing Emerson hard in his side to get his attention.

"Ouch," he protested. "You have *got* to learn to just tap somebody on the shoulder, dude. I swear I'm going to have a permanent bruise."

"One, I think you say 'dude' more than I do now. It's a crying shame and I plan to remedy that immediately. And two, we have a visitor."

"Oh," he said, finally catching on. He immediately elbowed Anthony, and within a minute everyone was watching the two Murphys. I felt goose bumps prickle up my arms and down my neck, a feeling I always got when I saw Murphy time travel.

"How's it going?" the new Murphy asked himself.

The Murphy in the present was studying this version of himself with narrowed eyes. "You're from five months ago, aren't you?" It was then that I noticed that the visiting Murphy was wearing a PE T-shirt with the words *Pleasant Wood Middle School* emblazoned across the front. He also smelled pretty rank.

"Yup," the visiting Murphy said as he helped himself to another slice of pizza off his future self's plate. "We are supposed to be running the mile. This is much better."

Current Murphy wrinkled his nose. "It's time to take that gym shirt home and wash it."

"Yeah?" Murphy said, giving himself a sniff. "You're probably right."

A second later Aaron was standing over the two Murphys, his face a storm cloud. Without saying a word he yanked both of them from their seats at the table and marched them out the door.

"Um, what was that?" Hudson said as the entire camp turned to watch both Murphys getting hustled away, Mr. Blue and Mr. Munkhouser hot on their heels.

"Other than confusing?" Gary said. "No idea. Looks like they're in trouble, though."

"But that doesn't seem fair," Hudson said. "He shouldn't get punished just for having a RISK factor."

I glanced over at Hudson, who was watching the Murphys with concern etched on his face. If this had happened at the beginning of camp, the odds were pretty good that he wouldn't have even noticed it happening.

"You're right," I told him. "It's not fair. But no one asked us our opinions, did they?" I felt even more sorry for my friend. Someone needed to take the attention off Murphy. That someone was going to be me.

The Swallowtails were in the process of clearing their plates, and I saw Amy stand up to retrieve the tray of brownies the kitchen staff had just set out, and I was moving before my brain had a chance to think through whether or not this was a good idea. I leaped onto the bench I'd been sitting on a second before and launched myself backward into a back tuck. I stuck the landing and immediately did a backflip that landed me right in front of Amy. The effect wasn't as good as if I'd been visible, but my clothes flip-flopping through the air would have to do.

"May I?" I said, dropping low into a bow before standing up to take the tray of brownies. I heard a few chuckles, and with a flourish I offered her my arm like I was escorting her to a ball and not to her table. Anyone else would have had no idea that I'd just done that, since my sleeveless shirt didn't really give many hints about what my invisible arms were doing, but not Amy. Amy saw my arm and looped hers through it with a smile. Holding the brownie tray above my head like a waiter at a fancy restaurant, I escorted her to her table.

"Is everyone in your family like you?" she said.

"Nope," I said. "I broke the mold. I have three older brothers as normal as mud. Crying shame."

"I meant can they backflip like you?" she said.

"Yeah," I said. "My mom went through a phase during the last Olympics and enrolled us all in gymnastics for a solid year. None of us became professional gymnasts, but the backflip and tuck proved useful on the farm. Confuses the heck out of the cows." Amy snorted and took her seat. Before I set the tray down on the table, I tossed it high into the air, did a fast spin, and reached out to catch the tray again, only to discover that instead of falling back to earth, it was now suspended ten feet above my head. It spun slowly once and then lowered itself neatly onto the girls' table. I glanced over my shoulder to see Hudson wink at the table of girls. I'd been forgotten as they looked right through me.

I sat down at our table with a huff.

"That backflip or whatever was cool," Emerson said.

"Thanks," I said. "I was trying to take the attention off poor Murphy. Or should I say Murphys, like plural? How does one talk about someone's present self and past self when they are both currently operating in the same chunk of time?"

"Stop," Zeke moaned, closing his eyes. "You're giving me a headache."

"Speaking of headaches," Gary said with a jerk of his head, and we followed his gaze to the doors of the dining hall, where five TTBI agents were standing in their no-nonsense black suits. They scanned the room for a brief moment and started making their way across the dining hall toward us.

"Who's that?" Hudson said.

"That's trouble," I said.

"The TTBI," Emerson said.

"The Time Travel Bureau of Investigation," Zeke clarified.

"Why do they look like they want to kill us?" Hudson asked.

"That's how they always look," I said as my stomach did a nervous twist. "Whatever you do, don't tell them anything about time-traveling Murphy. As far as they know, today was the first time we've ever had a future or past Murphy show up. Got it?"

"I think so," Hudson said.

"White Oak cabin?" a tall dark-haired TTBI agent said when he reached our table.

"No," Gary said with a straight face. "The Blue Spruce cabin, sir." I snorted and the sip of water I'd just taken went up my nose. I spluttered and choked while Emerson whacked me helpfully on the back. Meanwhile Gary stared at the officer with the straightest of straight faces, which made it that much better. I covered my laugh with a napkin, thankful that my face was invisible to the scrutinizing stare of the TTBI agent. He studied me for another second before turning back to Gary.

"Is that so?" he asked, his look of confidence wavering. "Where is the White Oak cabin, then?"

"Over there," Gary said as he pointed at the Red

201

Wood cabin's table on the other side of the cavernous dining hall. The TTBI agent immediately turned and started in that direction, his counterparts trailing him.

"I thought people who knew what was good for them didn't mess with the TTBI," Hudson said.

"I'm not one of those people. Just ask the principal at my school," Gary said with an evil grin as the TTBI agents finally reached the Red Wood table. "Shall we head out?" he said, turning to us. We all stood and made our way quickly through the dining hall in the opposite direction of the agents and out the back door. I was about to let out a whoop of triumph when we ran smack into Mr. Munkhouser.

"Going somewhere, boys?" he asked, eyebrow raised.

"With you?" I said.

"Good answer," he said. "Let's go." With a sigh of resignation, we followed Mr. Munkhouser toward the nurse's cabin, five very disgruntled TTBI agents falling in behind us.

Nurse Betsy did not like TTBI agents, a fact that she made no effort to hide as all of us crammed ourselves into the tiny cabin that acted as the medical hub of the camp. In fact, I think she was the only adult on campus who didn't seem to get a little twitchy around the guys in suits. Instead she made it crystal clear to them that they were on her territory and it annoyed her.

"Stop taking up so much space," she said as the TTBI agents attempted to arrange themselves in some kind of semicircle around us. "You goons have shoulders the size of Buicks. What did your mothers feed you as children? Elephants?" I watched our short and stout nurse push around the TTBI agents like they were a bunch of naughty campers she'd caught messing around with the Band-Aid stash. I sure did love Nurse Betsy.

"Ma'am," Mr. Munkhouser said to her, his voice stern.

"Don't you 'ma'am' me," Nurse Betsy said. "I don't have time for this nonsense today." She turned to the TTBI agents, her finger already shaking in their faces. "Protocol is sending one agent. One! Why did we get the whole kit and caboodle today? Don't you boys have something better to do than to get in the way of people who actually have work to do? Watch your heads," she added as she sent three prescription bottles and a notebook sailing off her desk. Four of the agents ducked, but one was a tad too slow and got clubbed in the back of the head with one of the bottles.

"Sorry about that," Nurse Betsy said, not sounding the least bit sorry as she sent four clipboards zooming like bats through an open door to the right. A small boy, probably a Red Maple guy, was sitting in a chair with an ice pack on his head, and a second later he was levitated up and sent through the same door as the clipboards.

"Was that boy here for an injury involving his RISK factor?" Munkhouser said as he attempted to maneuver his iPad up and into a working position in the crammed office. "Do you know what level he is?"

"That is classified," Nurse Betsy said, turning her accusing finger to Munkhouser, who cowered back a bit.

"Begging your pardon," Munkhouser said. "But I am the head of the Department of Summer RISK Management and Assessment. Nothing is too classified for me."

"Fine," Nurse Betsy said. "Then it's not classified. I just don't want to tell you because it's rude to ask that in front of a large group of people. Now, please, hush a moment so I can get this mess sorted out." She turned and raised an eyebrow at a stack of files that immediately zoomed through the air and into her outstretched hand. She turned back to Munkhouser, who was clicking away at the iPad, and narrowed her eyes. "No electronics allowed in here," she said. "It goofs up my equipment." Before he could protest, his iPad popped out of his hand and zoomed out the window like some kind of weird black bird.

Hudson watched all this with his mouth hanging open. I'd forgotten that he'd never really seen Nurse Betsy in all her levitating glory.

"She's pretty great, isn't she?" I said as she whisked a jar of lollipops out of the hands of one of the TTBI agents and across the room to her own desk.

"She's amazing," Hudson said in awe. "Does she ever lose control?"

"Not that I've ever seen," Emerson said.

"It would be pretty funny if she did," Gary said. "She'd send a camper flying out the window or something."

"I'd be happy to do that for you, Gary, so we could evaluate just how funny that would be," Nurse Betsy said to Gary without looking at him.

"Listen up," one of the TTBI officers said, turning to us. "We need to speak with you about the time-traveling incident that happened today."

"What time-traveling incident?" I said.

"Don't play dumb," another officer said. "The traveler in your cabin named Murphy appeared at your table not more than fifteen minutes ago."

"Oh!" I said, slapping my forehead. "That! Well, we'd barely even noticed another Murphy was there. I mean, it's pizza day. Have you tried it? Each slice is perfectly crispy on the outside and delightfully squishy on the inside, probably because they use about a pound of butter in the crust. If you really want to level up, though, go for the garlic dipping sauce. You guys look like garlic-dipping-sauce kind of guys, I think. I'm sure we could get you a slice without too much trouble."

"And how many times has another Murphy shown up here at camp?" the officer asked, ignoring my pizza manifesto entirely.

"Hmmmm," I said thoughtfully. "It hasn't happened at all this summer. I think it may have happened once last summer, but we never got to talk to him, did we, boys?" Everyone else murmured their general agreement, and I saw one of the agents pull out a pad of paper to write something down.

"Where is Murphy anyway?" I said, glancing around. "Like, the one that is supposed to be helping us at our next camp challenge? Not the past or future or whatever Murphy who showed up at lunch?"

"That's none of your concern at the moment," one of the agents said.

"Actually, it is," Mr. Blue interrupted as he crammed himself into the tiny cottage. "There is a camp-wide challenge about to start, and I'm sure he would like to participate."

"What he would like isn't really a concern of ours,"

the tall blond agent replied. "He and his time-traveling counterpart are currently being questioned, and their information is being documented. He will be released to your care once that has been accomplished to our satisfaction."

"What about the rest of the cabin?" Mr. Blue asked. "Are they to be documented as well? If so, their parents will need to be informed and I'll have a mountain of paperwork I need your assistance with." He crossed his arms over his broad chest, and his elbow hit a glass jar. It toppled off the shelf and shattered on the floor. Everyone jumped, and I saw each agent put a hand reflexively to their hip, even though whatever they usually carried there was conspicuously absent.

"What do you all think this is? A clown car at the circus?" Nurse Betsy yelled, and suddenly every item around the room jumped to attention to hover somewhat menacingly a foot in the air.

The agent closest to the shards of glass that were currently spinning ominously near his face cleared his throat. "I think we're probably done here, at least with the miscellaneous campers."

"Miscellaneous campers," Anthony grumbled under his breath. "Makes us sound like the contents of a junk drawer."

"We've been called worse," Gary pointed out.

"Wow," Hudson said as he reached out a finger tentatively to give the glass of water floating in the air beside him a gentle spin. "This would get like a million likes," he said.

"Well then, I'll just get these gentlemen out of your hair," Mr. Blue said. He turned to Nurse Betsy, who was standing behind her desk with a red face and her hands on her hips, and he smiled apologetically. "Sorry about taking over your cabin. Please send Murphy over when he's done here."

"Of course," she said. "I know how to do my job, unlike some people who apparently need five people to do the job of one." The stuff in the room gave an angry shudder, and Mr. Blue quickly herded us back out the door to where Aaron was waiting. Mr. Munkhouser shouldered past us to reenter the cabin, his cracked iPad under his arm, and I had a moment where I was actually worried about Nurse Betsy. In the next second one of the TTBI officers yelped, and a jar of Band-Aids was launched from the window, and I stopped worrying.

"All right, then," Mr. Blue said as he hustled us away from the cabin. "Glad that is over with."

"Nurse Betsy is a boss," I said.

Mr. Blue chuckled. "That she is, Hank, that she is. If I die tomorrow, I think she could single-handedly run

208

this entire camp and do it better than I could.

"Aaron!" Mr. Blue said, striding over to our counselor. "Please escort your cabin to the next camp challenge. It's about to begin."

"I hear they played a trick on the TTBI agents," Aaron said, arms crossed over his chest. "How many points should I deduct from their score?"

Everyone started yelling at once.

"What?!"

"That's not fair!"

"Those guys are jerks!"

"The jerkiest of jerks!"

"This isn't fair!"

Mr. Blue held up his hands to hush our clatter of indignation and looked over at Aaron. "Today was an unprecedented situation, and I don't believe that they should have any points deducted. However," he said, turning back to us, "if anything like this happens again, I expect complete compliance out of you lot. Murphy is here due to special permissions granted, and if we step one toe out of line, they could decide to revoke our time-traveling supervision license. Which would mean that Murphy gets sent home immediately. I don't believe you want that, do you?"

Everyone murmured their agreement. "Good. Then you boys need to hustle," Mr. Blue said. "The next challenge is beginning any minute, and you don't want to leave the Swallowtails on their own, do you?"

"Let's go, then," Aaron said, and started jogging down one of the paths that led into the woods. I hesitated a second and turned back to Mr. Blue, who was studying the nurse's cabin with a furrowed brow.

"Sir?" I said, and he turned to look at me in surprise.

"Yes, Hank?" he said. "I'd have thought you'd want to be the first one to the challenge so you could quote Shakespeare to the ladies."

"That's an excellent idea," I said. "But I had a question, though, if you have a minute."

"Oh?" he said, eyebrows raised. "What's that?"

"It's something that you said about Murphy and getting your license to monitor time travelers revoked," I said. "I was just wondering: Do you have a license for each of our RISK factors? Like, are you only allowed to have a kid at camp if you have a license for their specific RISK?"

Mr. Blue nodded. "Sort of. There is a lot of legal mumbo jumbo and a mountain of paperwork involved, but basically we have an umbrella certification to monitor some of the more common RISK factors. It's why you are allowed to spend your summer here instead of in a government-run facility." He gestured around him to the towering trees, log cabin buildings, and dirt paths, and I nodded as I mentally compared them to some of the other concrete and brick institutions that were allowed to keep an eye on kids like us during the months we weren't in school. The comparison was not a kind one, and I felt a rush of gratitude that I got to be here. "But in order to accommodate kids like Murphy we have to have a special certification, and if you keep disappearing things, we may even need to get special permission for you," he said with a wink.

"So, if something goes wrong with a kid like Murphy, you could lose your certification for him to come back?"

"Correct," Mr. Blue said. "Now, is that all? Your team is waiting for you."

"Yes," I said, "but also, no. I was just wondering. What would have to happen for you to lose your licenses to watch *all* of us? Hypothetically speaking, of course."

"Well," Mr. Blue said, his brow furrowing again. "Hypothetically, if something were to happen to a camper on our watch, we would be in danger of losing our certification. It's one of the reasons we are so hard on you guys when you do things like sneak out to light lakes on fire."

"Right," I said as I remembered that our punishment

for that little adventure had been scrubbing down all the boys' bathrooms with bleach and a toothbrush. It was *not* an experience I wanted to re-create anytime soon. The faint sound of a whistle being blown down by the lake came drifting up the hill, and Mr. Blue smiled.

"You'd better hustle," he said. "The challenge has probably already started." With that he turned and walked back toward the TTBI-infested cabin. I raced after the rest of my cabin.

As I ran, I went over my conversation with Mr. Blue. It confirmed something I'd been suspicious of ever since Mr. Munkhouser had shown up and started inter-rogating us after the canoe incident. If a kid got hurt at Camp Outlier, like the kind of hurt you'd get if your safety tether became untethered twenty feet in the air on a ropes course, then the camp could lose its license. Was that why the government had decided to post Mr. Munkhouser here for the summer? Was he a watchdog making sure that no one stepped a toe out of line? The thought didn't sit well inside my head. For one thing it made me feel a bit guilty as I recalled some of the stuff I'd helped orchestrate last year, which included jumping off a bridge and encouraging Murphy to lasso a pig. Had any of those things gone wrong, we might not have been allowed to come back to camp this year.

"Get the lead out!" Emerson called to me, and I put on another burst of speed to catch up, smiling at the irony, since Emerson's vest had actual lead weights inside it. I pushed my suspicions to the back of my mind. It was time for another challenge.

CHAPTER FOURTEEN

We arrived to the challenge about five seconds before it was about to start, which was probably the first place we went wrong. The Swallowtails were waiting for us impatiently as all the other teams milled around chatting in excited anticipation.

"What's the challenge?" I huffed as we came to a stop beside the girls.

"What took you so long?" Amy said.

"No time for chitchat," Gabby said. "We need to get to our spot before the whistle blows."

"What spot?" I said, but Amy had me by the arm and was dragging me after the rest of the group as the girls pushed, shoved, and dragged us through the trees.

"Wait, is that the maze?" Emerson said, and I turned to look in the direction he was pointing. Sure enough, barely visible through the trees, was a seemingly endless jumble of white rope stretched between the trees.

"Keep up!" Kristy yelled, running ahead of us.

"I don't understand," I said, glancing around. "We aren't anywhere near the maze entrance." I remembered traversing the mile-long maze the summer before. It was configured using thick white rope wrapped between the trees, and it could be baffling at times, forcing you to backtrack and try multiple routes before you could find your way out. It was also fireproof, something we'd all been grateful for with Anthony on our team.

"Do you really think they have the same maze every year?" Gabby said, rolling her eyes.

"Yes?" I said at the same time about three of the other guys said the same thing.

"There are five entrances this year," Amy said. "Each team enters the maze when the whistle blows, and the first team to get one of their members successfully to the middle of the maze wins the points."

Before we could ask any more questions, the sound of a whistle blasted through the air. The girls redoubled their speed, and we hurried to follow them. A second later we rounded a corner, and I spotted the opening in the maze. It was about five feet wide, and the white ropes on either side of the tree stretched out into the woods. I glanced to the left and saw one of the other teams in the distance entering the maze from their own entrance. The sounds of shouts and laughter rang out through the woods, and I felt my adrenaline jump in my veins. This was going to be fun.

We made it to the first split in the maze.

"Take the left, we'll take the right," Kristy instructed.

"You heard her, men," I said. "Charge!" This time I took the lead, heading at a sprint down the path to the left as it wound through the trees.

"Slow down!" Gary yelled, panting.

"Hurry up!" I called back. For a solid minute we followed the meandering path dictated by the white ropes as they zigzagged us this way and that through the forest. I rounded the next corner at full speed, took another step, and then the ground under my foot disappeared. I felt my stomach drop a half second before my body followed suit. I let out a yelp of surprise and braced myself for impact, which hit painfully. My ankle rolled sideways, but before I could even fully appreciate that burst of pain, I felt someone land on top of me, followed by three more somebodies as what felt like my entire cabin fell into the same hole I had. For a minute there was a lot of yelling and shouting as we attempted to untangle ourselves.

"What is this!" someone yelled.

"Sure looks like a big stupid hole," said someone else. A flailing elbow connected with the back of my head, and I squirmed in an attempt to free myself from the other guys without much luck.

"Do I smell smoke?" someone yelped.

"Do NOT set anything on fire, Anthony!" someone cried. That made us move a little faster, and a second later we were upright.

"Sorry! I'll put it out!" Anthony said. I glanced around, and to my surprise and embarrassment, I realized that what I'd thought was a giant hole was actually only about two feet deep by four feet wide. I looked up to see Gary standing at the edge of the hole holding his side as he laughed so hard his face turned purple. Next to him, Mr. Stink was chattering angrily as he peered down at Zeke.

"How is it that you always avoid stuff like this?" Emerson said as he levered himself out of the hole.

"It pays to be the slowest runner sometimes," Gary said with a shrug.

"It also helps to look where you're going," Hudson said, brushing himself off and climbing out of the hole after Emerson.

"This is quite a hole," Zeke said, turning to take it in.

"You better get out of it before Mr. Stink has a fit,"

Emerson said, and Zeke grinned and climbed out.

"I wonder what caused it," Gary said.

"Better question," I said. "How did I not see it?"

"Fire is out!" Anthony said triumphantly, and I turned to see him stamping on a smoldering pile of something no longer distinguishable. He climbed out of the hole, and I was the last man left.

"Come on," Hudson said. "We aren't going to win anything with you down there."

"Let's hope the girls' path was the right one," Emerson added.

"It wasn't," said a voice behind us, and we turned as one to see the girl cabin standing there with red sweaty faces.

"Why are you in a hole?" Molly said.

"I have no idea," I said. "But I think I should probably get out of it now." I took a step and yelped as my ankle throbbed painfully.

"What?" Kristy said. "Is there a snake down there?"

"No," I said, and grimaced. "I think I twisted an ankle."

"It does look puffy," Amy said, and I glanced down at my invisible leg and shrugged. I mean, I was just going to have to take her word for it. "How did you get into that hole so fast?" she said, cocking her head to the side. "I could have sworn I saw you in the trees by

218

us about five minutes ago."

"He got in the hole so fast by face-planting into it," Gary said. "It was lots of fun."

"Somebody get Hank out of the hole and help him back to the entrance," Kristy said. "The rest of us need to keep going or this delay is going to cost us a win, if it hasn't already."

"I'll stay," Hudson volunteered, and I glanced at him in surprise. I'd have put my money on Emerson the Faithful or Gary the Lazy volunteering for this particular duty. No one argued with this decision, and before I could say a word, everyone else had taken off again toward the center of the maze.

"Well," I said, turning to Hudson. "Are you going to levitate me out?"

Hudson shook his head, his face draining a bit of color. "No way. I'm not allowed to levitate people."

"Okay, then," I said, glancing around the hole one more time now that it was actually empty. It was weirdly symmetrical, with sides cut in perfect lines rather than the jagged lines of nature. The thing Anthony had caught on fire was still smoking a bit, and I bent down to take a closer look. It was pretty charred, but I was almost positive that it had been a white bedsheet once upon a time. I felt the hairs on the back of my neck stand on end. This shouldn't be in the maze, not unless it was put here on purpose. I sat back as my brain started ticking. Maybe it was because I'd just had a conversation with Mr. Blue about what would happen to camp if something happened to a camper on his watch, or maybe it was the ever-present memory of my airport bathroom visitors, or maybe it was even the fact that I was standing there with Hudson, the kid who time-traveling Murphy had told us needed to be kept in the loop because "the future of Camp Outlier depends on it," but things suddenly clicked together in my head. Maybe we didn't have the world's worst luck. Maybe somebody or something was trying to sabotage camp in order to shut it down for good? My brain flashed to last year when Emerson had time traveled with Murphy and Gary to a future where Camp Outlier was nothing but a vacant property where people could go deer hunting. Was this how that future was going to come about? I shut my eyes as I pictured my first visitors to the airport bathroom. Was that a warning about the camp challenges getting sabotaged? My mind then jumped to my second visit, and I felt my insides turn. Maybe getting sabotaged was what caused that visit too.

"Are you getting cozy down there or what?" Hudson said, and I forced my mind back to the present.

"Nope, get me out of here," I said. Hudson crouched

down and after a bit of fumbling managed to lever me up out of the hole. I hopped on my good foot for a second, regaining my balance. It was going to be a long walk back out of here. Hudson let me wrap an arm around his shoulders, and together we started to hobble back the way we'd come.

"So, are you not allowed to levitate people because you accidentally exploded someone?" I joked.

"I didn't technically explode a *someone*," Hudson said, and grimaced.

I studied him for a second. "What did you explode?" I said.

"My sister's goldfish," Hudson said.

"Yikes," I said. "I bet that didn't make it onto your YouTube channel."

Hudson snorted. "Not quite."

We walked on in silence for a second before Hudson glanced over at me. "Is it nice?" he said.

"Is what nice?"

"Being invisible?" he said. "I think it might be kind of nice." I stared at his stupidly handsome profile in flabbergasted surprise, and then got myself together and really thought about his question. Was it nice being invisible?

"I don't think I'd call it nice," I finally said. "Maybe if I could control when and how I went invisible, it would be nice. But it's hard not to be seen."

"You're still seen, though," Hudson said. "I mean, you have this larger-than-life personality. Everyone at camp knows who you are."

"No," I countered. "Everyone at camp knows who *you* are."

Hudson shook his head. "They think they know who I am. That's a different thing."

"I'm listening," I said.

Hudson sighed. "It's hard to explain, and honestly I didn't even realize it until I lost my phone, but I think I've been faking my life for a long time now. Creating this image of the person I thought everyone wanted me to be when, really, I accidentally explode goldfishes. That's why it would be nice to be you, I think. Invisible."

"Wait," I said, holding up a hand. "Goldfishes? Plural? Like more than one goldfish? What kind of fish murderer are you?"

"Just one goldfish," Hudson said, and then paused. "And possibly a squirrel."

"Thanks for not levitating me, then," I said.

"No problem," Hudson said. "Think your foot's busted?"

I shook my head. "Just twisted, I think. Nurse Betsy will have to check it out, though."

"She can examine an invisible foot?" Hudson said.

"She can do anything," I said.

"I believe it after what I saw today," he said. "She kind of gives me hope, you know? Like if she could get herself together enough to do what she does, maybe I could too someday."

I nodded. "It's possible. I think a lot of people get better at managing their RISK factors as they get older."

"Why do you think that is?" Hudson asked.

I shrugged. "I think it's different for everyone. Sometimes I think people just stop being afraid of it, like Emerson. You never knew him last summer, but he's a whole different kid these days. Other times I think people figure out their triggers? Murphy tends to time travel more when he's stressed. It's probably why he hasn't traveled as much this year as last year. Last year he didn't think he was going to survive the summer, and it docsn't get much more stressful than that." I swallowed hard, wishing I didn't know that fact firsthand.

Hudson shuddered. "I wouldn't trade him RISK factors if you paid me."

"Maybe you should talk to Nurse Betsy about it," I said. "I've never seen RISK factors so similar, and maybe she has some tips."

"Maybe," Hudson said thoughtfully. Together we hobbled along like some bad version of a three-legged race team, both of us lost in our own thoughts. Behind us a whistle blew, and the faint sound of cheering drifted through the woods.

"What are the odds that's our team?" Hudson said.

"Slim to none," I said, and frowned.

"Man, could we have any worse luck?" he said, shaking his head.

"I'm beginning to wonder if it's all bad luck," I said, thinking again about the burned bedsheet that I'd bet just about anything was covering that hole so that we'd round the corner and not see it. However, since Anthony had burned it to smithereens, I had no proof. Proof or no proof, something fishy was going on at Camp Outlier this year, and I didn't like it.

DEAR GRANDMA,

THE SUMMER IS FLYING BY! CAMP HAS BEEN GREAT SO FAR. YESTERDAY WE DID A REALLY FUN CRAFT WHERE WE MELTED DOWN OLD CRAYONS AND TURNED THEM INTO THE UGLIEST CANDLES YOU'VE EVER SEEN. THEY SHED SAND EVERYWHERE, AND IF YOU BURN THEM, THEY SMELL LIKE A DAY CARE. I MADE YOU THREE OF THEM.

REMEMBER HOW I TOLD YOU AT THE BEGINNING OF THE SUMMER THAT I THOUGHT WE HAD A GOOD CHANCE TO WIN THE CAMP CHALLENGE? WELL, WE DON'T. UNLESS BY SOME MIRACLE WE MANAGE TO CAPTURE ALL

THE FLAGS IN CAPTURE THE FLAG NEXT WEEK, WE'RE
OUT. AND I DO MEAN ALL THE FLAGS. IT'S OKAY,
THOUGH. THE WHOLE POINT OF CAMP ISN'T TO WIN THE
CHALLENGE. THAT'S JUST SUPPOSED TO ADD TO THE FUN
OF THINGS. KRISTY IS HAVING A HARD TIME GIVING UP
ON THE DREAM, THOUGH, AND SHE AND A FEW OF THE
OTHER GIRLS SPEND ALL THEIR FREE TIME DEBATING
OVER WHERE CERTAIN CABINS HID THEIR FLAGS.

AS FOR ME? I'M GOING TO LIVE IT UP THESE LAST FEW
WEEKS. I DON'T KNOW WHAT I'D DO IF I COULDN'T COME
BACK HERE NEXT YEAR. I MEAN, WHERE ELSE DOES A
GIRL WHO ONLY SEES THINGS BECAUSE OF ECHOLOCATION
FEEL NORMAL? NOWHERE, THAT'S WHERE. THERE IS A
KID NAMED HANK HERE WHO'S BEEN INVISIBLE FOR MOST
OF THE SUMMER, BUT I CAN SEE HIM. I DIDN'T REALIZE
THAT I COULD SEE INVISIBLE PEOPLE BEFORE, BUT I
CAN! WHO KNEW! I THINK WE MIGHT NEED TO SEE DR.
KIPTNICK WHEN WE GET HOME, THOUGH. SEEING HANK
IS ONE THING, BUT I THOUGHT I SPOTTED AN INVISIBLE
PERSON THREE OTHER TIMES THIS SUMMER WHEN HANK
WAS NOWHERE AROUND. I'M SURE IT'S NOTHING TO WORRY
ABOUT, THOUGH. REMIND ME TO INTRODUCE YOU TO HANK
WHEN YOU COME TO PICK ME UP. HE'S REALLY FUNNY.

LOVE YOU,
AMY

CHAPTER FIFTEEN

"**C**ome on, slowpoke," Gary yelled, and I rolled my eyes. Gary was always the last one on a hike, and I think he was relishing the fact that Nurse Betsy had wrapped my twisted ankle in so much bright orange athletic tape that my foot now resembled a traffic cone.

"Ignore him," Emerson said.

"There's one!" I said, and pointed to our left, where a tiny spark of light had just flashed next to a pine tree. Emerson took off like a shot, and returned a moment later with his hands cupped together around the tiny flashing bug. I carefully unscrewed the lid of the empty peanut butter jar, and he slipped it inside.

"What's the count now?" Hudson called, and I held the jar up to eye level so I could peer in.

"I'm going to guess about fifteen," I said. "They won't stay still long enough to get an accurate count." Hudson nodded and then dived sideways as he attempted to grab another one.

"Hard to believe he'd never caught a lightning bug," Amy said. She was holding on to the empty lantern the girls had found for their own lightning bug container, and I bent over to peer inside.

"That's pretty cool," I said. "The lantern adds more flare than the jar." We'd invited the girls on our lightning bug hike earlier at dinner, and they'd happily agreed. I turned back to see our two cabins fanned out down the path, everyone intent on the small bits of light that made their appearance up and down the underbrush. It was the magic hour where the sun was setting and the dark was creeping in, and I kind of wished that I could bottle it up just like we'd bottled up the bugs in our jar.

"Stay on the path!" Aaron called, and everyone scrambled back, at least momentarily. I tried not to roll my eyes at our counselor, who had insisted on accompanying us on this adventure and pretty much every other one this summer.

"I see one!" Hudson called, and leaped into a nearby bush. Kristy laughed and reached in a gloved hand to help him out. I sighed and realized that, even if I hadn't had a bum foot and could jump into the bushes, Kristy would never be able to see my hand to help me out.

"Whoa," Emerson said from beside me. "Now that's awesome."

"What?" I said, turning back.

"The jar," Emerson said, reaching out a tentative finger. "It's gone." I glanced down and saw that the jar holding the lightning bugs had indeed disappeared, although it still felt solid enough beneath my glove-covered hands.

"Well, these were a waste," I said, sliding the gloves off and pocketing them so I could feel the cool glass of the invisible jar under my hands. I'd have to tell Nurse Betsy that we needed to try new ones. Emerson was right: the effect of the invisible jar was pretty awesome. The lightning bugs seemed to be flying around in a self-contained circle right in front of me, and I held them up to eye level for a better view.

"'Whoa' is right," Molly said, walking over to us, her own lightning bug cupped in her hand. She quickly slipped it into the girls' lantern before turning back to inspect my invisible jar.

"What is it?" Amy said in confusion.

"The jar disappeared," I told her since invisible things were never actually invisible to her. "I should really have you come poke around my cabin for me before we head home in a few weeks. I'm still missing a lot of stuff, and I could use some help finding it. I'm getting dangerously low on socks."

"I could probably do that," Amy said. "By the way, what were you doing down by the lake yesterday? I saw you by the boathouse, but when I called your name, you ran away."

"I wasn't down by the boathouse yesterday. Murphy time traveled during archery, and I volunteered to watch the rock circle. Besides," I said, pointing to my wrapped foot, "Nurse Betsy said she'd hang me from a tree by my toenails if I got this thing wet, and I kind of believe her."

"Oh," Amy said. "Maybe I didn't see you, then?"

"Guys! I got one!" Murphy called, and we turned as he came running down the path, his hands cupped together in front of him. He was two steps away from us when he suddenly tripped over a tree root. He pitched forward and disappeared. The lightning bug he'd been holding flew up and away into the darkening treetops.

"Freeze!" Aaron bellowed, and suddenly he was there, his head turning this way and that as though our friend would reappear if he just looked hard enough.

"He time traveled," I said, although this seemed so obvious it shouldn't need pointing out. "We need the rocks to mark out the spot he disappeared so we can make sure the coast is clear for him to come back. I've never seen someone accidentally explode a squirrel, and I don't know about you, but I think I can live without that particular experience."

"You can say that again," I heard Hudson mutter, and I made a mental note to ask him if he'd ever exploded anything besides a goldfish.

Aaron acted like he didn't hear me, though. The sound of a snapping branch came from our left, and Aaron leaped off the path and after the noise. We stood there frozen for a second as the sound of him crashing through the trees faded into the distance.

"Well, that was unexpected," Kristy said, walking over with Hudson. "That's pretty cool, Hank. Can I hold it?" I passed her my invisible jar of twinkling bugs as I dug around in my backpack for the rocks Murphy had tucked inside before we headed out. I found them quickly and tried to hand them to Amy so I could zip my pack back up, but she was still staring at the woods where Aaron had disappeared.

"What's up?" I said.

She shook her head and looked down at me long enough to grab the rocks. "Sorry," she said. "I thought I saw something."

"It's cool," Zeke said. "Happens to me all the time."

We set out the rocks and settled down to wait for our friend or counselor to show back up. Murphy was the first to reappear, coming back with a pop about five minutes later, none the worse for wear. Aaron was still nowhere to be seen, so we headed back to camp with our lightning bug lamps held up to guide us. The woods around us were getting darker and darker by the second, and I felt a shiver go down my spine as I glanced into their shadowy depths. We met Mr. Blue on the path when we were still a few hundred yards from camp. I thought he was going to stop and talk to us, but he just waved at us as he headed down the trail at a jog.

"Is it just me, or are things weirder than usual this summer?" Anthony said as we turned to watch Mr. Blue.

"You can say that again," I said.

The next few days at camp flew by fairly uneventfully—well, as uneventfully as things ever got at Camp O. Anthony lit a few things on fire; Zeke had an X-ray vision episode that required Mr. Stink to spring into action, much to the delight of the girls in the Swallowtail cabin; and Hudson levitated marshmallows over the fire for s'mores, which even I had to admit was pretty cool. Meanwhile we did the regular camp stuff that made Camp O so much fun. We shot bows and arrows during archery practice, hiked, built fires, swam in the lake, went fishing, and collapsed into bed each night sunburnt and happy.

It would have been easy for me to forget that we were possibly being targeted by someone intent on ruining Camp Outlier for kids like us, except that every day we got to spend together in the sun and fresh air was a stark reminder of what next summer would look like if whoever it was succeeded. Mr. Munkhouser and his ever-present iPad seemed to be everywhere that week, making it all the more obvious that things might not be what they seemed this year. He was especially intrigued by my foot and asked me on more than one occasion if it had been caused by my RISK factor in some way. He was even there when Nurse Betsy cut off the tape and declared my invisible foot as good as new, his eyes squinted as though maybe if he stared hard enough he'd be able to see my foot. I got my ankle wrap off just in the nick of time, since that afternoon the next camp challenge was announced.

"Ladies and gentlemen," Mr. Blue called. "We have only one more challenge to determine the participants in the final camp challenge of the summer, and we thought it was high time to revisit an old camp favorite." He paused for effect, and everyone seemed to lean forward in anticipation. "Anyone up for capture the flag?" he said, and the room went nuts. I jumped onto our bench, pumping my fist as Mr. Blue waved his hands for us to calm down.

"Each team hid their flag at the beginning of the summer," he reminded us. "Unlike last year where the game went on for the entire summer, this time, you have one afternoon. The team that has the most flags when the buzzer sounds at six wins. Camp counselors will be spread out across camp to act as referees and to make sure things stay under control. Please refer to the map outside for each team's territory. Remember, if you catch another camper in your territory, you are allowed to put them in your team's jail until someone else from their team is able to tag them and free them. If you take someone's flag, you have to make it back to your own territory in order to be safe. Until that point, it's free game. And last but not least," he said with a meaningful look around the room that seemed to linger a tad too long on our table, "we have a few additional rules, which are as follows. One: no naked flag capturing or jailbreaking."

"Aw man!" I called out, and everyone laughed. Every now and then I could control when I went invisible, although not well enough, and I was pretty sure a few people had gotten a good look at one of my butt cheeks during a rather momentous jailbreak. I kinda hoped it was the left one. It was the better looking of the two.

"Two," Mr. Blue went on. "No lighting things on fire. Three: your flag should have been hidden somewhere that can be reached from the ground. We had some floating and flying last year that weren't exactly safe."

"Now that's an awesome rule," Emerson said, and I smiled as I remembered how we'd floated him up to the top of the Red Wood hiding spot like he was our own personal Emerson balloon. It was the reason we'd won the game. Mr. Blue went on, recounting a list of rules that would have seemed ridiculous anywhere but here and included such gems as no sliming an opponent to not using electric currents near water. He finally finished and blew his whistle. Everyone bolted out of their chairs and stampeded for the door. I was in the lead, and it wasn't until I was halfway across the courtyard in front of the dining hall that I realized that I had no idea where our flag was even hidden. I threw on the brakes and skidded to a stop so fast that Emerson collided with my back, and we both went down hard.

"Will you two stop horsing around!" Kristy bellowed at us, and I felt someone yank me upright by the arms with hands that burned. I yelped and sprang to my feet and out of her grasp. I thought about yelling at her for forgetting her gloves, again, but I stopped myself since I wasn't wearing my gloves either. Although, in my defense, it was ridiculously hard to keep track of invisible gloves. "This way!" she said, and charged off into the woods, the rest of the girls hot on her heels.

"You heard the lady," Hudson said. "Move!"

"Where did you hide the flag?" I yelled, but no one even slowed down.

"Do you really think I'm going to yell that information?" Kristy called back just as another team crossed in front of us and went flying down a trail that led left. We ran, zigzagging through the woods down one trail after another until we'd made it to the far side of the lake. Kristy skidded to a stop near the water's edge, and for a second I thought that maybe they'd sunk the flag like we had last year.

"Where's the flag?" Gary wheezed as he put his gloved hands on his knees.

"About a half mile that way," Kristy said, pointing to her right.

"Wait, what?" I said, looking around. "Then why are we here?"

"We're currently standing in Red Wood and Buckeye territory," Kristy whispered.

"What?" I yelped. "Why are we in Red Wood territory and not protecting our own territory?"

"It's called a strategy," Gabby said. "If we aren't in our territory babysitting a flag, no one will know where our flag is. Instead, we are launching an attack before anyone else has a game plan. We are going to divide up into teams and each go after a different flag."

"How do you want us to pair up?" I said with a sidelong glance at Amy. I liked being paired up with her, especially when I was invisible.

"Gary, Murphy, and Hank, you guys team up with Amy and Gabby," Kristy said, all business. "Molly, you're with me, Zeke, and Anthony." She quickly gave us the intel we needed about where each cabin's territory lay.

"You guys have the trickiest assignment," Kristy concluded, turning to me. "The Red Woods hid their flag out there," she said, jerking her head toward the lake. "It's hidden under the dock, from what I overheard one of the Buckeye girls saying on a hike the other day. Good luck." And then everyone seemed to be running in all directions, leaving Gary, Murphy, and me standing next to Amy and a very grumpy-looking Gabby.

"So," I said, rubbing my hands together as I turned toward the lake and the dock on the far side. "Here's how we do this."

"Whoa, you've got a plan already?" Amy said.

I smirked. "I was born with a plan."

The Red Woods were smart. They'd situated their flag at the very end of the long dock that stretched out over the lake. So the only way you could reach their flag was by getting past the massive guy who was currently sitting on said dock. It was brilliant, really. From his vantage point, he could see anyone who might be coming his way and easily tag them. Cue the invisible kid.

The plan involved me swimming underwater to the dock wearing nothing but my black basketball shorts and a long rope tied around my waist in order to make my getaway faster. Gary was surprisingly agreeable to the plan since it meant that his part of the adventure involved nothing more than sticking himself to the other side of the rope and staying safely on land. Murphy confiscated a rope from the side of the boathouse, and we were in business.

"So, we cause the distraction," Gabby said. "And you two get the flag."

"Don't get tagged either," Gary said.

"Shoot!" Murphy said as Gary yelped.

"What happened?" I said as I turned to see a very annoyed Gary holding the rope in one hand while his other hand was pressed to Murphy's shoulder.

"I slipped," Murphy said with an apologetic shrug. "Sorry."

"Sorry doesn't fix this," Gary said.

"How long will you two be stuck together?" Gabby said.

"Long enough for him to really regret slipping," Gary said.

"Right," I said, rubbing my hands together. "So, just the girls will be the distraction. I swim out and get the flag. Gary and Murphy, um," I said, glancing at my two stuck-together friends. "Just stay hidden, okay? If they catch you two, they catch me by proxy." I stared at them for a second, feeling the oddest sense of déjà vu, but brushed it off. We had a flag to capture.

The girls took off at a run, and I stripped off my shirt and shoes and slipped into the water wearing nothing but my shorts and the rope around my waist. The swim across the lake felt excruciatingly slow since I was trying to move the water as little as possible. Since the stuff that was visible was underwater, the only thing that would give me away was the ripples generated by my arms. Every now and then the guy on the dock would scan the lake, and I'd freeze until he'd turned back the other way. When I was about five feet from the dock, the girls launched their diversion. I heard yelling and whooping and a very impressive rendition of a Dolly Parton song coming from the trees to the left, but I didn't dare look. Instead I took a few quick powerful strokes that put me underneath the long wood dock that sat suspended on metal poles above the water. There was about a foot of clearance underneath, but I kept my head low since the underside of the wood was a lovely mess of spiderwebs, dead bugs, and spiders that made my skin crawl. A second later I spotted the flag nested neatly between two very large spiderwebs. I snagged it, careful not to disturb any spiders. Mission accomplished, I was just turning to paddle back when something yanked hard on the rope around my waist and I went under. For a few crazy moments I thought that somehow the rope that Murphy had snagged off the side of the boathouse was boobytrapped just like the maze had been, but that thought disappeared a second later when I found myself standing in a large white bathroom dripping water all over the tile floor. Beside me was a very angry Gary and a very worried Murphy.

I spit out a mouthful of lake water onto the floor. "What just happened?" I said.

"Time travel," Gary said as though the word itself tasted bad.

"Where are we?" Murphy said as he looked around, taking in the rows of bathroom stalls and the wall of sinks at the far end. A toilet flushed behind us, and we all jumped.

"We're in a bathroom," Gary said. "Gross." And then it clicked. I knew exactly where we were. Without wasting another second, I shoved Murphy and Gary toward the large empty accessible stall at the far end of the row.

"What are you doing?" Gary asked as he attempted to bat away hands he couldn't see. I ignored him, just managing to get the door to the stall shut a second before a door swung open and an invisible boy wearing a baseball hat and a backpack walked in.

"Wait, is that you?" Gary whispered.

"Yes," I hissed. "Remember? I told you guys that we traveled to the airport bathroom to warn me about something. I'm on my way to camp."

"Warn you about what?" Gary said.

"I wasn't sure at the time, but now I'm thinking that I wanted to warn myself about somebody sabotaging camp," I said.

"Sabotaging camp?" Murphy said. "Why haven't you mentioned this before now?"

"I haven't had a chance," I said. "Aaron has been breathing down our necks pretty much every second, and I don't really even know for sure if that's what's happening." I quickly filled them in on my theory about camp losing its licensing to watch kids like us if something bad happened. Then I ran through the list of mishaps this summer, from the ones that had happened to other cabins, like the Blue Spruce and Morpho cabins' canoe busting into pieces in the first challenge to the ones that had happened to us, like the hole in the maze. When I finished, both boys just stared at me.

"I don't know," Gary finally said. "Who would sabotage camp?"

"That's what we need to figure out," I said.

"So, we're warning past you about something we haven't even figured out yet?" Murphy said. "Seems like a bad idea. I mean, nothing really bad has happened yet." I bit my lip, wondering if I should tell him that in less than five minutes another version of himself would be visiting this bathroom with a much scarier message and decided against it. Murphy didn't need that on his conscience, and I didn't have time to go into it right that second.

"No time to discuss," I said, peering through the crack in the door. "Past me is heading to wash his hands."

"Hold it," Gary said. "You can't go parading out there as nothing but a pair of floating wet shorts. You'll cause a scene."

"Good call," I said, and quickly stripped off my soaking-wet shorts and the rope and handed them to Murphy. I also thrust the Red Wood flag at Gary.

Those accomplished, I slipped out of the stall and crept across the cold bathroom floor. It was freezing in there, and the fact that I was soaked and naked didn't help matters, but I dutifully slapped an invisible hand over my own invisible mouth and dragged my past self into the bathroom stall.

"Hurry up and get that rope back on," Murphy said nervously as my past self gushed and chattered at us. "I don't want to leave you behind."

"Right," I said, slipping it around my waist and double-knotting it. Murphy visibly relaxed a fraction once this was done and turned back to the Hank who was on the way to camp.

I tried to remember how this had all played out a few weeks ago, but the memory was already a bit fuzzy. The guys had been trying to warn me about something, but they hadn't managed to do it.

I was just opening my mouth to elaborate when there was a hard jerk at my waist. A second later I was back in the lake. I surfaced, spluttering next to the dock, and the Red Wood guy whipped his head in my direction.

"Somebody's in the water!" he yelled, and three more Red Wood guys came flying out of the trees. I gave up any attempt at stealth and opted for speed instead, paddling hard across the lake while Gary and

Murphy pulled on the rope, accelerating my progress. I made it up and out of the water a minute later and hit the ground running with Murphy and Gary in tow. There wasn't time for clothes or even to untie me, not with the Red Wood guys bellowing like angry bulls twenty yards behind us. We were running at full tilt for a solid minute before I realized that we had never asked the girls where our territory was. Thankfully Amy and Gabby burst from the trees to our right a second later, a pack of Buckeye girls hot on their heels.

"Tell me you got it!" Gabby yelled.

"Got it!" Gary called back as he held up the flag. "Couldn't let it go if I wanted to." With the girls' help we angled ourselves across camp and headed for our territory, which was apparently somewhere near the archery course. We eventually lost the Red Wood guys, and while the girls went charging on ahead to scout out the situation, the three of us paused to catch our breaths.

"That was a big waste of time." Gary gasped as he leaned against a tree.

"Tell me about it," Murphy said. "We didn't get to warn past Hank about anything." He turned to me accusingly. "You wouldn't shut up!" he said.

"Sorry," I said. It felt weird to apologize for something I'd done weeks ago, and I realized that Murphy must feel like this a lot. "Well, what's done is done," I said. "Where's that flag?"

Gary held it up and cocked a skeptical eyebrow at me. "Are we really going to just go on playing capture the flag like we didn't just time travel?"

"Shhhh," Murphy said, glancing around quickly. "The TTBI has eyes and ears everywhere, and if they find out about this, we could be in giant trouble. When Emerson and Gary somehow managed to come along while I was time traveling last year, they thought it was a fluke that couldn't possibly be repeated or I would have never been allowed to come back."

"This just keeps getting better and better." Gary groaned. "Why am I friends with you guys again?"

"Because you love us," I said with a grin he couldn't see. "Should we catch up with the girls?"

"Shouldn't we do something about this first?" Gary said with a jerk of his head at the rope around my waist and a very stuck Murphy.

"Yeah, sure," Murphy said, sounding distracted.

"No one will find out we time traveled with you," I said. "I promise."

"Same," Gary said. "I don't feel like going down for something as stupid as a capture-the-flag game."

"Well, even though we won't win, at least we won't be completely empty-handed," I said. Just then there was a whoop of triumph, and we glanced over as Kristy came flying into our territory with a flag held high.

"Whoa!" I yelled, pumping my fist in the air. We may not have won capture the flag, but with two of the five possible flags, we weren't dead last anymore either.

Dear Mom,
I miss you! Can you believe I'll be home in just two weeks? This summer has seriously flown by, and I have soooooo much to tell you. Our team is officially up to twenty-five points since by some small miracle we won the capture-the-flag contest, which puts us in third place! Did I tell you that one of the guys in the White Oak cabin can light stuff on fire? It's not quite as dangerous as what I do, but thanks to all the accommodations at camp, I haven't accidentally shocked anyone too badly. Anyhow, quiet time is almost over, so I better wrap this up. I hope these last two weeks of camp slow down a bit, I'm not ready for it to be over yet!
Sincerely,
Emily

CHAPTER SIXTEEN

The morning of the next challenge dawned clear and bright, a classic Camp Outlier morning. I stepped outside our cabin and inhaled, breathing in the sharp piney scent of the forest. It felt unreal that the summer had slipped by so fast. Time was funny like that, dragging when you wanted it to move and moving when you wanted it to drag. The morning sun was just breaking through the trees, the birds were making a lovely racket as they said good morning to one another, and I had a good feeling about today. For one thing, I'd made it to today, something I hadn't been sure I'd do after Murphy's ominous visit at the beginning of the summer. I knew I wasn't completely off the hook since he could have visited me from sometime after camp too, but it seemed less likely. I was going to choose to believe Emerson that we'd dodged that bullet back at the ropes course.

"Morning," Gary said, stepping outside in nothing but his bright yellow boxers. His clear gloves were conspicuously absent, and I took a step to the left just in case he forgot and bumped into me.

"A lovely morning to you too, good sir," I said, giving him a bow with a bit of a flourish. "It's a good day for a good day, don't you think?"

Gary stretched and yawned so wide I could see his back molars. "If you say so," he said.

"I always say so," I said with a decisive nod.

Gary studied me for a second—or at least the area where he could tell I was standing. "Is it weird that you've only been visible for like twenty-four hours this whole summer? I'm kind of forgetting what you actually look like, except for your giant nose. I'll always remember that giant nose."

"Thanks," I said dryly.

"You're welcome," Gary said, and sniffed as he took in Camp Outlier in the early-morning light. "Think we'll ever forget this place?" he said. "Like when we're old and boring and hate life?"

"First off, I don't plan on ever being boring or hating

life," I said. "I don't think all adults are like that. Look at Mr. Blue: he's a riot and I'm pretty sure he's old. Second, no, I don't think we will. I think it's like your first love: it's something you don't forget."

"What do you know about love?" Gary snorted. "You got one pity kiss at the end of last year, and I'm pretty sure Kristy hasn't given you the time of day since."

"I think Kristy is just a little wrapped up in the competition," I said.

"That's an understatement." He snorted. "Although I think she's more wrapped up in Hudson, so maybe you're just old news?"

"You should try making an impression on a girl when all she can see is your clothing," I said.

"True," Gary said, and then paused. "Are you worried that this might just be your new normal?"

"Do you mean am I worried that I'm invisible for good?" I said.

"Yeah," he said, yawning again. "Do you think you'd drop the 'inconvenient' part of your whole inconveniently invisible label and just be plain old invisible? Hudson thought you were the invisible boy for the first week, remember?"

"What about Hudson?" Hudson said, walking out of the cabin. He gave Gary a once-over and shook his head with a smirk. "Nice boxers there, Gare Bear."

"Watch it," Gary said, but there wasn't any real anger behind his words.

I thought about what Gary had said about Kristy being wrapped up in Hudson. I didn't like that thought. I leaned forward on the railing of our cabin, and a second later the entire railing disappeared.

"Whoa," Gary said. "That was wild."

"It's still there, though, right?" Hudson said, sticking out a tentative hand to touch the railing.

"Yup," Gary said, reaching out to touch the space where the railing had been just moments before.

"Gary, stop!" I said, but it was too late. He was officially stuck to the invisible railing.

"Great," he said glumly. "This doesn't look stupid at all."

Hudson and I stared at him for a second while Gary stood there in his rubber ducky–yellow boxers, his hand on top of a railing that was no longer visible, and then we both burst out laughing.

"He looks like one of those old-fashioned mimes." Hudson laughed, tears streaming down his face.

"Real funny," Gary said. "If I could reach you, I'd smack you. Now somebody go get Aaron, or I'm going to miss breakfast."

"Sorry, buddy," I said. "I'll get him." I turned back toward the cabin door and put my hand on the doorknob at the exact same moment that Hudson did, and to my horror, his hand disappeared.

"No way," Gary said, and I turned to look at Hudson, but Hudson was gone.

"What?" Hudson's disembodied voice said.

I couldn't say a word. I just stared at him in shock. What had I just done?

"Dude," Gary said. "You think I'm screwed; take a look at your hand." There was a moment of silence and then a surprised gasp.

"I'm invisible?" Hudson said. "You made me invisible? You can do that?"

"Apparently?" I said, folding my hands into fists and holding them tight against my sides.

"You made his clothes invisible too," Gary said, glancing over at me. "But your clothes never disappear; that's interesting."

"What's going on out here?" Aaron said, coming out the door a second later, followed by a curious Murphy, Zeke, Emerson, and Anthony in varying states of getting dressed for the day.

"What disaster would you like to hear about first?" Gary said, holding out his free hand like he was the ringmaster at a circus. Mr. Stink pushed his way through the crowd and walked over to sniff at the invisible railing.

"This is insane," Hudson said, lost in his own invisible world.

I tore my eyes away from Hudson as Mr. Stink sneezed once, twice, three times, and as one we all looked over at Murphy, whose face went from confused to horrified right before he disappeared.

"You didn't touch him too, did ya?" Gary said.

"No," I said, my voice cracking. "I swear."

"Cool, so just the normal level of insanity, then," Gary said. Turning to Aaron, he raised an eyebrow. "Bet you're ready for this nifty summer job of yours to be over. Now grab the acid, will ya? I don't really want to be stuck to this railing in my underwear when the Swallowtails come looking for us."

The next twenty minutes were a flurry of motion and chaos. Nurse Betsy was called up to help unstick Gary, and Mr. Blue arrived moments later to examine the still completely thrilled and completely invisible Hudson. The only improvement with Hudson happened when he changed out of his invisible clothes and threw on some visible ones, making it much easier to keep track of him. I stayed out of the way; my hands clasped into fists in front of myself lest I accidentally make anything else disappear. When he walked in, Munkhouser looked like he was going to have some kind of fit. He'd already made me a level five for turning the rope invisible at the ropes course, and I bet he was wishing there was a level above that. With my luck, he'd invent one. Nurse Betsy marched over to me after she finished wrapping Gary's hands and handed me yet another pair of gloves.

"Here," she said. "Let's see if you can keep track of these for more than a minute." I slid them on my hands, feeling uneasy. My RISK factor had never been something that other people needed protection from, and I didn't like the feeling. I looked across the cabin at Hudson and scowled as he balanced a fork on what I assumed was his nose, but could have definitely been his forehead. Show-off. Nurse Betsy had assured us that he'd reappear, and her nonchalant confidence about it had made me feel somewhat better. She'd also cautioned Hudson to be extra careful today since he was navigating a RISK factor he wasn't familiar with.

Murphy's red rocks were placed in a perfect circle that Aaron graciously said he'd watch so that the rest of us didn't miss the next challenge. I felt a stab of regret for my friend who was going to miss out and crossed my fingers that he'd make it back from wherever he'd gone in time to catch at least part of it.

Breakfast was rushed since we'd arrived more than a little late, and we'd barely eaten a few mouthfuls of cold eggs when Mr. Blue took the stage. The hall quieted down as all eyes turned to him.

"Good morning!" he said, and we all called back our own good-mornings. "It's hard to believe that we have arrived at one of the last challenges of the summer, but here we are!" There was a chorus of mixed cheers and boos at this, and he smiled.

"Well then," Mr. Blue said, clapping his hands. "Unless there are any more unexpected changes to our challenge roster, I think we'd better get started!

"I'm going to wait to give you the details on this one until after you've all changed into swimsuits and headed down to the lake," he went on. "I think you'll find this challenge just ducky." He gave us an overexaggerated wink, and I glanced at the rest of my cabinmates.

"Did he just say ducky?" I said.

"He did," Emerson confirmed. "Let's hurry up and get changed so we can see what we're in for."

With that we were out the door and hurrying back up the hill. I expected to see Aaron on the porch watching Murphy's circle of red rocks, but he was nowhere to be seen. In his place was Mr. Munkhouser with his nose buried in his iPad.

"Where's Aaron?" I said, glancing around.

Munkhouser looked up and peered at me over his glasses. "That is none of your concern, young man. What are all of you doing back here?"

"Changing into swimsuits," I said. I was about to tell him to send Murphy down to the lake when he got back when there was a loud pop and Murphy reappeared.

"Who won the challenge?" he said.

"Nobody yet," I said. "Get dressed. You're just in time."

"Really?" Murphy said, his face lighting up.

"Not so fast," Mr. Munkhouser said. "You need to report to Nurse Betsy first."

"I thought Nurse Betsy wasn't going to be around today," Murphy said. "She told me after she unstuck Gary this morning that she had to go somewhere and would be gone the rest of the day."

Munkhouser's forehead wrinkled as he tapped at his iPad and then he nodded. "That's correct," he said. "Well, please report to her as soon as she returns." With that he headed out of our cabin, and we scrambled into our bathing suits. In no time at all we were changed and charging back down the hill. We met the girls at the bottom and headed toward the lake as a team.

"Wait a second," Kristy said, turning her head from me to Hudson and back again. "There are two Hanks!"

"No such luck," I said. "Just one Hank and a temporarily invisible Hudson."

"Thank goodness," Gabby said. "One Hank is more than enough."

"Amen to that," Gary said.

Amy fell in step next to me just as we reached the concrete steps, and we headed down them shoulder to shoulder. Suddenly she chuckled, and I looked over at her, confused.

"What's so funny?" I said.

"Hudson keeps making the absolute weirdest faces at everyone." She giggled. I glanced over at the floating pair of basketball shorts and T-shirt that appeared to be prancing down the stairs.

"He's enjoying my RISK factor a bit too much," I said ruefully.

"Maybe," Amy said. "But it seems like he's loosened up for the first time all summer. I mean, I've talked to him a few times at challenges or whatever, and he's always kind of had the personality of a potato. But now . . ." She trailed off as we watched the floating pair of shorts and T-shirt do a spin before sidling up to talk to Gabby.

"But now he's got the personality of a potato chip?" I said, finishing her sentence.

"Something like that." Amy laughed. I watched Hudson goof off for a few more seconds and I smiled. Amy was right. For the first time since he'd come to camp he'd relaxed enough for the real Hudson to show through the shiny facade he'd created for himself. He'd told me that he'd been jealous of my RISK factor, and he hadn't been lying. It was an odd feeling to have someone wish for the thing you'd wished away more times than you could count.

"It would have felt fairer if we'd traded," I joked. "I'd have taken his good looks and levitating any day."

"I wouldn't be so sure," Amy said, and I glanced over at her with my eyebrow raised.

"Why's that?"

Amy shrugged. "I like your face the way it is. It has character. Besides, levitating is just a fancy way of throwing stuff. What's so impressive about that?"

"Thanks," I said. "I'm pretty sure you're lying, but I appreciate it." I glanced back over at Hudson just as he did a complicated spin move that almost sent him headfirst down the stairs and I shook my head. "I guess I'm not the only one who added a new trick to their RISK factor this summer," I said.

"What do you mean?" Amy said.

I held up my hands. "I make things invisible now, and you see invisible people."

She cocked her head to the side for a second, considering this, and then shrugged. "I don't think mine is a new trick," she said. "I just never had a chance to hang out around invisible people before now."

"Good point," I said. "We're a rare lot—usually."

"Usually," Amy agreed, and then bit her lip as she looked behind her.

"What is it?" I said.

She shrugged. "It's just that I keep seeing things this summer that aren't there."

"Um, didn't we just discuss that?" I said.

She shook her head and smiled a bit ruefully. "Sorry, that wasn't exactly clear. It's just that I keep thinking I see this invisible person around camp. At first I thought it was you, but now I'm worried I might just be seeing things. Unless you've turned anyone else invisible that I should know about?"

"Just that guy," I said, jerking my thumb over at Hudson as he burst into song. I was about to ask Amy more about the invisible person when I spotted someone down by the boathouse. I stopped and took a quick side step off the stairs so that the rest of our team could pass me. To my surprise Amy stepped off the path beside me.

"What's going on?" she said.

"I thought I saw Aaron down by the boathouse," I said.

"Well," Amy said. "I guess that's not *that* weird. The entire camp *is* down by the lake."

"Right," I said, but I stayed where I was, squinting through the trees and underbrush to our left where the boathouse sat. Amy stayed beside me as the rest of our team trooped down to the lake, leaving us alone in the underbrush.

"We need to hurry or we're going to miss the start of the challenge," Amy said.

"Right," I said, and then turned to look at her as something occurred to me. "These invisible people you think you're seeing," I said, "how often have you seen them?"

"Not people, just one person," she corrected me. "I'm pretty sure I keep seeing the same guy. That's why I thought it was you for so long."

"Right," I said. "Well, do you remember exactly when you saw him?"

Amy shrugged. "I've caught glimpses a lot this summer. At first I didn't pay much attention because I figured it was just you in the middle of pulling a prank or something."

Just then Aaron emerged from the boathouse, and I crouched down in the weeds. I was about to grab Amy so she'd do the same, but she mimicked my movement on her own, and together we squinted down at my camp counselor. I expected him to head toward the lake and the camp challenge. Instead he looked left and right, his face a mask of frustration before he went slinking away into the woods.

I quickly shucked off my T-shirt and crept quietly through the underbrush, making sure to stay low so my shorts were hidden. Aaron was making his way quickly through the woods, his own posture hunched. I froze as he suddenly turned and scanned behind himself, his eyes passing right over me. I held my breath as he stayed that way for a moment, and then he headed into the woods at a jog. There was no way I'd catch up to him in the thick underbrush, so I hurried back over to Amy.

"What was that about?" she said.

"I'll explain later," I said.

Just then there was an excited shout from down by the lake, and we both turned back to the stairs.

"Hurry," Amy said. "If we miss the start of the challenge, I'll never hear the end of it from Kristy." We practically ran down the steep stairs to the lake, and I had to force myself to stop chewing over the Aaron and invisible person mysteries and focus on navigating the steep concrete stairs. I'd seen what happened when a canoe went careening down these, and I didn't really want to reenact it.

A moment later the lake came into view between the thick branches of the surrounding trees, and I squinted at it in confusion. There was something weird floating on top of the water.

"What's that?" I said.

"You are asking the wrong girl," Amy said. "All I can see is what looks like specks of something floating on the water."

"Colorful somethings," I said.

We made it to the bottom of the steps, and I got my first unobstructed view of the lake, and I blinked in amazement. There, floating on top of the water, were hundreds of rubber ducks in every color of the rainbow.

The campers were strung along the beach, each of them huddled in their respective teams. Amy and I hurried over and stopped next to Emerson.

I looked around and noticed that Anthony and Kristy were already standing poised at the edge of the water, their shoes conspicuously absent as they looked expectantly toward the center of the lake. One of the camp counselors was standing up in a canoe holding a megaphone and a whistle. A second later the whistle rang out across the water, and Kristy and Anthony took off. Steam hissed up around both of them the second they entered the water, and I coughed as a small fog surrounded us for a moment before dissipating. Apparently when you submerged a girl with burning-hot skin and a boy who self-combusted, you got steam. Who knew? I glanced to my right and noticed that the Blue Spruce team was sending two boys into the water as well.

"What do we need to do?" I yelled over the general clamor of cheers and encouragement of the rest of the camp.

"Each team was assigned two duck colors," Emerson yelled back. "We're yellow and white. We can each grab only one duck at a time and swim it back to shore. The first team to collect all their ducks wins." He tore his eyes away from Anthony and Kristy, who had each retrieved a duck and were paddling hard to make their way back toward us, and looked me up and down.

"Where's your shirt?" he said, and then laughed and shook his head. "Never mind, forget I asked. Since we're an odd number we'll have to send two guys and a girl in on this last round."

"Simple enough," I said, glancing around for Amy and smiling when she nodded to confirm that she'd partner with me. I'd grown accustomed to her *seeing* me, and especially now that I didn't have a shirt on, I felt even more invisible than ever. Emerson had somehow gotten paired up with Gabby, just like in the ropes course.

"You're with me too," said a voice at my elbow, and I turned and jumped in surprise to see nothing but a floating pair of swim trunks standing next to me. For a second I wondered if I was looking in a mirror, but a moment later I realized it was Hudson and placed a hand on my hammering heart.

"You scared me," I said.

"That's kind of ironic," Hudson said.

"It kind of is," I agreed as I turned to watch Molly and Zeke take off into the water.

Hudson, Amy, and I took up our positions on the edge of the lake to wait for our turn. To our right was a basket already half-filled with white and yellow rubber ducks. I did a quick scan of the other cabins' baskets, but it was too hard to tell if we were ahead or not. I turned my attention back to the lake and grinned as Zeke swam for all he was worth. He reached out and slapped my glove-covered hand and Hudson's invisible one just as Amy got a slap from Molly, and we charged into the water. I dived in, stroking hard for the center of the lake, where a big mass of rubber duckies had drifted together.

"Why do I feel like we got the short end of the stick?" I huffed to Hudson and Amy as we swam. Everyone else had managed to grab ducks that were fairly close to shore, but now that the easy pickings were gone, we really had to hoof it.

"This is so cool!" Hudson said, and I glanced over at him, but of course he wasn't visible. The only thing that made it obvious that there was even a person there were the slight splashes from his arms. I guess it was

262

kind of cool, I admitted to myself, especially when you saw it from this perspective. Hudson veered off to the left for a white duck while Amy headed to the right for a yellow.

I was still paddling hard for the center of the lake when I saw the boat. Mr. Munkhouser was coming across the lake in a small fishing boat with an outboard motor strapped to the back, his trusty iPad clutched close to his side. He had his head up, his eyes squinted against the bright sun that was bouncing off the surface of the water, and he was heading directly for the spot where a newly invisible Hudson was swimming. I saw what was about to happen in a split second, and I changed my course, swimming as hard as I could for the oblivious Hudson.

I kicked hard, pulling at the water with my arms until my muscles screamed. I yelled, trying to warn Hudson about what was coming, to warn Mr. Munkhouser. A second later I heard Amy's own terrified scream as she spotted the impending catastrophe. The motor's roar was too loud for them to hear either of us, though, and I watched in horror as the oblivious Munkhouser steered for what he seemed to think was a clear patch of water from which he could observe the challenge. He had no idea that he was actually steering straight for two kids, one of whom wasn't used to navigating a RISK factor that could put him directly in harm's way without the harm ever realizing it. The roar of the boat's engine was getting louder, and I heard the yelling from shore turn from cheers to screams of horror as my teammates registered what was about to happen, but there was nothing that they could do because they were too far away. I didn't waste time or energy looking back at the boat. I just swam faster. The dark lake water splashed up around my face, and I didn't even notice how cold it was anymore. Adrenaline pumped through my system, and my heart hammered hard against my ribs.

"Hudson!" I screamed, still three feet away. "Duck! You're going to get hit!"

"I got my duck!" he yelled back as his invisible hand closed around the rubber duck he'd had in his sights. The boat motor was so loud, it seemed to be roaring inside my brain, and I knew I had seconds. I lunged for my new friend, closing the gap between us and shoving him under the water just as something connected with the side of my head and everything went black.

CHAPTER SEVENTEEN

When someone drowns in a lake, it isn't the same as when they drown in a pool. Pools are clear. You can see the person who is drowning and generally get to them quickly. Lakes aren't like that. Lakes are deep and dark and the visibility is utter garbage. If you go under in a lake, there is only a very small chance that someone will be able to locate you quickly enough to save your life. It's like looking for a needle in a haystack. If you're invisible and you drown in a lake, it's like looking for a needle in outer space. This was why a RISK factor could kill you. It made already dangerous situations more dangerous and deadly situations even more deadly. I learned this lesson the hard way when I was eight.

I'd been goofing off with my brothers down by the creek that ran through the back of our property. It had been one of those really great summer days full of catching frogs, slinging mud at one another, and fishing with the small chunks of hot dog we'd pilfered from the fridge when Mom wasn't looking. I finally felt like I was big enough to keep up with my three older brothers, and it had been great to just be "one of the guys" and not the little guy Mom instructed them to keep an eye on for her. Which, considering I'd been invisible that day, would have been a bit of a trick.

The problem had happened when I decided to do one last swing on the rope that my brother Phil had attached to a tree limb that stretched out over the creek. If you swung just right, you could Tarzan yourself from one creek bank to the other, and while my brothers could do it with ease, I was just a hair too little to manage it. However, that fact didn't stop me from trying. While my brothers were busy packing up our fishing gear, I'd gotten my hands on that rope, taken a running start, and launched myself. Halfway across my hands had slipped, and I'd careened head over heels into the creek. The fall had managed to knock me out, and the current had whisked me downstream before my brothers had even realized what had happened. It took the police and a search party that consisted of every neighbor in ten square miles to find me five hours later, washed up on the shore, alive but barely. It's hard to find an invisible kid wearing nothing but a pair of mud-covered swim trunks.

It turned out that five years later, that principle still held true. When I opened my eyes, I was lying on the shore of the lake, and to my utter amazement, I wasn't dead. Although, as I stared up at the faces of half the camp looking down at me, I had the very unsettling thought that this was exactly what my view would have been if I was lying in a grave. I felt my body heave, and suddenly I was vomiting what felt like half the lake onto the sand beside myself.

"He's getting the water out!" someone said. "That's good!"

"Is he going to be okay?" someone else—I think Emerson—asked.

"Quiet," the first voice barked. "Let us work. Can you keep the rest of these campers back? We need some space here." I felt a sharp pain as someone stepped on my leg and another someone tripped over my foot. I couldn't look to see who it was, though, because a second bout of water was making its way up my throat and out my nose and mouth. Someone had their hand on my neck, and when I finished yacking, I turned to look at a very scared-looking paramedic.

"Is he breathing?" someone else asked, and I felt hands fluttering around my chest as whoever it was attempted to find my pulse.

"I don't know!" the first paramedic said in frustration. "How do you do CPR on an invisible kid?"

"I think I found his neck!" the other person said, and I peered up at the man in confusion as he put a hand under my armpit.

What was happening? My brain felt muddled and confused. Who were these guys, and why was I lying on my back in the sand?

"His name is Hank," someone said, maybe Gary. "Not Invisible Kid. Hank."

"Hank? Hank? Can you hear me?" said one of the paramedics.

"Yes?" I croaked, and there was a collective gasp of relief from the crowd surrounding me.

"You're alive!" Emerson said, and I was suddenly being crushed in a hug.

"Yeah?" I said. "Was I not supposed to be?" My head was throbbing, and I rubbed it as I peered around trying to make sense of what had happened. One second I'd been swimming for Hudson, and the next I was waking up a hundred yards away from where I started. Suddenly I remembered.

"HUDSON!" I said, and attempted to sit up. My efforts were thwarted by the paramedics who clumsily pushed me back down on the ground.

"Is Hudson okay?" I said. "Did he get hit?"

"I'm fine," Hudson's voice said somewhere to my left, and I craned my head, trying to see him. His face appeared above me a moment later, and I felt some of the terror that had almost strangled me a moment before loosen. Hudson was okay. Hudson was alive. Hudson was visible again, I realized as I looked up into his worried face.

"Get back please, get back," said one of the paramedics as he felt around my face, apparently still trying to get a pulse.

"What happened?" I said as I batted the hands away.

"You drowned," Emerson said in a voice that sounded choked, and for the first time, I really looked at him. He was drenched, and his eyes were bright red and puffy as though he'd been crying. A quick glance around showed a lot of other faces wearing similar expressions of puffy-eyed panic.

"Possible concussion," one of the paramedics said

to the other, finally finding my head. He prodded my skull carefully with his fingertips and I winced as he hit a particularly tender spot on the side of my head.

"OW!" I said as I saw the paramedic pull back a hand that was now liberally coated in my blood.

"Where did this come from?" he said, glancing down at me. I thought about explaining that my blood was always invisible until it touched something else, but I felt another bout of water coming up my throat, and I turned to the side and heaved again.

"He must have a laceration," the paramedic said. "But I have no idea how deep it is or if it needs stitches."

"How in the world are we supposed to stitch up an invisible head wound!" said the other.

"You jokers are a real piece of work, do you know that?" Gary said, and I could hear the fury in his voice. "You know he's actually there, even though you can't see him? His ears may be invisible, but they still work."

"I drowned?" I said. "And you guys found me?" I said to the paramedic who was currently putting a stethoscope against my right elbow. I sighed and moved it into position over my heart. These guys didn't seem capable of finding their way out of a box, let alone finding an invisible kid in a lake of all places.

"No," the paramedic said, a look of relief on his

face at finding my heartbeat, "your friends did."

"What happened?" I croaked. My throat felt raw, and I wondered if I'd accidentally swallowed a frog or something.

"You and Hudson got hit by the boat and you both went under," Emerson said, "but only one of you came back up."

"It took us a second to figure out which invisible kid we were looking for," Zeke added. "I mean, you both had nothing on but a swimsuit. Stupid," he said, shaking his head.

"What was stupid was somebody taking a fishing boat out into a bunch of swimming campers," Gary said, and there was a murmur of agreement from the surrounding group.

"Then what?" I said.

"Well, we figured out that it was you, and we all started diving, trying to find you," Emerson said, "but we couldn't."

"You were under for a long time," Anthony said. "Minutes."

"It felt like years," Emerson said. "Everyone was screaming and crying and freaking out. Murphy disappeared in the middle of the worst of it. We don't even know where in the lake to put his red rocks."

"Huh? Murphy's gone?" I said, still confused.

Apparently almost drowning could do a real number on your brain.

Emerson nodded. "He disappeared about five minutes into our search. One second he was swimming next to me and the next second he'd disappeared. If I hadn't been looking right at him, I probably would have thought that he'd drowned too."

"Did I really drown?" I said.

"Yeah," Emerson said with a glance over at Hudson. "We thought you were a goner."

"Who found me?" I said.

"No one," Emerson said. "Even Amy couldn't see you in all that water." He sniffed and rubbed an arm across his nose. "You'd been under a really long time when Hudson decided to risk levitating you. He got you to the surface and Amy was able to spot you long enough for us to grab you."

"Oh," I said, lying back as I tried to make all the puzzle pieces of the story fit together.

"Your friends were pretty impressive," the paramedic went on. "I've never seen so many kids that could hold their breaths for so long." He turned for confirmation to his colleague, who was attempting to put a blood pressure cuff on my shoulder.

"It's true," he said, and I took pity on the guy and guided the cuff onto my arm so he could stop searching. He smiled in appreciation as he activated it and glanced up at my friends. "You must be able to hold your breath underwater for about two minutes," he said to Gary. "You were down there so long that I was a little worried we were going to have to find more than one kid."

"'Hold your breath for about two minutes,'" I repeated as the words rang a very familiar bell. I glanced around looking for Murphy and then remembered that he'd disappeared during the search.

"What was that?" the paramedic said, removing the blood pressure cuff.

"Nothing," I said, shaking my head. "Just glad my friends were able to hold their breaths for two minutes." I watched Emerson's face and saw the moment recognition dawned. Gary, Zeke, and Anthony realized the same thing a moment later, and if I hadn't almost died, their expressions would have been funny enough to make me laugh. I'd gotten the idea about holding our breath for two minutes from Murphy, and now, I realized, that might not have been a coincidence.

Just then Mr. Blue pushed his way through the crowd of campers with Mr. Munkhouser right beside him. I took in Mr. Munkhouser's disheveled hair, broken glasses, and soaking-wet polo shirt. He looked like he'd seen a ghost, and I felt a tug of pity for the man.

He hadn't meant to hit me with the boat after all.

"Is the boy all right?" he asked.

"The boy's name is Hank," I heard Gary growl somewhere to my left.

"I'm fine," I said as I tried to sit up only to have my head swim sickeningly. "I think."

The paramedic pushed me back down and turned to Mr. Blue. "We're having a hard time getting a good idea of his injuries," he said. "Can you turn him visible?"

This sent a ripple of unhappy murmurs through the surrounding campers because, of course, Mr. Blue could do no such thing. People who weren't familiar with kids like us sometimes said stupid things like that, and it always set my teeth on edge.

"We need Nurse Betsy," Amy said. "Where is she?" she asked Mr. Blue.

Mr. Munkhouser grimaced and looked away with a guilty expression.

"She's at a government-mandated RISK training seminar about an hour away," Mr. Blue said. "Her attendance was nonnegotiable." He glanced over at Mr. Munkhouser, making it perfectly clear who'd required her attendance at the seminar.

"Oh, she's not going to be happy about this," Amy said, shaking her head.

"You can say that again," Emerson said as he eyed Mr. Munkhouser with real concern. "She may actually kill you."

"You're not wrong," Mr. Blue said. "She's been notified and is already on her way back."

"You should probably run," I told Mr. Munkhouser. "She's scary when she's mad."

"No one is running," Mr. Blue said. "Especially not you until after you've gotten a thorough checkup from these fine gentlemen, although I'm sure Nurse Betsy will want to do her own assessment when she gets back."

"How did the paramedics get here so fast?" I asked.

"Well," Mr. Blue said, "thankfully I had the foresight to ensure that we had medical professionals on the premises just in case something were to happen."

"Nothing *would* have happened if a level five RISK child wasn't allowed in the water without a special accommodation for visibility," Munkhouser said, and I saw him glance down at a very waterlogged and very broken iPad.

"Or," Mr. Blue said, his voice stern, "you should have checked with the head of the camp before taking out a boat during a camp challenge."

Mr. Munkhouser's face turned red and he stood up a bit taller. "It's not my fault your equipment is faulty!"

he said. "I spotted the boy and would have been able to turn in plenty of time if the steering shaft hadn't been stuck!"

"The steering shaft was stuck?" Mr. Blue said. "Are you sure?"

"Either that or he ran over Hank for fun," Kristy said. "I saw him trying to turn the boat."

"Thank you, young lady," Mr. Munkhouser said, sounding relieved.

"Faulty equipment or not," Mr. Blue said, "you should have checked with me before taking out that boat." Before Mr. Munkhouser could respond, Mr. Blue was turning to address the rest of the campers, dispersing them back up the hill toward their cabins where hot showers and dry changes of clothes awaited them. I glanced back out at the lake that had almost claimed my life just as something splashed into the water. A second later Murphy's head emerged from the water and he whipped it this way and that, looking out over the empty lake in a panic.

"Over here! We found him!" Emerson called, already splashing back into the water toward our friend. Murphy seemed to take a second to register what Emerson was saying, but then he was swimming hard for shore. He stumbled up out of the water a minute later and staggered over to where I lay still surrounded by two fumbling paramedics. He shoved aside the one closer to him and fell to his knees.

"Hank!" he said. "You're alive!" He practically collapsed on top of me in a relieved hug.

"Have a nice visit to an airport bathroom?" I whispered so only he could hear, all too aware of the audience around us. He opened his mouth in surprised shock, and I smiled a bit ruefully. I was going to have to give him a talking-to about triple-checking that somebody was dead before terrifying their past self about it. I looked from Murphy's relieved face to Mr. Blue's concerned one and frowned. There was more to this story. We needed another midnight meeting.

CHAPTER EIGHTEEN

After the paramedics left, I was escorted to Nurse Betsy's cabin so she could give me a proper once-over. Murphy came along too, escorted by Aaron, who'd appeared out of seemingly nowhere as soon as the paramedics were packing up. Mr. Munkhouser attempted to follow me but received a very unfriendly door in his face from a very angry Nurse Betsy, who had no problem sharing her views on grown men who drive around in fishing boats like they don't have the sense they were born with. While Nurse Betsy got started, Aaron escorted Murphy into the small side room, where he would recap his time-traveling adventures for the TTBI. I watched the door close behind him, wondering if he'd tell the truth about his visit to the airport bathroom or if he'd make something up. He wasn't supposed to tell anyone their future, and since he'd managed to freak me out about mine for a large percentage of the summer, I kind of understood why that rule was a good one.

Unlike the paramedics, who'd fumbled around like they were blind, Nurse Betsy navigated her assessment of an invisible kid like the pro that she was. She started by pulling out a large container of baby powder and hair spray.

"Shut your eyes and hold your breath," she instructed, and a second later I was liberally coated in Aqua Net and then doused with baby powder. I sneezed but didn't protest, as this was a method my mom had used more than once in my childhood. I caught a glimpse of myself in the mirror of her office and smiled at the powder-coated ghost-Hank. Now that she could see me, Nurse Betsy lost no time making sure that all was well. She used small pieces of medical tape to close up the gash on my head, and made me do a couple different tests to ensure that I didn't have a concussion. When she seemed satisfied, she stepped back and carefully ruffled my hair, sending another shower of powder onto her pristine floor.

"Want me to call your parents?" she said. "Mr. Blue has already informed them of today's events, but

I know that, when something scary happens to me, I still want to talk to my mom." I thought about it for a second and then shook my head.

"I'm okay," I said, not feeling up to a lecture from my mom. "Really."

"Okay, then," Nurse Betsy said, and to my surprise she leaned in and gave me a long tight squeeze. When she stepped back, she had a white Hank print on the front of her scrubs, but she didn't seem to mind.

"What was that for?" I said, hopping down off the examination table.

"Everyone needs a hug sometimes, even overconfident campers who think they're too cool for it," she said.

"Oh, I'm never too cool for a Nurse Betsy hug," I said with a grin as she ruffled my hair again, sending a new flurry of powder down around my ears.

"Are you trying to grow a mop up here?" she said.

I shrugged. "It's hard to cut invisible hair."

"Want me to do something about it, sugar?" she said.

I grinned. "Only if you promise to call me sugar from now on."

"Can I call you sugar?" Murphy asked, emerging from the side room with Aaron.

"I'm heading up to the cabin to check on everyone else," Aaron said. "Murphy, please wait for Hank and escort him up as soon as Nurse Betsy's finished with him."

Murphy nodded and then raised an eyebrow at my powder-covered appearance as Aaron left.

"What's happening here?" he said.

"Nurse Betsy's going to make me pretty," I said with a grin. "Have a seat and watch the magic happen."

She scoffed as she grabbed scissors from her drawer and set to work. I watched as large chunks of matted and powder-coated hair fell to the ground. I picked up a chunk and rubbed it between my fingers until the powder fell away and it became invisible again.

"Make sure you sweep this up right away," I said. "There is nothing worse than invisible hair that you can't see all over your floor."

"Other than an invisible boy almost drowning because he can't be seen?" Nurse Betsy said.

"Maybe," I said with a shrug, and I realized again how close I'd come to today being my last day.

Nurse Betsy turned to Murphy and jerked her chin toward the door. "I forgot I loaned my broom and dustpan to Mr. Munkhouser this morning," she said. "Be a dear and run over to his cabin and fetch them for me." Murphy nodded and slipped out the door as Nurse Betsy brushed some more powder off her scrubs.

"And here I thought that mess with the TTBI a few

weeks ago was going to be the most exciting thing that happened this summer," she muttered to herself.

"Why did so many of them show up that day?" I said.

Nurse Betsy huffed. "I'd say to ask your friend Murphy, but he can't tell you a thing. That's one of the reasons they were here, to make sure that he was following the rules. Like having one of their junior agents in your cabin wasn't enough . . ."

"Wait, what?" I said. "There's a junior agent in our cabin?"

"Oh darn," she said, putting a hand on her hip and shaking her head in the worst imitation of regret I'd ever seen. "I wasn't supposed to say that, was I?" She stood there for a second and then gave an overexaggerated shrug and winked at me.

I stared at her for a second, my mouth hanging open in shock. Aaron! Aaron was an undercover TTBI agent?

"Close your mouth, sugar, or flies will get in," she said, reaching over and giving my chin a quick upward tap that closed my mouth.

"Aaron?" I said. "Really?"

"Well, the cat's out of the bag now. I guess Aaron will have to go be a top-secret jerk somewhere else next summer. I sure hope the TTBI doesn't come back to yell at me." She gave me a big dramatic wink, making it clear that she wasn't at all worried about that particular possibility.

"You may be the only person I've ever met that isn't intimidated by those guys," I said.

"They should be intimidated by me," she said.

"I think they were," I said. I remembered the levitating glass that had made the eyes of one of the agents about pop out of his head.

Nurse Betsy turned and sent a bottle of Advil and a glass of water zinging across the room and directly into my hands. "Take two of those," she instructed. "If you don't now feel like you've got an elephant tap-dancing around inside your brain, you will in an hour or so."

"Thanks," I said, and downed the pills. Its mission completed, the bottle flew dutifully back across the room and into the cabinet it had come from.

"You know how we have a new kid in our cabin this year that can sort of do what you do? Hudson? The one that I accidentally made invisible this morning?"

She nodded. "Oh yes, I've heard the girls talking all about Handsome Hudson. Think he'd let me be a YouTube star with him?"

"You know about that?" I said, turning to look at her.

"Sugar," Nurse Betsy said with a smile, "just assume

I know everything." She stood back to survey her work. Cocking her head to the side, she grabbed the baby powder and gave my head another good coating. I shut my eyes tight and held back a sneeze as she trimmed a few more pieces before finally stepping back with a nod of approval.

"That should do it," she said. "Definitely an improvement."

"Um, can I ask you a question?" I said, glancing down at my powder-covered hands.

"You can ask anything you want," Nurse Betsy said. "I make no promises about answers, though."

"This new thing that I do," I said, holding up my hands. "The making-things-and-people-invisible thing. Why do you think that started? I never did it before this summer. Do you think it will go away? I almost got Hudson killed today because he was stuck with a RISK factor he wasn't used to. Could Mr. Munkhouser make me wear those itchy gloves all the time even if they don't always work? Do my parents know about what I did to Hudson?"

"Well now, that's more than one question," Nurse Betsy said, propping a hand on her hip. "But I'll give you answers as best I can. As to why this started? Well, my guess is that you're going through something this summer that set it off. Some kind of shift occurred in the makeup of Hank that triggered it. If you get whatever it is sorted, your new little trick will probably either go away or you'll get a better handle on how it works. The gloves—well, sugar, they need to stick around as long as your new talent does. Just ask Gary or Kristy about the best way to navigate that nuisance. Your parents have been notified, but they didn't seem too concerned with the new development. And let's make one thing perfectly clear: *you* are not responsible for almost killing Hudson. There now, was that all?"

"Yeah," I said. "Thanks." I loved the way Nurse Betsy always gave it to us straight. No sugarcoating, no nonsense. It was refreshing. "Can I head back to my cabin now? I'd love a shower. I smell like a combination of my aunt Buella and a baby's backside."

"There are worse smells," Nurse Betsy said. "Just take a whiff of some of your buddies sometimes."

"You're not wrong," I said. "Thanks for everything."

"Sure thing," she said as Murphy walked through the door clutching a broom and dustpan. Nurse Betsy immediately sent them zooming around the room to clean up the powder and hair.

"What do you think?" I asked as I turned my head this way and that to give him the full effect.

"I'll let you know when you're actually visible again," Murphy said. "It's kind of hard to tell."

"Fair enough," I agreed, and together Murphy and I headed out the door and up the hill.

As soon as we were out of earshot of the cabin I glanced over at Murphy and raised a powder-covered eyebrow. "So, are we going to talk about what happened? I'm assuming you just lied through your teeth on your report." Murphy glanced around nervously and then grabbed my arm and pulled me over so our backs were against a nearby cabin.

"I'm so, so sorry," he said. "Like unbelievably sorry."

"For what?"

"For basically telling you that you died when you didn't," he said.

I shrugged. "How were you supposed to know that Hudson was going to levitate me off the bottom of the lake?"

"Wait, that's how they found you?" Murphy said. "I thought Hudson exploded some of the stuff he levitated?"

"He does," I said. "You should ask him about what happened to his sister's goldfish sometime."

"I guess if the choice was risking exploding you or never finding you, I'm glad he risked it," Murphy said.

"You can say that again," I said, and shuddered.

"Why didn't you tell me about the second visit?" Murphy said.

"Why would I?" I said. "Nothing changed about how I was living my life. I've always tried to live like today might be all I get. Besides, I told Emerson, so I had somebody watching my back."

"I could have watched your back too," Murphy said. "You sure watched mine last year, whether I wanted you to or not."

I shrugged. "I didn't want this hanging over your head all summer. One summer with a death sentence is enough for one lifetime I think. I'm alive. You didn't have a crummy summer, and Hudson didn't explode anyone. Besides, if we're talking about not telling people important information, how about you not telling us that Aaron was a TTBI agent?"

Murphy winced. "Nurse Betsy told you?" he asked.

"She's the best, isn't she?" I said. "Think she'll marry me someday?"

"No," Murphy said, and I laughed.

"Seriously, though, why didn't you tell us about him?" I asked.

"I kept looking for an opportunity, but that guy's got eyes in the back of his head. It's a minor miracle that he didn't figure out that I time traveled to an airport bathroom to hang out with you—twice!"

"That's been today's theme," I said with a grin. "Minor miracles."

"Munkhouser should get fired," Murphy said, shaking his head.

"It's not completely his fault," I said. "You weren't back yet, but he said that his boat was broken. Apparently, he saw me and Hudson, but he couldn't turn the boat."

"That's some really bad luck," Murphy said, shaking his head.

"Bad luck is one theory," I said. "But I think somebody busted that boat on purpose."

"Who would do that?" Murphy said.

"I have an idea about that," I said. "But I want to tell the rest of the guys and the Swallowtails too."

"Let me guess," Murphy said. "Midnight meeting?"

"Midnight meeting," I confirmed. "Now let's hurry up and get back to the cabin."

White powder fell off me as we hurried up the hill, and I got more than one strange look from the other campers I passed. It didn't bother me, though. Getting looked at never bothered me like I knew it bothered some of the other kids with RISK factors. It was *not* being seen that I couldn't stand. The sun was just starting to set as we made it back to the cabin. I paused right before going through the door.

"What are you doing?" Murphy said.

"Taking advantage of the situation," I said. "Give

me a second to get into character. This opportunity is too good to pass up."

With a bang, I threw open the cabin door and stood there, arms extended like a zombie, my head cocked to the side at an odd angle.

"SCROOGE!" I bellowed, and staggered into the cabin.

Zeke was standing closest to the door and he let out a bloodcurdling scream before leaping backward into Emerson, who barely managed to stay on his feet.

"Gah!" Gary yelped, and grabbed the closest thing to him to use as a weapon. It happened to be the toilet plunger that usually sat by the bathroom door in a bucket, and the sight of Gary standing there ready to beat me to death with a plunger was too much. I snorted and broke character.

"Sorry!" I said, holding up my hands. "It's just me! Put your weapon down!"

Everyone relaxed and even Gary laughed.

"What the heck happened to you now?" Gary said, thumping the plunger back into the bucket.

"Standard procedure," I said. "This is much better than spray paint, though. At least this will come off in the shower."

"Why did you yell 'Scrooge'?" Emerson asked as

Mr. Stink came over to investigate my powder-covered calves.

"You know," I said, bending down to rub him behind the ears. "Like in *A Christmas Carol*? Bob Marley comes in as a ghost and scares the daylights out of old Scrooge."

"I think you mean Jacob Marley," Anthony said.

"That's the best ghost you could think up?" Gary said. "You need to watch more TV."

"Maybe," I said, and I was about to ask about what had happened while I was at Nurse Betsy's when the door opened behind me and Aaron came in. My stomach did a quick flip-flop as I remembered what Nurse Betsy had said about him. He did a double take at seeing me and then almost as quickly scowled down at the floor. I followed his gaze and saw the trail of white powder I'd left behind myself.

"I'll sweep that up after a shower," I said.

"Good answer," Aaron said. "Hurry it up. It's lights-out soon." He turned to the rest of the guys and raised an eyebrow. "That means you guys too. Get those teeth brushed and get in bed." I grabbed a cleanish-looking pair of shorts and a T-shirt from the communal clothing pile and my towel and made my way to the showers. I caught sight of myself in the mirrors above the sinks out of the corner of my eye and felt my heart do its own nervous little jump. The powder had worn off in some places, giving the rather creepy illusion of my head being hollow, since you could see through it. No wonder my ghost trick had worked out better than I'd anticipated.

"What's wrong?" Emerson said, coming to stand beside me.

"My head looks like a piece of Swiss cheese," I said.

"It does," Emerson agreed. "It's kind of creeping me out too. Go shower."

"Already ahead of you," I said as I hustled into the shower. I poked my head around the corner a minute later to see him standing in his pajama pants and weighted vest, his face serious as he seemed to work something out in his head. I left him to it and ducked back into the shower. He was quiet for a second as I lathered up, the white powder swirling away down the drain.

"I thought we'd lost you for a few very scary minutes today," he finally said. "I was kicking myself for not doing more, I mean, you told me about Murphy's warning. I should have seen it coming."

"Nobody saw it coming," I said. "Which, if I had my choice, is how I'd want to go out too. Surprised."

Emerson snorted, and I could hear the smile in his voice when he replied. "Only you, Hank, only you."

"Don't say anything to Murphy about it," I said. "He already feels bad. Besides, if a certain government agency finds out that he's spouting off about futures willy-nilly, he'll be in hot water."

"Speaking of hot water, are you almost done?" Emerson said.

"Almost," I said, poking a now powder free and therefore invisible head back out of the shower to glance around. The coast was clear, so I whispered just loud enough for Emerson to hear me.

"We need a midnight meeting. Can you spread the word?"

"I'll try," Emerson said. "But Aaron is kind of everywhere. Besides, how are we supposed to get out? There's a locked door, not to mention the alarms on the windows. The only reason it worked last time was because the Red Maple guys were getting initiated."

"Let me worry about that part," I said.

"If you say so," Emerson said. I watched him go, and then I carefully stepped out of the shower, making sure to leave it running, and toweled off. Now completely naked, but also completely invisible, I tiptoed through the opposite side of the bathroom and opened the door to the Red Maple cabin. Eli was tossing a football around from camper to camper, and I ducked as it went sailing over my head. Thanks to the general clamor and chaos of it all, I was able to slip through the cabin and out the far door and into the night. I hit the ground running and raced back down the hill the way I'd just come.

My bare feet were tough from running around the farm without shoes, and I barely felt the rocks and sticks I ran over. The night sounds were starting to wake up around me, and the pink glow of a setting sun was just visible over the trees. I hit the bottom of the hill and pumped my arms hard as I headed up the girls' hill. Running naked didn't bother me. Getting bitten by mosquitos, who couldn't care less if I was invisible or not, wasn't my favorite. I slapped at the buzzing pests as best I could without slowing down my pace. I passed three different counselors, but thankfully none of them even glanced in my direction.

I made it up the girls' hill in record time and skidded to a stop outside the Swallowtail cabin. The lightning bugs were just starting to blink around the surrounding bushes like tiny UFOs as I peered through the screen to see all the girls sitting and talking or quietly reading books in their bunks. It was a sharp contrast to the chaos and noise that was currently happening on the boys' hill. Even from outside I could tell that their cabin smelled better than ours too, and I was just trying to figure out how to get their attention without terrifying them when someone was suddenly standing on the other side of the screen I was peering through. I jumped backward and barely swallowed my yelp of surprise.

"Nice haircut," Amy said, eyebrow raised, and I suddenly remembered that, to her, I wasn't invisible. I felt my face burn, and said a silent thank-you for the very thick shrubbery that surrounded the cabins and provided some much-needed coverage. Still, I'd never had a girl staring straight at me like that when I didn't have any pants on, and I quickly reached over and snagged one of the beach towels that was hanging over the railing of the cabin so I could wrap it around my waist.

"What are you doing standing in our bushes?" Amy said.

"We need another midnight meeting," I hissed. "Tonight."

Amy glanced quickly behind herself to make sure no one was watching her and then looked back at me. "Okay," she said. "We'll meet you guys at the truck again at midnight."

I shook my head. "It's not that easy this time," I said. "Aaron locks our door and the windows have alarms. We're going to need your help sneaking out."

Amy nodded as Kristy wandered over to stand beside her.

"Who are you talking to?" she said.

"Hank," Amy said.

"Is that my towel?" Kristy said, leaning forward.

"Forget about the towel," I said. "We need a meeting tonight, but we can't get out of our cabin."

"We can take care of that," Kristy said. "Just be ready at midnight, okay?"

"Consider it done," I said, bowing low.

"He bowed," Amy said helpfully to Kristy.

"Huh," Kristy said. "The towel just kind of looks like it's trying to fold itself. Interesting."

I straightened up and stood there awkwardly for a moment as Amy looked right at me. "Um," I finally said, "if you wouldn't mind turning around? I need to get back to my cabin, and I can't exactly take this towel with me."

"No problem," Amy said, turning quickly so her back was facing the screen.

Kristy looked at her in confusion and then busted out laughing. "Wait a second," she said, turning back to me. "You're naked, aren't you? Except you aren't to Amy! Oh, that's too good!" She snorted and the other girls in the cabin came over to see what was so funny. Now I had an entire cabin of girls staring at me with the exception of Amy, and I suddenly wished I'd thought this plan through a tad more before I launched myself naked into the night.

"Good night, fair ladies!" I called, quietly just in case there was a counselor nearby. "Glad I could provide some levity and entertainment to your night. Dream of me!"

"Girls?" I heard a voice call from inside the cabin. "What are you looking at?"

"A raccoon!" Kristy called, and the girls quickly turned their backs to me. That was my cue, and I chucked the towel back over the rail and took off at a dead sprint. The run down the girls' hill and back up the boys' hill was much darker, and I slipped through the Red Maple door completely out of breath. Things had calmed down and Eli was sitting against the far wall, feet propped up on a table while he was reading aloud a chapter from *The Hobbit*. He'd read the same book to us last year, and I smiled as I crept quickly through the room, the familiar story reminding me of last summer. There was something lovely about hearing that someone who seemed completely ill equipped for a grand adventure was going on one anyway. Besides, I agreed with the Hobbit motto of needing two breakfasts. I made it back into the bathroom, where my shower was still running and hopped back in. For the second time I covered myself in soap since running around in the dirt naked wasn't a super clean activity.

"Aren't you done yet?" Aaron bellowed less than a minute later as he popped his head into the bathroom from our cabin.

"Almost!" I called. "Hair spray and baby powder are a sticky combo!" I heard him huff in frustration and shut the door. I turned my shower off and dried myself quickly before throwing on shorts and a T-shirt. I ran my hands through my hair and looked into the mirror over the sink more from habit than because I really thought I'd see my own reflection, and to my shock, there I was, fully visible.

I jumped in surprise and then cringed as I realized just how close I'd come to being seen running around camp in the nude. Now that I could see my head again, I got my first really good look at my new haircut and the medical tape holding my head wound together and smiled, making a mental note to thank Nurse Betsy.

"Move it!" Aaron bellowed from our cabin, and I hurried through the doors and into bed to wait for midnight.

CHAPTER NINETEEN

The girls arrived right on time. I heard them before I saw them, and I sat up so fast that I cracked my head on the bunk above me. A second later I saw Emerson peer over the edge of the bunk.

"What's going on?" he whispered.

"Midnight meeting time," I said. "The girls are going to spring us."

"Nice," Emerson whispered, and disappeared back into his bunk. I felt the entire thing sway and shake a bit as he strapped on his weighted vest. Around the room I saw the other guys' heads pop up like gophers' out of their holes. The scratching noise came at the screen again, and I slipped out of bed and into my shoes. Aaron's muffled snores were still coming from the front of the cabin, and I felt a surge of pride at the guys as they all crept out of their bunks on silent feet.

The noise that had alerted me to the girls' presence came again, and I turned toward the big screened-in window just in time to see the alarm melt into a sticky silver puddle on the floor. A second later the screen slid silently up and out of the way as Kristy poked her head inside. She was wearing a black baseball cap pulled low over her white-blond hair, and she jerked her chin when she spotted us. One by one we each slipped out the window and into the night. I was just turning to shut the screen when it moved on its own, sliding back down and into place.

"Well done," Kristy said, and Hudson just shrugged nonchalantly.

"May we escort you lovely ladies down to the truck?" I whispered to the Swallowtails as I relished the feeling of being visible once again.

Kristy shook her head. "Follow us," she said. So we did. The girls led us into the woods beside the cabins and down one of the trails that led toward the lake. We followed silently, only stopping once to find Mr. Stink after he wandered off the path to investigate an interesting-smelling log. The moon was full, sending a smattering of silvery light onto the path through the trees, but we didn't really need it to see where we were going since Anthony's hair was on fire for most of the walk. The girls finally stopped beside the old firepit that sat just on the edge of the lake.

"Wait a second," Murphy said, glancing around. "Isn't this where . . . ?"

"Where we lit the lake on fire?" Anthony said. "Yeah, same place."

"We thought you'd appreciate it," Molly said, sitting down on one of the logs that surrounded the empty pit.

"Wait a second," I said. "You guys were supposed to meet us here that night, and instead Mr. Blue and Eli came down on us like a herd of elephants. I never got to ask why you didn't show up."

"Yeah!" Gary piped up. "Did you guys tattle on us or something?"

Kristy laughed, as did the rest of the girls, and I felt my indignation rise as I recalled the oh-too-vivid memory of me and the rest of the guys scrubbing out the bathroom with nothing but toothbrushes and bleach.

"Oh, we were there," Gabby said. "We were about halfway down the hill when we heard Mr. Blue and Eli on the trail. They were looking for you guys, so we hid, and a second later we saw you yahoos light the lake on fire. It seemed like a good mess to avoid, so we headed back up the hill and into our bunks with no one the wiser."

"Pretty slick," I said.

Gabby shrugged. "We sure thought so."

"Well then," I said, rubbing my hands together. "Let the midnight meeting begin. We have a lot to discuss."

"Careful," I heard Murphy mutter beside me.

"You should be one to talk about careful," Gary snapped. "If you'd given us the heads-up today, Hank might not have almost died!"

"Easy," I said, holding up a hand to calm Gary down. "He did warn me. In fact, he warned me a bit too well since he overshot the mark and predicted my death."

"Whoops," Murphy said, shrugging helplessly.

"It's fine," I assured him again. "No one expects you to be a human Magic 8 Ball. Especially when you've had a TTBI agent literally breathing down your neck— and ours—all summer." This statement was met with cries of surprise and outrage from the group, and I flapped my hands at everyone to quiet them down.

"Aaron!" the guys all shouted.

"Shhhhhh," I said, glancing around. "Yes, Aaron. Nurse Betsy told me today, but Murphy has known for a long time." I glanced over at Murphy and he nodded.

301

"Ever since I time traveled at the canoe challenge," he said.

"The challenge that went horribly wrong after the Blue Spruce's canoe fell to pieces in their hands," I said. "Which brings me to the real reason for this meeting. Someone is trying to cause something bad to happen this summer at camp."

"Are we sure you aren't that someone?" Gabby said, eyebrow raised. "You sure seem to be in the middle of a lot of the messes."

"She's right," Zeke said. "You might be jinxed."

"Fair point," I said. "We can keep that as one hypothesis, but I have a different one if you'd care to hear it."

"Hypothesize away, oh invisible one," Kristy said.

"I think," I said slowly, trying to get the words just right, "I think that our team in particular has been targeted by someone trying to cause a disaster here at camp. A disaster that would put the camp's future as a safe haven for RISK kids at, well, risk. Did you know that Mr. Blue has to have a special certification in order to allow RISKs at camp? And he needs a special license for really special kids like Murphy?"

"Really?" Gary said. "I'd have guessed he just got one big license that said, 'caretaker of the strange and stranger,' and called it a day."

"I knew that," Anthony said. "There was a lot of paperwork involved last summer when I wanted to come here."

"Well," I said, "apparently, if something bad happens to one of us, Mr. Blue could lose that certification, not to mention any special licenses, and we wouldn't be allowed back at camp next year. It's one of the reasons I think Mr. Munkhouser is here this summer, to keep an eye on things and to report back if anything goes wrong. Remember how Mr. Blue covered up what happened at the ropes course when he showed up? If something goes wrong or someone gets hurt or worse . . ." I trailed off, swallowing hard as I remembered the feeling of vomiting out half the lake.

"So if you'd succeeded at drowning today, then none of us could have come back?" Kristy said.

"Maybe," I said.

"So, who is sabotaging camp?" Molly said.

"At first I actually thought it might be Aaron, since he wasn't acting like a normal camp counselor," I said. "But now that I know he's a TTBI agent, his sneaking around is making more sense." I shook my head. "No, I think that the somebody sabotaging camp is invisible." I glanced over at Amy, who suddenly sat up straighter as she looked at me.

"Again, are you talking about yourself?" Gabby said.

303

"No, I think there's another 'somebody' that's invisible," I said. "And I only know this because of something Amy said. Want to explain?"

"Well," she said, "I'm not sure how to explain it. I mean, during a big chunk of the summer I kept spotting someone invisible lurking around camp, but for a long time I just thought it was Hank up to no good."

"Completely valid assumption," I said. "However, it wasn't me. Which means somebody else is sneaking around camp, and I have a feeling that this invisible someone is the person behind all the mishaps this summer. If we can catch him, then we can put an end to it once and for all."

"Okay," Emerson said. "Any idea how we do that?"

"Well," I said with another glance at Amy, "the best way I know to catch an invisible person is to make them visible. I have a plan if you guys are up for it." There was a general murmur of agreement as everyone leaned forward, and I quickly explained what I'd been rolling around inside my head. If we pulled this off, we might just be able to save camp, and spend our last two weeks of summer living it up.

"I mean, it's no juggling dishes in sparkly vests, but it just might work," Hudson said when I was done explaining.

"I think we got it," Kristy said, yawning widely.

"Can we call it a night?" Amy said, stifling her own yawn. "I'm whooped."

"You can say that again," Gabby said. The rest of the girls murmured their agreement and stood up.

"Try not to light any lakes on fire tonight, okay, boys?" Molly said with a wink.

"Someday you guys are going to have to tell me everything that happened last summer," Hudson said as we watched the girls disappear into the woods.

"Make you a deal," I said. "If we survive this summer, I'll write you a book about last summer. For now, though, let's cross something off the old Life Lists. We've been far too neglectful of those this summer, and it's high time we correct that. Who is up for a midnight swim?"

"You have *got* to be kidding," Emerson said, his jaw dropping. "We literally fished you off the bottom of that lake hours ago. Now you want to go swimming in the dark?"

"A ship in harbor is safe, but that's not what a ship is built for," I said.

"What's that mean?" Emerson said.

"It means last one in is a rotten egg," I called as I yanked off my T-shirt and basketball shorts and headed for the lake at a run wearing nothing but my favorite polka-dotted boxers. I pounded down the dock and did a double front flip into the water. I hit the cold water feeling vibrantly alive from the tips of my toes to the top of my blessedly visible head. The weight I'd been carrying with me since the first day of camp was gone. I surfaced and turned back toward the firepit where the rest of the guys were watching me.

"You only live once, guys," I called. "Do it now, or do it never. Tomorrow isn't a guarantee." That did it, at least for Emerson. He splashed into the water a moment later, followed by everyone else. Gary was the exception and chose to walk to the end of the dock and plop down to dangle just his toes in the water.

I glanced over at Emerson and nodded my head once. He nodded back and together we dived under the water and swam for the dock. Poor Gary didn't know what hit him as we launched out of the water, grabbed his feet, and pulled. He crashed in, fully clothed, and came up sputtering and yelling. We laughed and ducked as he splashed water at us and vowed to stick bugs in our bunks. He got over it quickly, though, and shucked his own sopping-wet T-shirt and shorts up onto the dock. Together we paddled out toward the middle of the lake, where the full moon was reflecting like a huge round cheese on the still water.

"I can't believe you chose to cross this one off the

Life List tonight of all nights," Emerson said as he swam beside me.

"Just had to get back on the horse," I said.

"You mean almost drowning today?" Emerson said.

"Yup. If I didn't get back in this water, fear was going to get a foothold, and I try real, real hard not to give fear footholds in my life."

"Huh," Emerson said thoughtfully. "And here I just thought you were nuts."

"Nutty as squirrel poo, my friend," I said with a grin. "Besides, when are you ever going to get a chance to swim in a moon again?" We all paused as we reached the center of the moon's silvery reflection and stopped to tread water.

"I'm not going to lie," Hudson said after a minute. "Camp is actually shaking out to be better than I'd thought it would be. I just wish I hadn't lost my phone so I could capture this," he said, looking up at the sky. "Wow, I don't think I've ever seen so many stars."

"If your phone was here, you'd miss the best part," I said.

"Oh?" Hudson said. "What's that?"

"Experiencing it," I said. He opened his mouth like he was going to protest and then shut it again to look back up at the moon. "Oh, and I don't think you lost it

307

as much as I made it disappear," I said, since today felt like a day to confess all the things.

"Huh?" he said, glancing over at me. I held up my glove-covered hands and wiggled my fingers.

"Sorry," I said. "In my defense, when I made it disappear, I didn't know I could make things disappear."

Hudson shrugged. "Don't be sorry," he said. "It's been kind of nice not to have it this summer."

Without even consciously summoning them, I found myself quoting the lines Mr. Blue had said to us at the beginning of camp. "'Two roads diverged in a wood, and I—I took the one less traveled by. And that has made all the difference.'"

"Why are you quoting Mr. Blue?" Emerson asked.

"I'm not quoting Mr. Blue," I said. "I'm quoting Mr. Blue quoting Robert Frost. I was just thinking that not living life handcuffed to a screen might be the road less traveled by for our generation, and that it may just make all the difference."

"Maybe," Gary said. "If I'd never come to camp, I don't think I'd have ever unplugged long enough to even realize there *was* another path."

"Same," Hudson agreed. The other guys all murmured their own agreement, and I realized that here was yet another reason why we needed to make sure camp was here next year and the year after that.

"Here's to the path less traveled," I said. "May it make all the difference."

"Maybe it will," Hudson said. "Speaking of a difference, I really liked being invisible today, though. It was freeing to just be me."

"You know you can be you without the invisibility, right?" I said.

"Maybe," Hudson said. "I'm just starting to figure out who that might be."

I could have stayed in the moon's reflection all night, treading water, laughing, telling stories. Life Listing always resulted in the best adventures, and I realized that I'd been neglecting my list. Nothing like almost dying to make you appreciate life more, I thought a bit grimly. The slow brightening of the horizon finally signaled us that it was time to get moving.

"We'd better hustle," I said as we paddled back toward shore. "If Aaron wakes up and we're gone, we will be in big trouble."

"Worth it," Zeke said, and everyone chimed in with their agreement.

We made it back to the dock and hoisted ourselves out. Goose bumps erupted up and down my arms and legs as I ran back to the firepit in my underwear. I reached the spot where I'd left my clothes, only to find that they weren't there.

"Uh-oh," I said as Hudson and the rest of the guys skidded to a stop beside me.

"Hey!" Gary called from the dock, and we all turned his way to look. "Someone took my clothes!" I was about to yell back that ours were gone too when I saw a note stuck to a tree. I walked over and pulled it off. It had one word in swirly, girlie handwriting: PAYBACK.

"Uh, guys?" Hudson said, and I turned back to see his head cranked back as he stared up into the trees around us. There, knotted together and hanging in long looping ropes around the branches of the trees, were our clothes.

"Payback," I said out loud, and flipped the note so the rest of the guys could read it.

"Good to know they don't hold a grudge," Gary said as he rubbed his hands up and down his arms. It had taken the girls a year, but they'd finally gotten their revenge for the prank we'd played on them last year at the very end of camp. We'd snuck up their hill and tied all their clothes together, exactly like this, and had Emerson string them through the trees like Christmas lights.

"No fair," Murphy said, his teeth chattering. "They dumped water pitchers over us last year for that. They can't get revenge twice."

"They can, and they did," I said, a bit impressed despite the fact that I felt like a human icicle.

"Somebody find me a rope," Emerson said glumly. "I'll get them down."

"I got this," Hudson said, and narrowed his eyes at the long cable of our clothes that was hanging a good twenty feet above our heads. It shivered and then slowly began to undulate in the air like some sort of weird clothes snake.

"So much better than floating me up there like a party balloon," Emerson said.

Hudson moved his hands, and the clothing rope did an intricate twist and spin in the air ten feet above our heads.

"Stop showing off and just give us our clothes already!" Gary said. "I'm freezing over here!"

"All right," Hudson said. "One second." Before he had a chance to lower them any farther, though, there was the sharp snap of a stick in the woods to our right, and Hudson jerked his head toward it like the rest of us. The clothes snake jerked too, and I watched as it went flying through the air and flopped into the lake. A second later Mr. Stink came trundling out of the woods holding a large earthworm in his jaws, and we all relaxed. For a second there I'd been certain that we were about to reenact last year and get busted by Mr. Blue and Aaron.

"Great," Gary said dryly as we watched the long

rope of our clothing floating on the surface of the water. He turned to Hudson, arms over his chest. "Why is it that this never happened on your YouTube channel?" he accused.

Hudson sighed. "Because I redo something over and over again in order to patch together usable footage."

"That seems like a lot of work," Gary said.

Hudson nodded. "It's exhausting."

"Well," I said, rubbing my hands together, "at least the lake our clothes just landed in isn't on fire this time."

Murphy snorted. "How is it that you always look at the bright side, Hank?"

"Seriously," Gary said, and shivered. "It's annoying."

I shrugged. "Because I've made it a habit."

"Can we please move this along?" he said through chattering teeth.

"Guess we'd better go fish those out," Emerson said, moving back toward the lake, where our clothes were slowly starting to sink beneath the surface. The sound of a cabin door slamming in the distance made us all jump, and I glanced up at the horizon, where the sun was starting to creep up over the trees.

"No time," I said. "We need to get back to the cabin, like five minutes ago."

"But we're in our underwear!" Zeke hissed. "People will see us."

"Not if we hustle," I said. "Now move it!" I turned and sprinted up the hill. It took a second, but I heard the guys pounding behind me as we made our way through the pale light of dawn toward our cabin. As we ran, trying our best not to trip or laugh at the ridiculousness of it all, I knew that the rest of the summer was going to be a really good one, and I wasn't going to let anyone screw that up for us.

CHAPTER TWENTY

"What is wrong with you guys?" Aaron said at breakfast as he looked at each of our faces.

"What's that?" I said, shaking myself. I'd been half asleep, my head propped on my hand, and I looked across the table to see that Gary had given up and was snoring with his head flat on the table next to his oatmeal. I gave him a swift kick to the shins, and he jerked awake, looking around groggily. Everyone else looked just as rough, and I made a mental note not to pull another all-nighter anytime soon. The adrenaline of racing through camp in our skivvies and sneaking back into our cabin had worn off and exhaustion had set in. The girls in the Swallowtail cabin were grinning at us, and I stuck out my tongue at them. The camp challenge board had been cleared off, and I glanced nervously at the vacant pegboard. What did that mean? Was the challenge officially over because of what had happened?

Thankfully Mr. Blue took the stage a few minutes later and put at least a few of my questions to rest.

"Good morning!" he called, and we all chorused back our hellos. "Well," he said, clapping his hands together. "Let's hope that today is a much less eventful day than yesterday."

"Hear, hear!" I called, and everyone turned to look at me. I grinned back, grateful to be visible with a decent haircut for once.

"We have decided that in light of the recent dramatics surrounding the final camp challenge to postpone it until further notice," he said. "Instead we will enjoy our last few days at camp." He paused and swallowed, glancing down at the floor for a second, and I shot a worried look at the rest of the guys. What was going on?

"This place is incredibly special," Mr. Blue went on, an emotional hitch in his voice, "and while I hope it is here for years to come, the future is never promised, so, please, make sure that you make the most of the rest of your summer." With that he turned and walked off the stage. There was a smattering of applause as everyone

315

looked at one another, trying to figure out what exactly that speech had been about. Our table, however, knew exactly what that speech had been about. We ate in silence until Aaron excused himself to use the restroom. We watched as he made his way across the dining hall and disappeared behind the door at the far end.

"That did *not* sound good," Murphy said.

"You're right," I said. "And where is Munkhouser?"

"There," Emerson said, and we turned as the man in question walked in. He looked none the worse for wear from the events of the previous day, and he held a large silver laptop tucked under his arm.

"He didn't miss a beat, did he?" Emerson said.

I nodded as I watched Munkhouser take his customary seat next to Mr. Blue. He'd been tracking every mishap and misfortune for the entire summer on his ruined iPad and that laptop, and even if our plan did work and we captured the person responsible for all the problems, he still had a pretty convincing case against camp. I cocked my head to the side and glanced over at Hudson.

"Hudson?" I said. "As our local techy guru, how easy would it be to destroy Munkhouser's files from this summer?"

Hudson shrugged. "If he has it backed up somewhere, impossible. If he doesn't, we'd just have to ruin the laptop since his iPad bit the dust yesterday."

"Camp Outlier is a technology dead zone, remember?" Gary said. "He doesn't have it backed up somewhere; I'd almost guarantee it."

I smiled and glanced over at Gary. "I was really hoping that's what you'd say. Are you up for causing a little extra trouble during phase one of our plan this afternoon?"

"Do you even have to ask?" he said with a smirk.

"Explain to me again why we're breaking into Nurse Betsy's cabin?" Zeke said later that afternoon as we crouched in the bushes beside the dining hall.

"Because we're dumb," Gary said. "That's the only explanation. Like really supremely, incurably dumb."

"Or we decided to follow yet another Hank plan," Murphy said.

"Same thing," Gary said.

"Excuse me," I said. "So far this summer almost all of my plans have worked out. Have you had to scrub even a single toilet with bleach and a toothbrush yet?"

"Really?" Gary said. "Scrubbing toilets with a toothbrush is our benchmark?"

"Shhhhh," Emerson said with a nervous glance over his shoulder. "I really don't like the idea of stealing supplies from Nurse Betsy of all people. If she catches us,

317

she won't just get mad or call our parents, she'll chuck us out the window. We've seen her do it too! Remember those TTBI agents that made her mad?"

I laughed. "That was great." When no one else laughed with me, I got serious again. "Let's not think of it as stealing. We're just borrowing the stuff we need because if we told her what we were up to, she'd stop us."

"Easy for you to say," Emerson said. "You aren't the one sneaking into her cabin."

As we'd discussed, Gary and I were the distraction, and if there was one thing I was good at, it was being a distraction. We needed something big enough to draw Nurse Betsy out of her cabin and bad enough that Mr. Munkhouser would feel the need to stick his long nose into things, and I had a pretty good idea how to do that.

"So, tell me again what I'm getting stuck to if your hands don't work right?" Gary asked as we jogged the short distance across camp to the nature cabin. Inside this little cabin were cages of bunnies, lizards, snakes, two rats named Taco and Rocko, and an odd assortment of frogs and toads.

"You said no live animals, right?" I said.

"Right," Gary said. "I don't need you sticking me to a rabid squirrel."

"Shame," I said. "If my hands work, then it's just the laptop. If they don't work, I may need to stick you to a fish tank or a turtle shell or something."

"A turtle is a live animal," Gary said.

"Technically, I'd only be sticking you to the shell of a live animal," I said.

"Hank . . . ," Gary said, making my name into a warning.

"All right, all right," I said, putting my own gloved hands in the air in resignation.

"Let's hope this works," he said, flexing a gloved hand. "With our luck we'll just get in more trouble with Mr. Munkhouser for not wearing the proper safety equipment."

"That's the goal," I said with a wink. "I just wish my new ability was as reliable as yours," I said.

"No, you don't," Gary said, and there was something about his tone that made me not push it any further. We arrived at the nature cabin and walked inside to find about half of the Swallowtail girls there. Gabby and Emily each had a sleepy lop-eared rabbit in their arms, while Molly fed a big turtle a piece of lettuce. Kristy was there too, although she'd obviously forgotten her gloves since her bare hands were clasped firmly behind her, dutifully not touching anything. There was

319

something in her face, though, that made it clear that she really wished she could be holding an animal like the other girls were.

I glanced around the small cabin. There wasn't a counselor in sight, which was good since the whole point was luring out Nurse Betsy.

"Thanks for meeting us here," I said.

"No problem," Gabby said. "Abby and Emily are by Nurse Betsy's cabin, ready to sound the alarm. Are you ready?"

"Ready for what?" said a voice behind us, and Gary and I jumped about a foot as Aaron walked through the door.

"Abort! Abort!" Gary whispered under his breath, but I ignored him. Aaron showing up wasn't ideal, but I worked well under pressure. Besides, we had no way of telling everyone else what was going on.

"Hi!" I said to Aaron, improvising. "Ready to hold a rat! Gary here has always wanted to check it off his Life List."

"I have?" Gary said.

I nodded. "Yup, and today is your day, my friend." With that I quickly made my way over to the rat cage, where Taco and Rocko were investigating the carrot that someone had dropped in their cage. I knew they were friendly, but I still hesitated a half a second. There was something about a rat that gave me a bit of the heebie-jeebies, which, of course, is why they were perfect for this.

"Hank," Gary whispered, warning in his voice. "I said no live animals."

"Just keep your gloves on," I said while simultaneously slipping my gloves off and dropping them next to Rocko. "Oh no!" I said with overexaggerated panic. "Shoot! I think these gloves don't work either." Reaching my hand inside the cage, I pulled out Taco the rat. He immediately disappeared. I reached in with my other hand and pulled out Rocko, who blinked and disappeared too. I turned, not surprised to see that everyone in the cabin was watching us, and I held up the invisible rodents. A few of the girls took a nervous step back, and Gary let out a very impressive scream. Everyone jumped and looked his way, and I took advantage of their distraction and carefully put both rats back in their cage.

"Sorry," Gary said. "I don't like invisible rats."

"Ouch!" I called loudly as in my hands I carefully squashed the ketchup packets I'd snagged from the dining hall. "I just got bit by an invisible rat, and they got loose. Help!" Chaos erupted as everyone stampeded to get out of the cabin. Even Aaron hightailed it with impressive speed.

Gary walked over to stand next to me, his arms crossed over his chest. "You're a terrible actor," he said. "Your special effects with the ketchup were subpar at best."

I shrugged. "It worked, didn't it?"

He glanced around nervously. "You didn't really let invisible rats loose, did you?"

I shook my head. "Of course not."

"QUICK!" I called after the retreating campers. "Somebody get Nurse Betsy!"

A minute later Nurse Betsy came flying into the cabin, her blond hair standing out in a wild halo around her face. She spotted us instantly and narrowed her eyes.

"Why does it always seem to be you guys?" she said as she placed her hands on her hips.

"Because you're super lucky," I said, and grinned as I plucked Taco out of his cage and offered him to her. "Invisible rat?"

Nurse Betsy was finishing bandaging the finger that I swore up and down was throbbing from the rat bite that hadn't actually happened when Mr. Munkhouser came in. He was sweating with large dark rings under the arms of his polo, and he looked around the dim cabin before spotting us.

"What happened here?" he said, popping open his laptop.

"Somebody took a boat out and almost killed an invisible RISK kid," Gary said dryly. "Oh wait, that was yesterday."

Mr. Munkhouser looked up, glancing from me to Gary to Nurse Betsy and back again before looking down at his computer. "That was most unfortunate," he said. "I apologize. However, had you had the proper equipment and safety measures in place, that never would have happened."

"That's where you're wrong," Nurse Betsy said, her voice sharp. I glanced over at Gary. I hadn't planned on this particular confrontation, but I was pretty pumped to have a ringside seat.

"Pardon?" Mr. Munkhouser said, glancing up at her over the rims of his glasses.

"What I mean is that you can have all the safety measures in the world, and things will still happen to RISK kids simply because they're kids," she said, propping her hands on her hips. "To think otherwise is just plain foolishness."

"Ma'am," Mr. Munkhouser said. "Your job is to

bandage boo-boos, and mine is to regulate an entire population of extremely dangerous children. You do your job, and let me do mine."

Nurse Betsy stared daggers at him, and I was really hopeful that she was about to put his scrawny, condescending self right through the wall, but after a second she turned to us, her face flushed red with anger.

"Boys," she said. "When you're done answering Mr. Munkhouser's questions, please report to my office. I need to check your boo-boos." With that she slammed out the door, and I said a silent prayer that Hudson and Emerson had had time to grab the stuff and get the heck out of Dodge before the wrath of Nurse Betsy came down on them. I watched her stomp away down the hill for a second before turning back to Mr. Munkhouser.

"Everything okay in here?" Aaron asked, and I saw behind him the rest of the White Oak guys as well as the Swallowtails. Emerson leaned around our counselor's shoulder and gave me a big conspiratorial wink. I smiled: they'd gotten the stuff.

"All good," I said. "Anyone have any interest in holding an invisible rat that bites?"

"Pass," Hudson said, shaking his head.

"Are you sure?" Gary said. "I'll even loan you my

gloves." Before Hudson could say anything Gary had whipped off his gloves and tossed them to Hudson, who caught them.

"Phew!" he said. "These things stink." He went to hand them to Gabby, who held her hands up and took a giant step back to avoid them.

"Gross!" she said as her shoulder slammed into Gary.

"Whoops!" Gary said, and he tripped forward, two bare hands held out. A second later both of his hands were firmly stuck to the laptop.

"Oh man!" he said. "Look what you made me do!" Mr. Munkhouser stood there sputtering as Gary lifted the laptop with his sticky palms and turned to him with a smile. "I'll return this after Nurse Betsy gets it off. The acid we use should do wonders for it." With that we marched out and down the hill, a protesting Mr. Munkhouser trailing. I smiled, pleased that things were going the way I'd planned. I glanced over at Kristy and raised an eyebrow to silently ask her how her end of things was going. She nodded and gave me a thumbs-up.

"Wow," Nurse Betsy said when she met us at her cabin door. She looked Gary up and down, surveying the damage. "It looks like you're doing a fabulous job handling this population of dangerous kids." She shook her head back and forth before smiling at Mr. Munkhouser with a few too many teeth to be friendly. "Now if you'll excuse me, I have some boo-boos to attend to. Come on, darlin'," she said to Gary. "I know how to do *my* job." I hid a grin behind my hand as Nurse Betsy ushered him inside.

We still needed to catch whoever was *sabotaging* camp, but getting rid of the last of Munkhouser's records of this summer's mishaps would go a long way toward *saving* camp for the future. Phase one was officially in motion, and I could only hope that phase two would work out half as well.

CHAPTER TWENTY-ONE

"Good evening, campers!" Mr. Blue bellowed that night at dinner.

Everyone chorused a greeting back to him, and I shot a glance over at the Swallowtail table. Like ours, their faces were tight with anticipation. Amy chose that moment to look at me, and I mouthed the word *relax* as big and obviously as I could. She cocked her head to the side and I mouthed, *Act natural.* She nodded, finally getting the message, and I saw her elbow Gabby in the ribs and whisper something to her. I sat back, thankful for my once-again invisible face that allowed me to convey messages on the sly to the one person who could see me regardless of my invisibility. I was almost thankful for its reappearance this time, since keeping my own face relaxed would have been a trick I wasn't sure I was up to at the moment.

"It was brought to my attention that we can't end camp without finishing off the challenge competition," Mr. Blue said with a raised eyebrow at the Swallowtail table. Kristy beamed back at him. I'd chosen the right girl for that particular job, that was for sure. Kristy could talk a turtle out of its shell if she put her mind to it, and I made a mental note to congratulate her after this was all over.

"Tomorrow morning, we will be embarking on the final camp challenge of the summer!" This was met with a fresh chorus of cheers, and I shifted excitedly in my seat. "Tomorrow morning, a backpack full of supplies and a list of items will be dropped off at your cabins' front doors," Mr. Blue went on. "Working as a team, these items need to be collected as quickly as possible. The first team to collect all their items and return to the dining hall will earn a whopping forty points."

There was an excited murmur around the hall as everyone mentally added that forty points to their own score. I didn't have to be told that forty points would push us over the edge and put us in the lead despite our rough start. I shook my head and refocused. Winning didn't matter; we had bigger things at play here. Now that Mr. Blue had set out the bait, it was time for us to set our trap.

For the second night in a row, we slunk across the floor of our cabin and toward the window with the melted alarm. We were about halfway across when a shadow appeared in front of us, blocking the moonlight. Murphy yelped in surprise and jumped backward, knocking Gary and Anthony to the ground.

"Going somewhere, gentlemen?" Aaron said, and I felt my heart sink. I was still mentally scrambling with what to do next when suddenly I saw two bedsheets free themselves from the bunks behind Aaron's back. A second later they were wrapping themselves around our brawny counselor's shoulders and chest, pinning his arms to his sides and hauling him backward and toward the nearest bunk.

"Whoa," Gary said as the sheets rapidly tied themselves to the bunk despite some pretty impressive thrashing from Aaron. Aaron was just opening his mouth to yell when Hudson sent a large sock sailing across the room and directly into his open mouth.

"Color me impressed," I said as I surveyed our bound-and-gagged counselor.

"We are going to get into so much trouble for this,"

Murphy said, shaking his head.

"Definitely," I said. "You may get to scrub a toilet with bleach yet, my friend."

"What happens when someone comes in and sees him?" Emerson said. "The whole plan will be ruined."

"Allow me," I said, carefully taking off my newest set of gloves from Nurse Betsy and placing my bare palms on Aaron's bare shoulders. He flickered and then disappeared, clothing and all.

"Why do you think I can disappear other people's clothes but not my own?" I asked.

"Because RISK factors are weird," Gary said. "Let's go."

With one last glance at invisible Aaron, we slid out into the night. We made our way down the hill and into the woods beside the dining hall without incident. The girls were already waiting for us, bathed in a warm yellow glow from the light bulbs Emily was holding in each of her hands. I breathed a sigh of relief when I saw them. I'd been worried that something was going to hold up the girls.

"Okay then," I said, rubbing my hands in anticipation. "Let's save camp, shall we? Hudson, hand out the supplies, please." He grabbed his backpack and pulled out the cans of hair spray and baby powder that he'd managed to steal from Nurse Betsy's supply cabinet.

330

"We don't have enough for everyone to have their own, so we are going to have to divide this up," I said. "Two guys and two girls to a group and one jar of powder and can of hair spray. We'll spread out to improve our odds of spotting him."

"And once we spot him?" Gary said. "Then what?"

"Then you make him visible," I said, holding up my powder and hair spray. I quickly sprayed my own invisible arm with the sticky spray and then liberally shook the powder over the top to demonstrate.

"That part I get," Kristy said. "It's the next part that makes me nervous. What if this guy is dangerous? I mean, he can't be in his right mind if he's trying to sabotage camp, right? What if he catches us?"

I rubbed the powder off my arm, returning it to its original invisible state. "Don't let him catch you," I said.

"It's hard to catch something that you can't see," Amy said, and I glanced at her and raised an eyebrow.

"Yeah?" I said. "That's why we have the spray and powder?"

Amy shook her head and looked at everyone else. "I have an idea," she said. "But I'm not sure if you're going to like it."

"What's the idea?" Molly said. "I'm game for just about anything if it helps catch this guy." Everyone murmured their agreement except for Gary, who crossed

331

his arms over his chest, looking skeptical.

"That's what I hoping," Amy said, and then to my surprise she looked directly at me. "Hank?" she said. "Do you trust me?"

"Um, yeah?" I said, still unsure where exactly she was going with this. Before I could protest, she'd peeled one of my gloves off my hand and pressed my hand to her own bare shoulder. She blinked from view. "Who's next?" came her disembodied voice.

"Me!" Hudson said, stepping forward with a wide grin on his face. I felt someone grab my hand and a second later Hudson was invisible too. To my utter amazement, one by one my friends each stepped forward and disappeared. Even Gary, who I'd have bet money on pitching a fit, held out his arm without saying a word.

"This is spooky," Emerson's voice came from my left a minute later.

"Not to me," said Amy's voice on my right. "I can still see you all perfectly. Now, let's get started before Hank's invisibility trick wears off." There was a very confused flurry of motion as everyone attempted to find their assigned group without actually being able to see one another. Thankfully Amy was there to help shove people where they needed to go, and in no time I was standing with Amy, Murphy, and Gabby as the rest of the groups headed to their assigned positions. Emerson's group headed down to the boathouse while Kristy and Hudson led their team to the girls' hill, and Zeke and Anthony headed to the boys' hill. I watched the small flicker of flame floating in midair where I assumed Anthony's head was for a second before refocusing. I turned to where I thought Amy might be.

"Ready?" I said.

"Let's do it," Murphy's voice said, and I saw him pick up our powder and hair spray.

Since we didn't know what exactly was going to be sabotaged for this challenge, we'd decided that our best chance of catching this guy in the act was spreading out and covering as much ground as possible. My group was heading for the supply cabin, the small building where everything from extra toilet paper to campout supplies were kept. I had no idea what items were going to be on the scavenger hunt tomorrow, but I did know that the backpack of supplies that would be dropped off at each cabin were probably in here. It wasn't until we were halfway down the hill that I realized that I'd never put back on the glove Amy had taken off. I flexed my fingers before balling them into a tight fist. It had been both thrilling and unnerving to watch my friends disappear one by one. It had also been kind of funny to listen as they enjoyed trying out a RISK factor so different from their own. I realized that tonight, my friends were really going to see what it was like to walk a mile in my shoes. I glanced to my left as we passed Nurse Betsy's cabin, followed by the cabin where Mr. Munkhouser was staying. He'd probably see RISK factors a lot differently if he had the same opportunity. The idea was an intriguing one, but I pushed it aside as we reached the supply cabin.

I was about to open the door when it swung inward on its own, and I jumped about a foot.

"Relax," Amy whispered. "It's just me."

"Sorry," I said. "But it's really weird being on the other side of your own RISK factor."

"I can see that," Amy said.

"You can always see," I said, shaking my head as I followed her inside. Murphy and Gabby came right behind us, shutting the door quietly behind themselves. I was about to suggest that we hide when I realized that I was the only one who'd need to do that, since everyone else's clothes were just as invisible as they were. I grabbed my T-shirt and shorts with my bare hand, but nothing happened. I huffed, wishing this thing that I did was a bit more reliable, before I stripped off my camp T-shirt. Deciding that I might as well cover all my bases, I also kicked off my shoes and socks so I was in nothing but dark gray basketball shorts. That accomplished, I glanced around and spotted the large orange water canister that we used to refill our water bottles on hot days. I stepped in and crouched down, wedging myself tightly inside.

"Can you see me?" I asked.

"Nope," Murphy said. "That was really cool."

"Now what?" Gabby asked.

"Now we wait," I said.

"I thought you might say that," I heard Gabby say as the bench to my left let out a loud protesting creak as she sat down. I was about to suggest that she sit on the metal cooler instead since it seemed sturdier when I heard Murphy let out an exasperated cry a second before I heard a familiar pop.

"Murphy?" I hissed, glancing around the dark cabin.

"He's gone," Amy said. "Time traveled."

"Well, that stinks," Gabby said. "Now what?" Before I could respond or start to figure out what to do, there was a second loud pop. I was about to open my mouth to tell Murphy that I was glad he was back when I felt someone press a cold hand over my mouth.

"He's here," Amy whispered in my ear.

The hairs on the back of my neck stood on end, and I knew that she wasn't talking about Murphy. I stayed crouched in the water container as whoever it was made their way across the cabin. I squinted, wishing that I could have borrowed Amy's RISK factor just for tonight. The sound of hard-soled shoes on concrete echoed inside the small cabin, and a second later one of the backpacks that were lined up on the far wall moved, its top opening as the contents inside were rifled through. I glanced over to see where we'd set down the hair spray and powder just as the hair spray silently floated past my ear. Amy was on the move, or maybe it was Gabby. Our invisible visitor grabbed the next backpack, and I held my breath as the floating hair spray can moved closer from the left just as the disembodied jar of powder moved in from the right. There was a moment when they stayed suspended, a few feet from the upended backpacks, and then Gabby's voice rang out.

"Now!" she cried, and there was a hiss of spray and a flurry of powder followed by a surprised shout. A figure suddenly appeared, or at least his top half, coated in hair spray and powder. Gabby and Amy were slightly visible too, their bodies faintly outlined in powder and spray.

I yelled and leaped out of the canister to charge the invisible man just as he grabbed a nearby shovel and took a swing at Amy's head. She ducked, and the shovel swung over her head to thunk harmlessly against the cabin wall. I dropped a shoulder and tackled him just like I'd tackled my older brothers on countless occasions. There was a second of confused flailing as he attempted to get out from under me.

"Gabby," I yelled, "grab him! Or better yet, sit on him!" She tried, but the man still had the shovel, and it made contact with my shoulder a second later. The hit made me lose my grip, and in a second the man was up and running for the door, powder flying off him in all directions.

"Come on!" I called, but Amy was already ahead of me, sprinting out the door as the man made a beeline up the hill.

"Get help!" I yelled to Gabby before running after Amy. I heard Gabby yelling as she raced over to Nurse Betsy's cabin and began pounding on the door. Around me cabin lights flickered on. Amy was in front of me, her outline getting more and more faint as the powder that had sprayed on her flew off in all directions. Unfortunately, the man we were chasing was becoming more and more invisible by the second as well, and I saw him scrub at his arms and hair as he ran, further loosening the powder and hair spray combo. He was faster than us too, and he started to pull away as he headed for the woods.

"There he is!" Hudson yelled.

"Where?" Kristy cried, and I looked over to see

where my friends were, only to realize with frustration that I had no idea. However, the man we were trying to catch didn't have a clue either, and I saw him trip and go sprawling as someone, maybe Gary, let out a yell of triumph. The man tumbled, and more powder flew off so that he was now almost completely invisible.

"Hudson!" I called as an idea came to me in a flash.

"What?" he yelled back as the man made it to his feet again.

"The hair spray and powder!" I said. "Levitate it!"

"Right!" Hudson said, and a second later I saw the hair spray and powder go flying out of someone's hands and into the air. They headed right for the man, but a moment before they made it to him, they started to shake violently.

"Uh-oh," Hudson said just as the can of hair spray and container of powder exploded. For a moment every-thing was enveloped in a thick haze of powder, and I coughed, flapping a hand in front of my face as I tried to see where the man had gone. To my surprise, when the powder finally started clearing, all around me were the powder-covered outlines of my entire team. The effect was so distracting that for a second I couldn't figure out where the man we'd been chasing had gone. Then I spotted him racing toward the trees that ran along the edge of the hill that held the boys' cabins.

"There he is!" I said, already taking off, even though I realized that he was going to get away. He was too far ahead, and once he was in the cover of the dark trees, we'd never spot him again, powder or no powder.

Suddenly the man came to an abrupt stop, falling backward as though he'd just slammed into an invisible brick wall.

"Not so fast," Aaron's voice said, and a second later the man was flipped over onto his stomach, his hands pinned behind his back as our invisible camp counselor slapped a pair of neon-yellow handcuffs around invisible wrists.

"How'd he get out?" Emerson said, coming to stand beside me.

"No clue," I said.

"Probably his RISK factor," Anthony said. "He's super strong, remember?"

"However he got out, I'm really glad he did," I said.

"What's going on?" Mr. Blue said, and I turned as our bright blue head of camp came racing up the hill, Nurse Betsy at his side, her head full of bright pink curlers.

Trailing behind them was a pajama-clad Mr. Munkhouser looking utterly baffled. "What in the world?" he said as he took in the circle of powder-covered campers in various states of visibility.

"Got him, sir," Aaron called, and Mr. Blue hurried to his side.

"Got who?" Mr. Munkhouser said as he pushed his glasses up his nose and peered up the hill.

"Got the guy who's been sabotaging camp," I said. "The busted canoe, the hole in the maze, the ropes course, your busted boat, all of it."

"What's going on?" someone said right next to Munkhouser, and he jumped about a foot and squealed in surprise.

"Sorry," said Murphy's disembodied voice.

"Is that you, Murph?" I said. "Are you back?"

"If you mean am I back in the present, then yes," Murphy said. "But I'm still invisible. Um, how did this happen?" he said, and I had a feeling he was getting his first really good look at our powder-covered team.

"Not being able to see anyone is getting real old real fast," I said. "Hey, Hudson," I called. "Did you explode all the powder and spray, or is there some left?"

"Here," Amy said, holding up two canisters.

"Go spray down Murphy, would ya?" I said. "All this invisibility is making my head hurt."

"That's weirdly funny," Emerson said next to me, and then sneezed, sending out a small cloud of white powder into the air.

"Murphy time traveled?" Aaron's disembodied voice said. "So that explains it."

"Explains what?" I said, glancing over at the spot where I thought our counselor might be.

"He's three feet to the left of where you're looking," Amy said as she coated Murphy in hair spray and powder.

"Thanks," I said, adjusting my eyes to what I hoped was the right spot. The man in Aaron's custody thrashed against the handcuffs, and powder showered down around him, leaving the dirt white.

Mr. Blue turned to Nurse Betsy and raised an eyebrow. "Could you procure some more hair spray and powder for me?" he said. "I'd like to make sure our captive stays visible."

"I would," Nurse Betsy said with a meaningful look at me, "but I've got a feeling that my supply cabinet is empty."

"I've still got some left," Amy volunteered, and I glanced over to see a powder-covered Murphy rubbing at his eyes. Apparently Amy had been a bit over-enthusiastic in her coating efforts. Nurse Betsy nodded, and a moment later the canister and hair spray were whizzing through the air. Aaron's captive coughed as powder and hair spray flew, and I saw the extra powder cover our counselor just enough to make him visible.

"Man, I wish I was that good." Hudson sighed, and I glanced over to see him watching Nurse Betsy in envious awe.

"I'm glad you're not," I said. "I needed you to explode that stuff all over. Why do you think I told you to levitate it?"

"How'd you know I'd explode it?" Hudson asked, crossing his arms over his chest. "Sometimes I don't, you know."

"Oh, I know," I said, and smiled. "But you almost always do when you're stressed out."

"I do?" Hudson said.

I nodded. "Think about it. You stopped exploding stuff when I made your phone disappear."

"Huh," Hudson said. "Now there's an interesting thought."

I left him with his interesting thought and went over to where Mr. Blue was standing with our powder-covered captive and Mr. Munkhouser. Aaron was talking rapidly into a cell phone, and I could already hear the faint sound of sirens in the distance. If I didn't act now, my opportunity for some answers was going to be gone for good.

"So," I said, "who are you? And why have you been messing with our camp all summer?"

Instead of answering, the man just spit, but I was quick and stepped to the side so it hit Munkhouser instead. Munkhouser gasped and then gagged as he attempted to wipe the glob off his pajamas.

"This is a time-traveling criminal," Aaron said, coming to put a firm hand on the man's shoulder. "It's why I was stationed here at camp this summer."

"Really?" Murphy said. "It wasn't because of me?"

Aaron smiled. "It was also because of you," he said. "This man is what we call a worm. He can time travel only into the hole that a time traveler like yourself leaves behind. Which means that every time you disappeared this summer, you left a time-traveling door wide open for criminals like him to come through. We'd been tipped off that something was going to happen here at camp this summer, and the TTBI wanted feet on the ground."

"But why was he messing with camp?" I said, still not understanding.

"Because this place is an abomination," the man said, breaking his silence for the first time. Murphy jumped about a foot at the sound of his voice, and I heard Emerson gasp and Gary yelp.

"So," Gary said, walking up to stand beside me. "The future still doesn't like kids like us, is that it?" I think he was about to say more, but I spotted Murphy's elbow dart out and go directly into Gary's ribs. Gary grunted and closed his mouth, finally getting the picture.

"What do you mean 'still'?" Aaron asked.

"He didn't say still," Murphy said. "He said 'bill,' as in all the new rules and laws and stuff us RISK kids have to follow."

"Except here," Kristy chimed in. "Here we just get to be kids."

"You aren't kids. You're just a bunch of social rejects, burdens on society," the man snarled, and Mr. Blue's face clouded over.

"Aaron, I feel this man is in breach of the TTBI's mandates against discussing the future, am I right?"

"One hundred percent," Aaron said, and a wadded-up sock appeared seemingly out of thin air before being thrust into the man's invisible mouth. Just then four black SUVs with sirens squealing came speeding into the empty field beside the dining hall. "Here comes my backup," Aaron said.

The next ten minutes were a flurry of activity as TTBI officers swarmed in to take possession of the man. Murphy was led away by two of the officers, but he was back within ten minutes. Nurse Betsy bustled around to ensure that each of us was in one piece, curlers flying. She was in the middle of inspecting Emerson's skinned knee when he flickered and became visible again. A quick glance around showed each of our team members blinking back into the land of the visible. I looked down at my own hands and sighed. Apparently my own invisibility seemed to be here to stay.

"You're special again," Amy said, coming up beside me. To my surprise she deftly took one of my invisible hands in her own and squeezed.

"Special?" I said.

She nodded. "You're one of the only people in this world that I can really see. That makes you special."

"Gee, thanks," I said. "Good to know my mom isn't the only one that thinks that."

"Aw man," Hudson said, and I glanced over at him, all too aware of Amy's warm hand still held in mine.

"What's wrong?" I said.

"I'm visible again." Hudson sighed.

"Thank goodness," Kristy said, smiling her widest, most winning smile at him. He smiled back a bit ruefully.

"I'll make you invisible anytime you want," I said, and he grinned. "In fact," I said, "I think I might just have found a use for this new trick of mine." I leaned over and very carefully brushed a finger down Emerson's weighted vest. It disappeared, and he glanced down at himself in surprise.

"That's awesome," he said. "You may have to do that more often."

"Me next!" Gary said, holding out his hands with their shiny cellophane gloves. I obliged, carefully rubbing a finger down the plastic, and they disappeared too.

"It's like RISK camouflage." I grinned. "I should open a business."

"Not tonight you won't," Nurse Betsy said. "It's off to the showers and then bed with you lot." She ushered us back toward our cabin. We complied, and I fell into my bunk ten minutes later, powder free and exhausted.

"We did it, didn't we?" Emerson said sleepily from above me. "We saved camp."

"I think so," I said. "That guy we caught, you recognized his voice, didn't you?"

"Yeah," Emerson said. "I'm not positive since I couldn't see him, but I think he was one of the hunters that we ran into last summer. The ones that didn't think RISK kids were worth having around."

"Huh," I said. "Well, he's caught now, so we should be in the clear. Right?"

"Only time will tell," Emerson said.

346

"I'll let you know what it says," Murphy said with a laugh that ended in a yawn.

"Sounds good," I said, already closing my eyes. We still had our last challenge the next morning after all, and we were going to need our beauty sleep.

CHAPTER TWENTY-TWO

We lost the scavenger hunt challenge—by a lot, actually. We'd all been so tired from our middle-of-the-night adventuring that I think we were half asleep for most of it. It didn't matter, though, not really. Even Kristy applauded the Red Wood and Buckeye cabins when they accepted their award the next night at dinner. It would have been nice to win, I mused as I took another bite of my pasta, but I was just happy that we still had two weeks left of camp to live it up without impending doom or a mysterious sabotage hanging over our heads. The only problem was that Mr. Munkhouser seemed just as uptight as ever, recording every RISK mishap with precision in his notebook.

"You know," I said, glancing down at my gloved hands, "I think it's time that Mr. Munkhouser walked a mile in a RISK kid's shoes."

"Oh, this is going to be good," Gary said, rubbing his hands together in anticipation.

When dinner was over and we were dismissed up to our cabins for free time, I made sure I fell in line behind Mr. Munkhouser, who was so busy questioning a Monarch girl about her skinned knee that he didn't even notice when Anthony set his notebook on fire.

"Careful!" Kristy said, swooping in to grab the notebook out of his hand so she could stomp out the fire.

"Whoa!" I said, giving an overexaggerated yell as I pretended to trip over her, pitching myself forward and into the confused government official. Mr. Munkhouser yelped as I placed a bare palm flat on his arm. Mr. Munkhouser flickered and vanished.

"Whoops!" I said as I quickly jammed my glove back on my hand. "I guess these gloves aren't working either."

"What isn't working?" Mr. Munkhouser's voice said, sounding more than a little disgruntled as a disembodied hand picked up the charred notebook.

"Is everything all right?" Mr. Blue said, rushing over.

"We're fine," I said. "My gloves just aren't working great again."

349

"Safety protocols should always work," Mr. Munkhouser blustered, and we all just stared as the newly invisible man went about the business of inspecting his ruined notebook.

"He doesn't realize it, does he?" Kristy said.

"Wait for it . . . ," Gary said, holding up a finger. A second later Mr. Munkhouser let out a scream of surprise.

"There it is!" Gary declared.

"What? How?" Mr. Munkhouser said, and I watched as his pen suddenly snapped up to eye level as he tried to see his invisible hand.

"Look who it is!" I said, and we turned to see Nurse Betsy come bustling over with a can of hair spray and a container of baby powder in her hands.

"That was fast," Murphy muttered, and I shrugged.

"I may have tipped her off a bit," I said. "I felt like we owed her this one after stealing her supplies and the mess with the invisible rats."

"Nice," Hudson said approvingly as Mr. Munkhouser went stomping down the hill, half visible from his thorough coating of powder.

"Not as nice as exploding powder and hair spray over half the camp," Gary said.

"Whatever." Hudson grinned. "At least I didn't

350

get stuck to an invisible railing in my underwear this summer."

I snorted as Gary scowled at him.

"Want me to make you invisible again?" I said, holding up a bare hand. "You may need to hide for a while after that comment."

Hudson shook his head. "It was fun for a bit, but then almost getting killed kind of ruined it for me. There has to be a middle ground between being internet famous and invisible, right?"

"Yeah." Gary sniffed. "It's called being normal."

"Well, you'll never be that," I said, throwing one arm around Hudson's shoulders and another around Gary's, "but we wouldn't have it any other way."

"That was cheesy," Gary said.

"The cheesiest," I agreed. "Speaking of cheese, how good was that mac and cheese tonight? Who's up for a swim before lights-out?"

The girls fell into step with us, and together we headed toward the lake. Hudson was laughing about something with Kristy, and for the first time all summer, I didn't feel a familiar pang of jealousy.

"What are you smiling at?" Amy said, walking over.

"Just thinking that it's nice that someone knows when I'm smiling," I said.

"We all know that you're smiling," Gary grumbled as he shouldered past me to walk next to Gabby. "You've been visible for the last ten minutes."

I glanced down at my hands and saw that he was right. I was back, and I waited for the rush of relief that always came when I reappeared. But just like that pang of jealousy, the relief was gone too. Maybe it was my near-death experience, or maybe just the elation of figuring out how to save camp, but I realized that I wasn't scared anymore of disappearing and never coming back.

"Hey, Hank! Catch!" Gary called, and I turned, hands up ready to catch whatever he was throwing my way. To my surprise, I didn't see anything. Instead, I felt something furry brush against my cheek followed by tiny claws, and I let out a bloodcurdling scream and ran for the dining hall, because that's what you do when someone tosses you an invisible rat.

Dear White Oak men (Or should I say Blue Spruce men? Too soon? We can adjust to the new name next year),

Here are your instructions until we meet again for another epic summer. The same rules as last year: memorize it, then shred and flush.

A little time-traveling bird told me that it might be a good idea to learn all the choreography to the 1990s boy band classic "Tearin' Up My Heart" by *NSYNC. Okay, that's a lie. But I have a really sweet plan for next summer. Trust me.

Keep working on dancing in general (see above). I heard a rumor that there may be a camp-wide dance next summer.

Practice those juggling skills. . . . Next year it gets more exciting. I don't want to give anything away now, but live animals are involved. (Don't worry, no invisible rats. Probably.)

Everyone send me their updated email address and a phone number where we can FaceTime. I want to keep in touch with you yahoos. Just be careful, Hudson: no one wants you showing back up with the personality of a potato next summer. Take the road less traveled. . . .

Keep brainstorming ideas for initiation night. We only have a few more years until it's our turn in the Red Wood cabin.

Live it up and Life List it up. We slacked this summer on the Life Lists, and

I expect all of you to make up for lost time. Age twenty-five years or don't even think about showing your face here next summer. (That's harsh. I don't mean that. But do it.)

See the attached photo. Apparently, the girls had a camera the night of our midnight swim, and it's not every day you get a picture of you and all your best friends in their underwear. It's a gem. I'm framing mine.

Sincerely,

Hank

PS Can't wait to see all you knuckleheads next year. I miss you all already.

AUTHOR'S NOTE

Dear reader:

There is nothing better than going back to camp with your best friends, is there? Well, maybe getting to write another book set at your favorite camp from the point of view of one of your favorite characters . . . that might be better.

Welcome back to Camp Outlier, where the adventures are wild and maybe just a little dangerous. When I got the go-ahead to write a book to accompany my third novel, *Float*, I wasn't sure who should tell the story. I wrote *Float* from Emerson's point of view, and while he started camp as a socially awkward kid who couldn't control his floating issues, he ended camp as a confident kid with friends and a zest for life—despite the floating issues. His story was complete in my mind. He'd learned about living life outside his comfort zone, he'd made friends for the first time in his life, and he'd even caught the eye of Molly, the girl camper who turned into a cocker spaniel. When I started writing *Float* back in 2013, I always anticipated it being the first of a series, and that every book would be another year at camp from a different camper's perspective. I imagined that Gary's book would be called *Stuck*, that Hank's book would be called *Disappear*, that Anthony's book would be called *Ignite*—you get the idea. So now that the opportunity was here . . . whose story should I tell?

After momentarily entertaining the idea of writing the book from the point of view of one of the girl campers, I decided that my best candidates were Gary, Hank, and Murphy since they were the three characters that I'd developed the most in *Float*. I almost immediately threw out Murphy. I'd just gotten done writing a time-traveling book called *Glitch*, and I was worried that a story from Murphy's point of view would feel too similar. Plus, time-traveling books are tricky and give you (and your editor) lots of headaches. That left Hank and Gary as my options for protagonists.

Hank is my favorite character I've ever created. He's funny and weird and spent a large chunk of his time in *Float* running around naked, but I was worried that he wouldn't be as funny if the reader was in his head. Gary was also a good candidate since he's as grumpy and sarcastic as I think we all wish we could be. However, I was worried that his head might be *too* grumpy for a reader to reside in for an entire book. Plus, his journey was going to have to lead him toward being a more polite and positive person, and I wasn't ready to give up grumpy Gary yet. He was just too much fun. So, it was a toss-up!

What finally made my decision was the story that started bubbling up in my imagination. Hank loved being the center of attention, but what if, for some reason, he wasn't this summer? How would he handle that? In fact, what if a new camper showed up who stole his spotlight right out from under him? Enter Hudson, the new kid at camp, who would make Hank's invisibility something that bothered him for the first time in his life. Besides stealing Hank's spotlight, Hudson served another purpose—he addressed an issue that really wasn't an issue when I first started writing *Float* almost ten years ago . . . cell phones. I enjoy the privilege of going into elementary and middle schools to talk about writing and reading and chasing your dreams, and every year the number of kids walking around with their eyes glued to screens seems to increase. While technology is great (I wrote this entire book on my laptop!), I'm so worried about my young readers who are spending huge chunks of their precious lives staring at a screen when the big wide world is just waiting for them to have adventures in it. Childhood is terrifyingly short, and so many kids seem to be missing it entirely in the name of beating that next level or filming the perfect video. Hudson's journey in this book is one that I hope some of my readers are inspired to take. Hank quotes Robert Frost's poem "The Road Not Taken" and mentions that maybe, for his generation, the road not taken is one without a technology addiction. A road where adventures are had out in the sunshine and not in a virtual world. Where friendships are made over shared experiences in nature and not through messages on social media. Dearest reader, I hope that you get to experience going to camp someday, but if Camp Outlier is the only camp you get to attend, I hope that you still walk away understanding the value of friendships forged by shared experiences and adventures lived in the real world and maybe choose to take that road less traveled too. I think, like Robert Frost and Hudson, you'll find that it makes all the difference.

Until next time,
Laura Martin

PS. *Float* was written in 2013, which was my last year before becoming a mom, and I blame the overuse of the word *butt* in that book on my kid-less status. Now that I have four (kids, not butts), you'll notice that word is used a lot less in this book. Which, considering my main character is the ever-naked Hank, is kind of an impressive trick. I apologize or you're welcome . . . depending on where you fall on the derriere debate.

ACKNOWLEDGMENTS

I have so many people that I need to thank for letting me return to Camp Outlier for another year! I'd been dying to come back ever since I finished *Float*, and I owe Tara Weikum for loving *Float* and its cast of misfits enough to want to see what happened to them in their second year! Thank you for continuing to champion another book by Laura Martin. I'm so grateful for the opportunity to continue creating worlds with dinosaurs, sea monsters, and floating kids.

A huge thank-you, as always, goes to my agent, Jodi Reamer, for helping me continue to navigate the world of publishing. I'm forever grateful that you're in my corner, and I can't wait to see where this journey takes us next. Thank you to my mom for editing every book that I write, regardless of my ridiculous deadlines, so that I can send it on without any embarrassing typos. I owe my dad a thank-you as well for having all those harebrained adventures that first endeared *Float* to so many readers.

A huge I-couldn't-do-it-without-you thank-you goes to my husband, Josh, who has continued to support this dream of mine. Thanks for being the leader of Team Martin.

I always like to end my acknowledgments by noting that none of this, not one book, not one word on a page, would have been possible without God. I'll forever be grateful for the gift of words He blessed me with, and for the opportunities He's provided for me to use that gift.

Ephesians 3:20–21

Now to him who is able to do immeasurably more than all we ask or imagine, according to his power that is at work within us, to him be glory . . .